MW01534118

THE GOLDEN AGE OF *Charli*

RSVP

JENA C. HENRY

THE GOLDEN AGE OF CHARLI
RSVP

iUniverse books may be ordered through booksellers or by contacting:
iUniverse
1663 Liberty Drive
Bloomington, IN 47403
www.iuniverse.com
1-800-Authors (1-800-288-4677)

Author Photo by Charles Mader

ISBN: 978-1-4917-6963-8 (sc)
ISBN: 978-1-4917-6962-1 (e)

Library of Congress Control Number: 2015912309

Print information available on the last page.

iUniverse rev. date: 08/21/2015

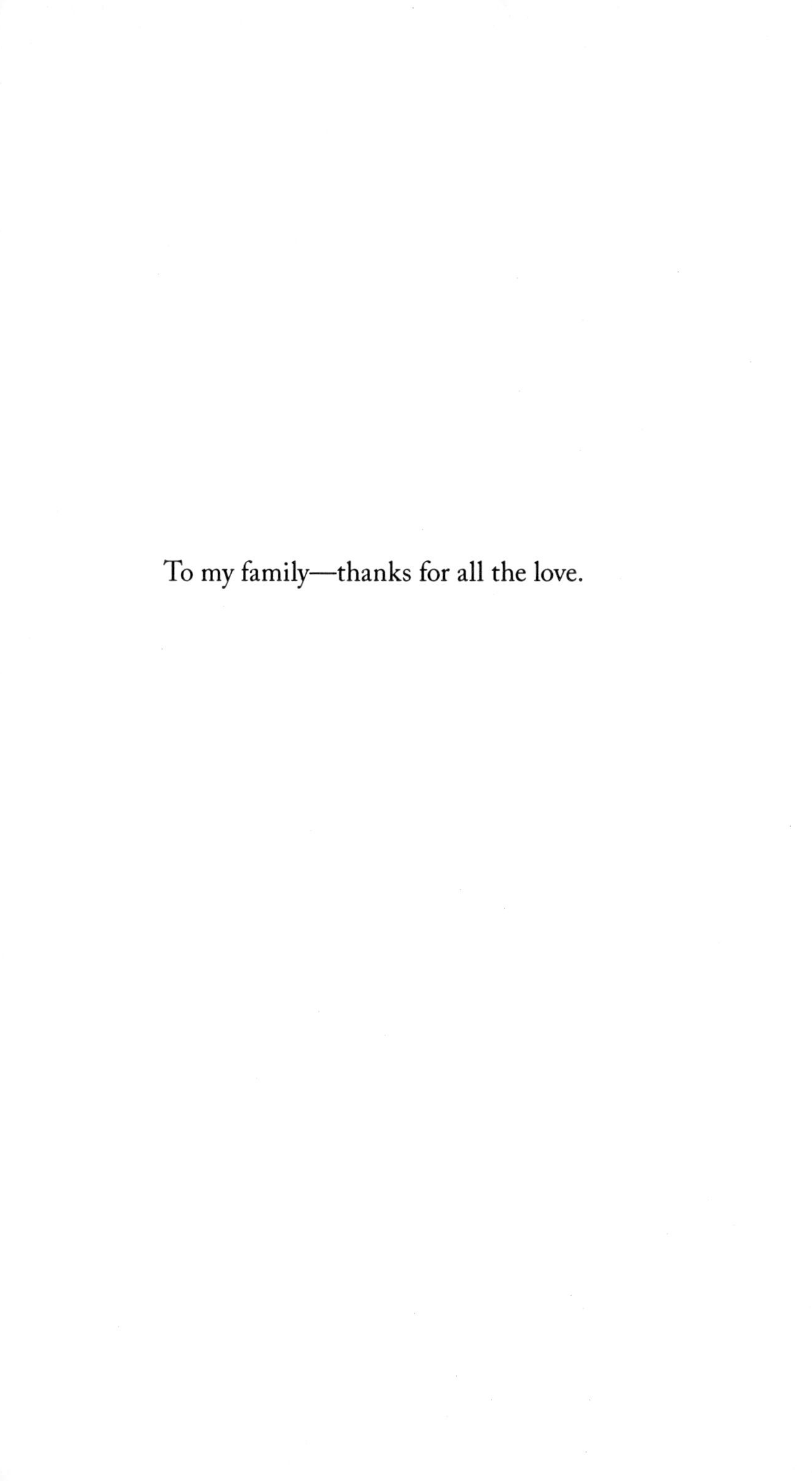

To my family—thanks for all the love.

Prologue

I jerked awake, arms and legs tangled in the sheet and comforter, my pillows in a heap on the floor. *What happened? What did he say?*

Where am I? Oh no, not again. Not another nightmare, another shadow on my day.

If I were wearing a red-bordered name tag, it would read, "Hello! My name is Charlotte Angstrom Eddy McAntic." At school, I'd enrolled with my given name, but I'd changed it to Charli as a preteen. Now I answered to hon, Mom, Auntie, "Where are you?" or "Help!"

When I had been a teenager, at the dawning of the Age of Aquarius, my friends and I had been convinced that we wouldn't live, or didn't want to live, past the age of thirty. But of course I had survived to cross that infamous, untrustworthy threshold. I'd spent my thirties, forties, and even my fifties in peace and harmony aligning marriage, mortgage, careers, and children.

I'd married Pud, a no-nonsense, hardworking, establishment-type guy. Somewhat surprisingly, based on his serious, no-frills demeanor, he'd parlayed a math degree into an exciting career supporting open-wheel auto racing.

I'd started out as a free spirit but had ended up taking the more traditional route. I'd earned a law degree, focused on contracts, and then dedicated myself to my favorite jobs—wife and mother. Our two boys were young adults now, almost launched, although still within the orbit of Planet Home.

Thanks to love, the stars, and a little help from my friends, the seasons gently went round and round.

So why was I having bad dreams?

1

The Golden Years

N*o, no, come back! What was he saying?*

"It's over. I love golf. I am going to live at the clubhouse and golf all the time."

Please stay! Give me a chance!

Wait, what is happening? Where am I?

Stop! Wake up! I was groggy and unsettled. *Is Pud leaving, or was it a nightmare?* The scene had been so vivid; it had been as if I were streaming a high-definition episode of my life. Slowly, my terror faded. I timidly opened my eyes. *Crazy dream! Whew, everything's all right now. Or is it?*

Golden years of retirement? A time to savor the sunset years together? Where's the gold? And more importantly, where's my husband?

Every day, my husband cruised down the retirement path—straight to the golf course. I was stuck at home without him. Pud had embraced his new life, but he had stopped embracing me. I wasn't part of his happily ever after.

I awoke to my daily reality show, *Retirement, the Twilight Zone*.

My day had dawned with a jolt, and I was not used to such a turbulent start. Before the arctic chill of Pud's retirement had blown into my life, I'd sprung out of bed every morning with a smile on my face and exclaimed, "Thank you, God, for another beautiful day!" Sixteen hours later, as my husband and I would turn in for the night, I would close with, "Another great day!" In between these upbeat bookends had stretched the hopeful gift of my day, waiting for me to fill it with abundant possibilities.

My daily affirmations were not formal prayers or religious moments but personal cheers of thanks and joy for another day of opportunities. I rejoiced about all the bounty that the new day would bring. I enjoyed caring for my family and my home, volunteering, and seeing my friends. My life may have been old fashioned and humdrum by today's standards, but I liked trying out a new recipe, weeding the garden, and texting my sons. What could be better? Well, one thing could be a lot better. I wanted to share my days with my husband too.

I aimed to be joyful. Most of my screen names and usernames contained some form of the word *joy* to remind me every day to be a positive person. I believed that something wonderful was always around the next corner. From a first grader who had daydreamed during reading circle and then discovered an exciting game on the playground to a shy teen who had bought an ice-cream cone and then flirted for the first time with the guy behind the counter, I'd always known that something thrilling would be around the next turn.

But now, my husband was newly retired, and some of my home responsibilities had eased up, as well. Yet my personal positivity was challenged. Was there really something amazing ahead for us at this point in our lives? I didn't even know how many miles or corners remained for us, let alone thrills.

Pud and I had been in harness for over thirty years, creating a home, raising a family, being responsible. After all that, I had to admit that I was bewildered by the way Pud and I were getting along now. Not only was Pud leaving me and heading to the golf course morning, afternoon, and early evening; even when he was at home, he was quiet and withdrawn. We didn't talk very much, and I didn't feel close to him. When he was away at the golf course, I was lonely. When he was home, I was even lonelier.

We seemed to be at a distance from each other. We were like people passing each other on a walk, smiling politely and saying nothing beyond "Hi," or like acquaintances waving across a busy restaurant. We were cordial but not close—and certainly not husband-and-wife close anymore.

Who was this stranger in my house? I suppose when Pud had been working and I had been more involved with my home and children, we had grown used to going our different ways. Pud had traveled so much for his job that we literally had been physically apart for much of the time. Had we also separated emotionally through the years?

I'd had high hopes that when Pud retired, we would have fun together. But what exactly should we do? Just take it easy and binge watch multiple TV seasons? Or have contests to see who could read the smallest print without reading glasses, or who could count his or her pills into the plastic compartments faster?

I didn't seriously expect that we would spend dreamy hours of bliss in twin hot tubs sighing at the ocean view like in the TV commercials, but I did crave some romance now that we had time together after the busy years. I yearned to hold hands as we smiled and looked deeply into each other's eyes. I desired to lovingly stroll together into our golden years. Pud was strolling, all right—hand in hand with a golf club.

Part of me understood that the guy had worked hard his whole life and certainly deserved the opportunity to indulge his golf passion, and I could even go so far as to say that I was glad he had something interesting to do and wasn't just hanging around the house with the retirement blues. Truth be told, we lived on a golf course, so I had to expect some golf. But the other part of me wasn't expecting golf to be a new forty-hour-a-week job.

The men's league was on Tuesday; Wednesday was a men's group at another course in town; Thursday, Pud and his buddies traveled to different courses around the state; and Friday, Saturday, and Sunday were mandatory golf days. What about me? What was I supposed to do? Sit on a bench at the clubhouse and wave as he made the turn?

Some of our friends assumed that I golfed and that I enjoyed golfing with Pud. Wrong on both counts. We'd attempted to hit the links together early in our marriage, but I was too much of a type A personality and competitive. Pud was just as type A as I was, and when I'd had trouble learning the game, he'd become an impatient teacher. I had been his frustrated student. Pud was a scratch golfer and relished the competition with his male buddies. I'd given up and decided that I had better things to do than spend four hours on a Saturday afternoon on a good walk spoiled.

It was time for me to get up, but the dream had left my thoughts swirling and careening like an out-of-control carousel. *Carousel? Oh, that was part of my bad dream too.* There was something about clowns leaning from carnival horses and waving signs as they went round and round.

What had the signs said? Pud, stay home! You can't make him stay home! *What should I do?* I needed to catch the brass ring of blissful married retirement. *Charlotte! You need to stop tormenting yourself. Take a deep breath, and think calmly.*

As I put on my T-shirt and jeans, I realized I wasn't the only wife in the world with these problems. One of my girlfriends had faced a similar scenario. A few weeks earlier, Pud and I had met Karen and her husband, Bill, for drinks, and they had described how they were preparing to be empty nesters. We'd howled as Karen had related how she had informed Bill that he needed to come up with activities to do together. After some thought, he'd suggested a nightly walk around the block. She'd scoffed and snorted. "He should have known that a sedate stroll would be too boring and bland for me."

"So did you agree on something to do together?" I'd asked.

"We ended up going to a pottery class, and we are making an entire set of dinnerware. I designed the plates," Karen had said.

Bill had added, "I can actually throw clay now. I am making the bowls, and it took me four weeks to make two bowls that were actually the same size." He'd cupped his hands to show me the size variations he had experienced during his learning curve.

"How many bowls have you finished?" I'd asked with interest.

"Just the two."

I must have looked puzzled.

"So far."

I wondered if the solution to a happy retirement was for Pud and me to develop a joint hobby like Karen and Bill had. I doubted that pottery would get my husband excited, and we already walked around the block with the dog every evening. I remembered that a community education course catalog from a local school district was lying in a pile of catalogs and ad flyers on our kitchen table. I could leaf through the fall semester offerings to see if there was a class that Pud and I might like to take together.

I stopped pondering and moping. I still hadn't found the solution to my retirement blues, but it was time I started my morning and acted like my user name was *joy* and not *complain*. My nightmare of Pud leaving me still lingered and darkened my day, but I pressed on.

I switched my mind to my chores. I made the bed and walked to our kitchen, poured a cup of coffee, and left it to cool while I headed to the laundry room. I began the process of herding the laundry from washer to dryer while I also planned my grocery list. Pud was in the kitchen, viewing the credit card bill on his computer. I was surprised he was still home. I thought he would have left to golf by now. As I climbed over the dog and passed Pud with my clothes basket, he turned to me and said, "Um, last night with Dan and Mark went well, I thought."

I glanced his way, nodded my agreement, and almost walked on, involved with my own concerns, but then I stopped and realized that Pud had actually spoken to me in a conversational tone. Most of our talks these days were terse queries: "Did you get the mail?" "Did you remember to renew your license?" But this morning, Pud sounded friendlier.

I turned to him with a smile. At the time, this seemed to be a simple break in my organized routine, like catching the momentary flash of a darting indigo bunting out of the corner of my eye, quickly forgotten. Later, I would learn that our chat was not routine or merely a serendipitous day brightener but the seed of something special.

"Yes," I agreed. "Dinner was delightful. I had fun with you." I stopped myself before I added, "About time we did something together."

Dan and Mark were our landscaping team. They had finished a big backyard project for us. We had taken them out to eat at a nice restaurant in downtown Cleveland to celebrate the project and to let them know that we appreciated them as responsible and talented young men.

"They have been so diligent and creative about our patio project. It was a big job, so it was nice to thank them. I enjoy encouraging young people, don't you?" I shifted the laundry basket to my other hip and then, caught up in the conversation, I put it down.

"Oakley, uh, do you need to go out? Mom, the dog baby says she has to go potty."

"What? Okay, Oakley. How is my beautiful Mrs. Pet Dog? I'll let you out, my sweetie." Oakley the dog was the most beautiful and loving beast in the whole world. She was a large, sturdy retriever mix with fluffy golden-and-white fur, bright chocolate eyes, a tail that thumped love and joy with each beat, and a smile that melted my heart.

"Pud, it's a new world for you and me, having time together to do special things like that," I continued. I let Oakley back in, and she leaned against me as I gave her a welcoming pet.

Although it developed slowly, this talk turned into a both-of-us-talking-at-once chat. An animated conversation was a gift I loved to receive from Pud. Our exchanges stalled when he didn't answer or when he responded with a nod, sigh, and a slight compression of his lips. Other times, he tuned me out while he shouted his wisdom to the television commentators. Pud had never been a chatterbox, but our retirement communication had dwindled to the intermittent static and blurts of a distant AM radio station.

This particular morning, our signals were tuned to the right frequency. We laughed and relived the dinner we had relished with our young friends. Pud seemed to enjoy our spirited and good-natured chat. And, as we would discover, our conversation would lead to many more rollicking activities.

"I wish our boys would join us sometime. They would have liked that steak place we went to last night," I added. I was proud of our young adult sons, but at times, I missed their boyhood days when they had been part of every family happening. Our two were my alpha and omega, literally my *A* to *Z*; our older son was August, and our younger boy was Zimmer. August recently had graduated from college and stayed busy with his first career job. He lived in Cleveland near his work but stopped by our house during the week or on the weekends, mainly with his laundry or to get together with his local friends. Zimmer was still in college but currently had left the nest and journeyed to Australia for an internship.

"Well, uh, they'll never go out to eat with us," stated Pud emphatically like a judge pronouncing sentence. "Did you, uh, remember to mail in the car registration? And why are the Fergusons getting a divorce?"

"What? I thought we were talking about last night," I said. "I enjoyed hearing about Dan's job and goals for his landscaping business. I really like the idea of us being positive and encouraging, and it's fun to share a special meal."

"What special meal? I thought we weren't, uh, going to cook tonight."

"We can make something if you want to. I meant our dinner out with Dan and Mark, the landscaping guys. I enjoyed taking them out to eat and getting to know them better."

I returned to my laundry staging area. I assumed we were done chatting. I squinted at the symbols on the dryer, decoding an appropriate cycle for Pud's shirts. Since he retired, he wore golf shirts every day. He decided to save money by washing his own shirts and eliminating the dry-cleaning bills—except I was the one who generally washed them. I selected the washing cycle and temperature and put in the fabric softener. I opened the dryer and felt to see if that load was finished. With all my clanking and concentrating, I missed Pud's grand pronouncement.

"I have an idea."

2

The Lightbulb

Pud's given name was Stewart; he had been named after his dad. He'd begun life as Junior, but on a trip to visit his grandma, his name had been changed forever to the nickname *Pud*, short for *Pudding*. The family story was that little Junior had been sitting at the top of the stairs at Grandma's house, and Grandma had caught him ready to throw an antique music box. She'd loved his cute little chubby face, so she'd called to him, "Junior, my sweet, widdle pudding, don't throw Grandma's box, pudding dear!"

Stewart Junior had thrown the prized object despite Grandma's tender pleas. His older brother and sister had hooted about the name Pudding and begun teasing and taunting "widdle pudding." The name Pudding—or Pud for short—had stuck, so I guess that was his punishment for throwing the clock.

Pud still fit him as an adult. He had an open, friendly face, and he was the kind of guy that people adopted as an extra son or brother. But he was not a jiggly pudding. His beliefs about how to live a correct life were solid and black and white, with zero shades of gray. He was dependable with a big dose of common sense.

Pud had left his computer and switched on the business channel when I came back to the family room. "Did I hear you shout something? Or what's wrong? I was back in the laundry room."

"I didn't say anything. Oh, wait. I forget. Oh, now I remember. I had an idea. It was something about us, about us eating out. I have to get going soon and meet Sam at the clubhouse; we are getting our grips checked."

I moved the coupon junk mail off the kitchen table, set aside the continuing-ed flyer, and folded the towels that I had taken from the dryer. We had a small laundry room, so it worked best to fold things on the kitchen table. "Okay, well, if you have time, I would like to hear your idea."

I kept folding, and Pud got up and turned off the TV and rounded up his cell phone and keys. "Oh, I know what it was. Why don't we keep on going out to eat? We can invite other people. We can take out your niece and nephew, your sister's kids, whatever their names are, for dinner."

"What did you say? You mean Robin and Chester?"

"Uh, that's what I already told you. Let's take Robin and what's her husband's name out to a nice place like we did with the landscaping guys."

"Would we go to Cincinnati? Robin and Chester? Or would we take them out when they came home to visit?"

Pud put on his jacket and red cap and walked out the door. "We can go there, if you want. Make a little trip out of it," he called back to me.

I realized that Pud had left without kissing me or saying good-bye. I ran out to the garage and yelled as he drove his golf cart away, "I would love to go to Cincy and see Robin and Chester! You had a great idea!"

As I went about my day and trimmed my to-do list, I continued to think about Pud's idea. His idea germinated in my mind and sprouted other ideas. I didn't even mind being by myself all afternoon. I thought about my family and not about scary, taunting clowns.

I'd grown up in northeast Ohio, in Akron, "the Rubber Capital of the World." Pud and I now lived about twenty miles from where I had been born. We resided south of a small town in a quiet, well-appointed development. The streets in our neighborhood wound around a clubhouse, pool, and golf course. Large, contemporary, two-story homes with fabricated stucco and stone predominated. The dwellings mirrored the personality and characteristics of their owners, our place included. The houses, like their inhabitants, were well made, solid, and pleasing, but not glamorous or trend setting.

Pud had moved a bit farther from his childhood home than I had. He'd grown up in a tiny crossroads town in western Ohio. People in other parts of the country assumed that Ohio was mainly farmland, and that indeed was the Ohio where Pud had grown up, the heart of farm and 4-H country. After college, Pud had moved near Akron and begun his first job at a sports marketing group. Because he possessed and enjoyed advanced math skills, he'd created a niche for himself, handling analytics and data. Through the years, he'd specialized even deeper into tire metrics and found a perfect fit for his love of numbers and sports in auto racing. His passion and his career had focused on consulting with race teams.

Cleveland was the nearest big city. We had the benefits of living in the suburbs but with easy access to the arts, sports, and fine dining that a larger city offered. Not to be outdone by Akron, Cleveland billed itself as "the best location in the nation." I wasn't sure that America agreed with that assessment anymore, and we all complained about the snow, cold, and dreary days, but our less-than-ideal weather and average scenery made it easy to find loads of better choices when we wanted to vacation. The mantra of northeast Ohio was, "There are no hurricanes, forest fires, or avalanches." There were also no palm trees or mountain vistas, but we did have green grass, trees, and valleys and places to hike, changing seasons, and Lake Erie.

Pud and I had moved to our present home when our boys had been ages six and nine. By that time, I had left my position as a legal contract writer with a health benefits company to be a SOM, a stay-at-home mom. The busy years of Little League, Scouts, choir, piano lessons, school sports, homework, and school had begun here and been augmented by swimming, fishing, and playing with friends. It had been a safe and tranquil place for the boys to grow up. A lady up the street had lamented that civilized neighborhoods were tough on raucous, untamed boys. I'd agreed, but I had hedged my bets by choosing our house by a home with four boys, three of them triplets. Who would notice my two boys swinging on the lamppost?

Oakley the dog came and snuggled by me as I ate my lunch. She wanted a bite of my ham sandwich, but I think she wanted company too. She licked up some errant bread crumbs and ran and got her bone and brought it back. I gave her a bite of my sandwich.

"I'm a good mommy, aren't I, Oakley sweetie?"

I gave her a big hug. She was such a good buddy.

I finished lunch and then buckled down and paid the bills. Some were online payments, but for some, I had to track down stamps and envelopes. I took them down to the mailbox and waved to my neighbor as she pulled down her driveway.

The fresh air was invigorating, and I decided to make a cup of chai tea, sit outside, and look through a magazine for decorating ideas. Oakley and I plodded back to the house, and I dropped off the junk mail in the trash can. I made my tea and settled outside. I inhaled the lovely aroma and considered the neighbor I had just seen. I didn't see anyone on our street much anymore except coming and going.

Oakley and I snuggled on the lounge chair. When we'd first moved here, all the houses on our street were being built and settled at the same time. We neighbor ladies had bonded while our kids played. We'd gone for walks and relaxed at the pool together for hours while our kids had had splash contests and cannonball fights. In the evenings, we'd gotten together for wine and chatted until the husbands had come home late from work.

But now, fifteen years later, the kids were leaving for college and jobs, the husbands' careers were winding down, and some couples went south for the winter or moved away permanently. New neighbors, almost a generation younger, took their place. The neighborhood picnics and block parties dwindled and stopped. We nodded to folks in passing, no longer sharing confidences and struggles. A gal up the street waved to me every time she drove by, but she'd never stopped to tell me that she was driving to chemo treatments. I'd found out she was ill from her social-media site.

When the boys had been young, some days had been happy and some days had been cranky and filled with shouting and arguments, but each day I'd tried to do something good and positive for my kids. We'd gone to children's museums or browsed at toy stores, visited farms and fairs, and driven around and followed a blimp. At home, we'd grown lima beans in glasses, crafted T-shirts with puffy paint for Father's Day, dumped vinegar and baking soda in science experiments, and baked cookies and sprinkled the entire kitchen.

"A penny for your thoughts, and I think you need to be drinking something stronger."

"Uh, what? Oh, hey there, Nicki."

Nicki was my next-door neighbor and truly was a rocket scientist. She was a physicist who worked at NASA near the Cleveland airport. She was also skinny, blonde, and perkily pretty.

"It's so good to see you," I said. "How have you been? And yes, let me get us something stronger."

"I can just stay a few minutes," Nicki said. "I came home from work early because the girls are coming back from college, and I wanted to get things ready. I saw you sitting here looking glum, so I decided to come give you a kick in the—"

"White or red?" I asked. "Or both?"

I brought out some glasses and two bottles. Oakley and Nicki's dog were prancing around together in the green space between our yards. "You picked a good day to come home. It's getting really nice out—must be at least seventy. So how are your girls?"

We settled down with our glasses and got caught up with each other's families. Then Nicki told me about the Fergusons.

"Did you hear they really are separated? Debbie found her high school lover boy through her social media, and now they are living together."

"Geez," I said. "Are you kidding?"

Nicki called the dogs back, and I poured us some more wine.

"So, Pud is retired now. Wow. How's that going?"

I gulped my wine. "You know, you caught me thinking about all that. I was sitting out here realizing how fast the years have gone, and now the kids are grown and retirement is finally here," I began.

"I knew you looked way too serious out here. That's why I came over."

"I'm so glad you did. Do you want some cheese? I'll get some in a minute. You know, when the boys left, I wasn't too sad to see those childhood days end, because I was satisfied it had all gone so well. I adored my kids when they were little, but now I am thrilled to see them graduate and take on the world. Don't you love it now that your girls are creating their own lives?"

Nicki followed me into the house. I put some blue cheese and brie on a plate, and we brought it back outside.

"I do love to see the girls thrive at college, but in all honesty, it's nice to have them away," Nicki said. "We were starting to clash. All they think about is boys. Now I have time for myself and for Ian."

"I hear you. I am not sure what to think about retirement. When the kids were at home, I was occupied with them, and you know how Pud traveled all the time. We lived separate lives. I looked forward to sharing more time with Pud once he retired, but all he does is golf. Pud might as well still be a thousand miles away on a trip."

"That's not all bad to have him out of the house."

"Ha! And another thing—we aren't close. I feel so distant from him. Not to get too weird with you, but we aren't romantic at all."

"Men! Sometimes they are animals; sometimes they are on another planet." Nicki gave me a hug. "The girls just texted, and they will be here soon, so I gotta go; I am running out of time to get things done, but good to see you!"

I hugged her back.

Oakley was asleep on the patio, and I decided to sit outside a few more minutes. The sun went behind some clouds, and the temperature and my mood cooled. I thought about Nicki. What had she said? She had to get going because she was running out of time?

Now I had too much time with my silent husband. We had nothing to talk about except bills and taxes and what day was trash day. Pud loved his golf. I wondered if he still loved me.

I had fantasized about languid hours of afternoon delight. Well, we were getting older; maybe I should be happy with an afternoon nap together. I put down my glass and magazine. I wasn't focusing on the bathroom design tips. To be fair to Pud, I was naive to think he would spend every moment with me. I didn't want every hour to be together, but I longed for his companionship and attention.

I carried the wineglasses in and put them in the dishwasher. Oakley barked. Pud opened the door and yelled in that he was going to mow the lawn. I shouted, "Okay!" as the door slammed behind him. Pud was a fastidious mower. His stripes in the grass, whether horizontal, vertical, or diagonal, rivaled a professional baseball field. I had to give him credit for taking care of our yard.

My mood brightened as I cooked. I was looking forward to sitting across the table from Pud at dinner. I wouldn't have to search for conversational tidbits tonight; I was excited to talk to him about our Cincinnati plans. Planning a trip should give us enough to talk about to get through dinner.

Pud finished the mowing and came in and washed up for dinner. He greeted the dog but didn't say anything to me as he passed me in the kitchen. Maybe I needed to jump and twirl in circles for him like Oakley did.

I put the scalloped potatoes and meatloaf on the table. We served ourselves. "Thanks for mowing the lawn. It looks beautiful."

"Yes, the fertilizer seems to, uh, be working."

We passed the salt to each other. "Golf was good?"

"Yes, I beat Sam and had nine pars, four birdies, and three bogies and two double bogies. I hit my ball in the water on seventeen, or I would have had a par."

We lapsed into silence. I dropped my fork, and the noise startled us. I remembered to get the mixed vegetables out of the microwave. Pud left the table. Was he done all ready? He really didn't want to spend any time with me.

I called to him, "Pud, I thought more about your idea of going to Cincinnati."

"I was downstairs getting wine; I'm coming. What did you say?"

"Oh, wine sounds good. I was saying how much I liked your idea about visiting Cincinnati, so what do you think of adding to it? Why don't we keep it going? Now that all the nephews and nieces are getting older, we can get to know them as adults, as friends, instead of as a pile of children on the couch that don't talk to us at Christmas. Let's get to know all of them."

"Uh, we don't know them? What did you say? I don't get it."

"You had a great idea to take Robin and Chester out to dinner. I was thinking, let's *get to know* all of them. Let's get beyond the polite visiting at the holidays and get closer to all the nieces and nephews."

Pud rummaged through the drawer for the corkscrew. I reached around him and found it for him.

"Do you want some wine?" he asked.

"Yes, but just a little. I had some already when Nicki stopped by," I said.

"Who? Oh, Nicki from next door?"

"Yes, but I want to talk about your idea. I think it will be really neat to visit Robin and Chester. But let's keep on going. Why don't we make the rounds this year and take all the young cousins out for a special evening? They are all young and trying hard, and it would be so much fun to treat them to a gourmet meal."

"Okay, sounds good. So, what are you thinking? This Napa Valley cab is really good."

My sister, Sibby, had three children, and her new husband, George, had two children, so there were five altogether that we called the "young cousins."

"Well," I continued, "we have five young nieces and nephews and their significant others, right? We can plan to visit each of them. Let's try to do it all this year. How cool will it be to show them all how much we love them by treating them to a fabulous meal?"

"Fine with me. Oakley, is it okay with you? Let's see if we can fit everyone in this year. We would start with Robin and Chester in Cincinnati, right?" said Pud. "I think we are pretty busy until fall."

"This is such a great idea. Good job, Pud."

"We could schedule the Cincinnati trip for October," Pud continued. "The last tournament is in September, and there may be a few good weeks to golf, but by October, they are doing course maintenance, and by November, the course will be closed. I, uh, forget where everyone else lives."

I ignored the importance of golf in our schedule. "Well,

Annie goes to college near Chicago, and Lindsey and Erik live right in Chicago, so we can hopefully see them together. I suppose we'd want to go there in nicer weather, so maybe the spring, unless there was a break in the winter weather and we could drive to Chicago in February. After Chicago, we can see Buddy in Indiana, and I am not sure what Byron is doing."

Then we both remembered at the same time. "Oh, we have our big trip to Marco Island scheduled for this winter too!"

After Pud had picked his retirement date, we'd decided to plan a special celebration getaway. Friends had told us that they loved the Marco Island and Naples area, and the beaches, warm weather, and upscale dining and ambience had seemed like a perfect fit for us. The trip was a reward for both of us. Pud had successfully completed his career, and I couldn't wait to leave my household routine and savor a luxurious time with him.

We examined our calendar again and made sure we picked a free weekend for our adventure to Cincinnati.

Pud asked, "So we will be taking them out to eat, right?"

"Yes. Let's go to the best place in town. We want them to feel loved and wanted, and you know what that means to us—the best food and wine, fine dining!"

Silence.

"Does that sound okay? We take them out to the best place we can find?"

Pud nodded.

"This is going to be such a great way to get to know Robin and Chester as adults, as friends. They aren't little kids anymore sitting at the little kids' table that we just ask the obligatory 'how is school going?'"

Pud nodded again and looked at his social-media account on his phone.

"One more thing. We are going to be warm and welcoming, positive, and encouraging."

Pud rolled his eyes. "Sounds good, Mom. Oakley says it sounds good."

"Okay, I have to think of a name for our project. You know how I like to give my goals a formal name. It makes it seem real and important to me," I said.

"Do you want some more wine, and, uh, um, did you feed the dog?" asked Pud.

"Yes, and I might as well strike while the iron is hot. Before I forget, I will text Robin and get our first trip set up," I said.

I texted:

> Hi Robin and Chester—how are you?!?! We are planning our autumn fun and were thinking we would like to take a trip to Cincy and see you!!!! We will stay at a hotel and take you both out for a snazzy dinner!! Thinking about early October. Thoughts?!?! Ly!!! Auntie Charli and Uncle Pud

I hit send, finished my wine, and wondered what would happen. The text reply dinged. I dropped my phone and then grabbed it and clicked it open, reading:

> Hi! We're doing well! I'm currently preparing for a big exam on Wednesday which is always fun. But we would love that!

As Pud, the retired race-tire engineer and analyst, would say, "The wheels are spinning. Here's where the rubber meets the road." A few more texts confirmed that

Robin and Chester were indeed up for a visit from us. We set a date in early October without any trouble. We launched Project RSVP, as I had decided to call it. Our goal was to build camaraderie with our family's young adults.

Pud and I smiled at each other. We smiled at each other! Our early morning routine chat in between laundry and golf had sparked Pud's great idea. By evening, we had set on the course of getting to know all the young cousins better. We would support and encourage them. We had contacted Robin and Chester and confirmed the first date. We smiled at each other once again and finished our wine with a satisfied glow.

3

Press On

When I had been seventeen, I'd plunged into the world of commerce. After years of babysitting, I had been hired for my first real job. I'd worked the lunch hour, the rush, at our local fast-food stand, famous for its golden arches. Those were the days of twenty-five-cent hamburgers and shakes, before wraps, premium sandwiches, and lattes. Those were also the days that I made a $1.10 per hour.

It was my first experience with how a business was organized and operated. I enjoyed learning all the rules, such as greeting and thanking the customer for coming and remembering to "suggestive sell." I learned how to scrape out the huge cans of ketchup before they were discarded. Every tablespoon of sauce saved affected the bottom line, multiplied by thousands of stores every day. I even liked using the time card. Crew members were required to watch training tapes during breaks. I believe I was the only worker who looked forward to the tapes.

The lunch shift was also my first time dealing with people who weren't my family, friends, or familiar faces. The older workers had laughed at me on my first day as I'd fought the shake machine; I'd splattered everyone, but I'd stayed upbeat and decided to focus on the positives. My coworkers had been people to get to know and new lifestyles and values to consider.

One day at a crew meeting, my McDonald's manager had distributed a notice on parchment paper to everyone:

> Nothing in this world can take the place of persistence. Talent will not; nothing is more common than unsuccessful people with talent. Genius will not; unrewarded genius is almost a proverb. Education will not; the world is full of educated derelicts. Persistence and determination alone are omnipotent. The slogan "press on" has solved and always will solve the problems of the human race.
>
> —Calvin Coolidge

I couldn't remember why the manager had given this to us. It might have been his holiday present. This inspirational quote changed my life. The idea that personal persistence had a direct effect on outcomes, that I could plan to succeed, had been a bombshell launched into my docile and dependent life. I'd once worried that I lacked skills—I couldn't sing or sew—but now I'd realized that determination could be a vital talent. I'd decided that I would press on. Class by class, I'd finished college and law school, and I'd focused on faithfully completing small steps and goals in my law career too. My ability to organize and focus had enhanced my contract-writing skills, and when I'd moved on to my motherhood career, my attention to detail had enhanced those eyes in the back of my head, as well.

As I'd grown older, I'd learned that persistence worked just as well for all the mundane tasks that cropped up in everyday life. Bit by bit, a whole driveway could be cleaned of snow, a mountain of laundry could be washed and folded, or two hundred daffodil bulbs could be planted. Persistence had led to resolve, and my fortitude and determination muscles had grown stronger.

Even in my new retirement life, I'd discovered that being scheduled and organized was satisfying. After my morning coffee and news check on my tablet, I did the time-sensitive work first, mainly for the nonprofit boards I served on. I finished a report, scheduled appointments, or returned calls and e-mails. I moved on to housecleaning, or as my mother used to say, "ready up the house," followed by a coffee break, and then on to errands, such as the grocery store. I accomplished this by lunchtime.

Then in the afternoon, I tackled a bigger ongoing project. My current major task was to clean out closets and the basement. I didn't want to leave the boys with a big mess when I died. I announced my daily goals and schedule to whomever happened to be around the house. Pud didn't listen to me, and if the boys ever took note, they did that eye-roll thing when I reviewed the day's campaign.

I was halfway through my morning schedule when I heard a muffled roar and realized it was Pud. He seemed to be shouting from far away. I was in our closet sorting through my winter clothes and reviewing what I wanted to take on our upcoming trip to Cincinnati and then Marco Island. I walked toward the Pud pandemonium with an old Christmas turtleneck decked with holly and drunken reindeer halfway on, stuck at my nose and eyes. I bumped into him, and he yelled, "You scared me! I almost spilled my Coke!"

"Where were you, and what were you yelling about?"

"The garage. Oh, uh, I couldn't get the caps off my golf cart batteries, and I remembered something I wanted to tell you."

"Okay, what was it? I was back in our closet."

"Well, now I … now I forget. Just a minute. I have to go to the bathroom."

"Okay, I'll wait for you," I said.

Ah, forgetting … the bane of old people. Retirement was different from the other life milestones. The earlier markers had been self-explanatory—graduation, followed by all the firsts: job, career, marriage, home, children, and busy lives. I'd looked forward to the blessings of each waypoint, and I'd known what to do.

But I didn't know the script for the golden years. What was expected of me? Was the retirement I shared with Pud nothing more than the penultimate milestone, the B roll before the end? Years filled with forgetting things and running to the bathroom all the time? I realized what the final alternative was, but looking forward to silver-hair shampoos and hernia surgery didn't compare to dreaming about courtship and family life. I wanted this period of life to be exciting, just like the previous markers of life.

We tried to joke about getting old with our nonretired friends. "How are you doing now?" they asked.

"Fine, for old people," we replied. When we said that, we wanted the response to be "No, you aren't old! Ha-ha! Why would you say that?"

But they didn't laugh incredulously like we expected. Our friends didn't disagree with our age assessment at all.

Instead, they looked at us, puzzled, and lamely mumbled, "Well, as long as you're having fun!" Then they continued, "What's it like having Pud underfoot? Bet you can't wait to get him out of the house. He'll have to get a job as one of those greeters with a red vest." I had to face it; everyone thought we were officially old.

I didn't hear Pud come back; I was so wrapped up in my own thoughts. I was also wrapped up in my turtleneck. I tugged it down so I could breathe, gulped, and then said, "I was in the closet sorting through seasonal clothes and also trying to decide what to take on our road trip next weekend."

"What, uh, road trip?"

"The one to see Robin and Chester in Cincy! Next weekend! *Remember?*"

Thanks to the Internet, our plans for our Cincinnati trip were in place. A few nights earlier, we'd poured our wine and spent the evening cuddled by the computer, plotting our reservations. Pud had divided the duties.

"I will look up hotels on the computer, and you can use your restaurant app on your tablet to find a restaurant." He'd clicked away. "There are six Hywet Hotels places in Cincinnati."

We used Hywet Hotels because we saved their reward points.

"Do you know Robin's address so we can see which is the closest?" he'd asked.

I'd looked it up. "Show me on the map where they live, and I can keep that in mind when I look for restaurants."

"How about the Cityscape? It looks like it's 3.4 miles from their place. See? It's south off the highway."

"It looks north to me."

"No, *no!*" Pud had yelled. "See? It's right here. North! It will be easy to get to their place."

"Oh, okay. You said *south*."

"No, I didn't," had been his exasperated reply.

"Okay, I finally got the restaurant app to work. Here is a four-dollar-sign place that features steak, fish, and sushi, and it looks like it has a great wine list. Here's the location. Do you think it's in the right area?"

"Let me see." Pud hadn't had his glasses on, so he'd squinted mightily. "Looks like it's twenty-eight minutes from their apartment. Too far."

I'd looked. "No, it says twenty-three minutes."

"I can't see without my glasses."

"I understand. No biggie. We are doing pretty well with our plans. Here are a few more with three dollar signs or four dollar signs and over one hundred five-star reviews. I'll e-mail Robin and Chester and give them some choices."

We'd experienced spurts of crankiness, but overall, our planning time had been enjoyable, and we'd finished our reservations and our wine in good spirits.

Now that Pud was on track with the weekend plans, I left him to his golf chores in the garage. I took my turtleneck back to our bedroom and tossed it in the charity bag. I gave up on three pairs of jeans that were too snug. I decided to save the purging of shoes and purses for another day.

I made a cup of coffee, cinnamon dolce, and stepped out to relax on our patio. The day was mild enough when the clouds let the sun take center stage, and the lounge-chair cushions had almost dried out from the latest rain. My favorite plant, the Harry Lauder's walking stick, was especially full and gnarly, and as I looked up, the gentle birch trees tickled the passing clouds.

Our big, fluffy yellow dog ran up and shook her bone at me. I grabbed her ears and scratched her ruff. I loved her big, sparkly brown eyes, pudgy brown nose, floppy ears, and merry demeanor. She had been a short timer at the animal pound when we'd adopted her. In fact, she had been at her expiration date.

Oakley had proved my premise that nice surprises were always right around the corner. One day, I'd had the urge to get a dog, and I'd found her picture on the county animal shelter's website. Zimmer was always in the mood for a new pet, so he'd gone to the pound to check. An hour later, he'd come back, and a seventy-five-pound, untrained but very enthusiastic beast had bounded into the house and out the open sliding door.

We'd panicked. "Oh no, she's gone! Why didn't you keep her on the leash?"

"I did!" Zim had insisted. "She's so strong she broke the dang clip when she pulled."

"Call her!" I'd yelled.

"Mom, we haven't even named her yet!"

He'd anxiously gone outside to search for the dog, and in no time, he'd found her happily sitting on our front porch, joyously waiting to be let back in the house. She hadn't run away!

"Good girl!" Zim had said as he'd opened the door, and the dog had shot into the family room, jumped over the couch, and knocked me down. It had been love at first sight for all of us.

Pud walked around the corner and found us. "Oakley, are you and, um, uh, Mom sunbathing together?"

"Yes, for a minute, and then we are going for a walk. Are you heading off to the golf course? Have fun."

"I will. I plan to use the trimmer this afternoon. So, uh, will you remind me to go get more oil for the mower?" With a wave and an air kiss, he zoomed out on his golf cart.

It was so relaxing, sipping my coffee and watching

Oakley snuffle her soccer ball around the yard. We wouldn't have many more nice days to enjoy outside. I took a minute to go over the plans for the weekend. I looked forward to seeing Robin and Chester and going on a road trip with Pud.

I had always enjoyed getting to know people, making time to learn about their lives, listen to their problems, and then laugh or cry together. Sort of like my mom. For years, every time we'd gone to the mall together, we'd lingered at the cashier stand, as a clerk, no longer a stranger but now a bosom buddy, had poured out her heart to my mother. Mom had held many a friendly therapy session with saleswomen, ladies ahead of us in line, and people walking through the door with us at the department store entrance. I'd always groaned impatiently, wanting to get to the jeans department. Now I appreciated the satisfaction that comes in connecting with others.

I hoped that we would have a positive time with our niece and nephew. Young people faced so many challenges now, finding jobs and living in these expensive times. Robin and Chester were newly married and trying hard, and I wanted to treat them to a fun evening.

I had known my niece Robin and her siblings their whole lives. I had been there for all the birthdays, holidays, and school events, but at family gatherings, the kids had played with each other, and Sibby and I and the other grown-ups in the family had camped out in the kitchen and gossiped and visited. I knew them as "the kids," but I didn't have a real relationship with Robin and the others.

Pud and I would now get to know Robin and Chester and the other "cousins," as we called my sister's kids, as individuals. What would we have in common? Would Pud have a good time? I knew he would enjoy the dining part of the trip, but he could be impatient and so rigid in his thinking. He enjoyed arguing and playing the devil's advocate, and he delighted in skewering wimpy, half-baked beliefs, especially ideas developed after 1950. Could he relate to Robin and Chester? I wanted this visit to be a positive show of love to our family, and I prayed it would be a success. I also wondered if our time together would be a step in thawing out the chilly feelings between Pud and me.

Oakley wanted Mom to go inside, so I finished my coffee, and we walked through the backyard and into the house to finish our chores. Pud would be out golfing for three to four hours. I liked to be home to greet him. I had time to pick out my clothes for the special Robin and Chester weekend.

"Then, Oakley, we can fit in a walk."

As we hurried back in the kitchen, both of us tried to squeeze through the door at the same. The dog romped, and her tail swiped the jars and bags of dried beans that I had out on the kitchen table. I had forgotten they were still there. That had been yesterday's project: to put dried beans and various lentils into mason jars to decorate the kitchen counter. Now all the bean types were mixed up on the table and floor. I would have to sweep up and sort all the beans.

"Oh, well, nothing like persistence," I told Oakley as I gave her a love pat.

4

Cheers!

Whenever I went on a road trip, I remembered the story of the box. The boys had been little, and we had been headed to the grandparents' for Christmas on a rainy, gray day on a bleak county road. Suddenly, up ahead, we'd all seen something tan and small in the middle of the road; it had crouched on the centerline. As we'd come closer, Pud had shouted, "That damn cat needs to get off the road!"

At the same time, the boys had shouted from the backseat, "Watch out for the cat!"

I'd looked up, gasped, and shrieked, "You're going to hit the cat!" We'd shuddered as we'd watched the creature start to run across the road.

It wasn't until we'd been a whisker away from hitting the unfortunate animal that we'd all realized it was a cardboard box. In the rain, the wet shape had looked remarkably like a moving feline. It had been like one of those word or drawing puzzles, where if you looked at it one way, it was a cat, and then your mind could see it another way as an ordinary brown box. We still laughed about Dad and his cardboard-box cat.

Now it was another drizzling, gray day, and Pud and I were packed and ready to start our road trip to Cincinnati. The big weekend was here! As we headed to the highway, we passed Pud's golf course, and he looked to see if any hardy golfers were starting a round.

Pud said, "Uh, at least it's raining this morning; should be, should be okay to golf tomorrow when we get back." But what I heard was, "I would rather be golfing." Was golf always number one in his life?

"Do we have everything?" I replied evenly.

"Yep, yep. It's all in the back."

We drove past the farm 'n' feed store that looked like a fun place to stop and browse, except I always forgot about it as soon as we passed.

"Well, we should have a nice drive down. What is it, about three hours? And that will give us time to have a little happy hour in our room before the evening begins," I said.

"Happy hour. Oh darn. We, uh, forgot to pack the wine. Should I turn around?"

We turned around. Our neighbors probably chuckled at how we always had to return for something. I joked with our boys not to immediately fire up the meth lab when we left the house, because we would be back within ten minutes and would catch them in the act.

Pud ran in and grabbed the wine bottle; fortunately, he found it on his own, and we were on our way again. We both noted the ambient temperature, thirty-six degrees Fahrenheit, and then turned on the 1940s channel on the satellite radio.

"So tell me again: what are Robin and … you know, whatever her husband's name is … doing? Does he have a job? And is, uh, Robin finishing her first year?"

"Chester. Chester has been working at his media job for I think about six months now. Robin has finished two years at pharmacy school. I think this is her last year of classes, and then she begins internships next year. This will all be good to ask them tonight."

We spied a blue rest stop area sign. Pud looked at me. "Should we stop?"

"What's our motto? Never pass up a bathroom."

Back on the road, Pud told me to watch for a bridge that he remembered had a pretty view of a valley. He also pointed out cows, a hawk flying, corn that was still standing, and slow trucks in his way. We saw a police car with lights on pull over a car on the northbound side of the highway.

"There's someone who's having a bad day," noted Pud. Pud always said that when he saw someone pulled over. "Look, the odometer is 31031.0!" he added.

I told him about my thoughts for Christmas presents for the boys, and he said, "I need to check on my, uh, Medicare."

Deciding that it was better to ride quietly and ponder my own thoughts, I dozed awhile.

I opened my eyes when Pud said, "Look!" A truck on the opposite side of the highway rolled by carrying a huge windmill blade. We always seemed to see at least one blade on a road trip. We had met our quota and could check that off the day's list.

I asked Pud, "So, do you miss work?"

Silence. Pud was occupied reaching in his pockets, checking for his phone and wallet. He steered with his knees, which always alarmed me.

"Pud, do you miss work?"

"Oh, I miss the travel and working with the race teams. It was exciting to go to the track. But I don't miss going to the office."

"Well, think how many years you worked. Over forty years, right? I would imagine that you would really feel a loss."

"Forty-two years, three months, and twenty-one days."

"I'm sorry, what?"

"I didn't work forty years; it was forty-two years."

"Oh, right. So, retirement is okay?"

Pud fiddled with the GPS and dropped his sunglasses. He didn't answer me; he never could multitask.

We neared Cincinnati, and Pud said, "Look for the hotel. We are about a mile—"

The GPS lady interrupted, "In one mile, turn left. Your destination is on the right. In one-half mile, turn left. Your—"

"Okay, we get it!" I yelled. "What am I looking for?"

"Big Bush Suites," Pud said, and then he repeated louder, "Big Bush Suites."

"I don't see it."

"In one-quarter mile, turn left. Your destination is on your right."

"Where the hell is it?" muttered Pud. "We should be right at it."

"Recalculating."

We drove around the block. Pud groped for his phone. He looked at his e-mail and swerved into the next lane and back.

"Don't check your e-mail while you're driving," I said helpfully.

"I wanted to double-check our reservation."

"Recalculating. Turn left onto Gotham Parkway. Recalculating."

"Yes, we are staying at the Cityscape. Where is it?"

Long pause while I recalculated.

"Oh, I thought you said Big Bush Suites. I think there was a Cityscape back where we were."

We all recalculated. Pud made an illegal U-turn, and we raced back to our hotel. After some discussion as to what would be the best parking space—the GPS lady did not share an opinion—we parked and headed into the lobby. Fortunately, the couple ahead of us complied with Pud's unspoken directive to check in promptly, and we had our room keys in just a few minutes. The desk clerk made an extra effort to be friendly to Pud. He proudly told her that we were in town to take our niece and nephew out to dinner.

We rode up the elevator, and as was my custom, I turned the wrong way down the corridor. Pud took off the correct way, and I wrangled my suitcase, made a quick about-face, and trotted behind. Pud rested his arm on my shoulders as we settled into room 315. I was startled by his touch but welcomed the warmth. He was my hero, my dependable, good-looking guy that the ladies noticed. He was tall, a little stocky, with thinning hair, but he had blue eyes that still had their effect on me. And now, he was comforting me with his closeness.

"Oh, sorry I bumped you; I was trying to reach my backpack around my suitcase."

Oh. Well, maybe his embrace wasn't the start of an arousing moment, but it was still a connection. We arranged our suitcases, and Pud turned on the TV. I leafed through the *Welcome to Cincinnati—the Queen City* pamphlet and then dug out my e-reader.

"We have time for wine, I think. Okay?" Pud said.

As Pud opened our wine and found plastic cups in the bathroom for our happy hour, I called to him, "Remember on our honeymoon? We were out in Long Beach, and we were watching the football playoffs in the bar—"

"What are you, uh, saying? I can't hear you."

"Remember Long Beach, and we were watching the game, and there was a turnover near the goal line, and we got mad and thought our team had lost as usual, so we went back to our room because it was our honeymoon, and then somehow we realized that the game had gone into overtime, and we quickly threw our clothes back on and went back to the bar?"

"Hmmm, how do you get this Internet connected?"

Pud struggled with the Wi-Fi, and I tried to get organized. I looked over the little gift bag we had prepared for Robin and Chester. I hadn't originally planned to bring them a gift or anything more creative than candy, but the previous weekend, we had enjoyed the annual wine-dinner festivities at our dear friends' home. Along with other colleagues from the auto-racing world, we'd shared an extravagant evening of many courses of fine wine and small plates of gourmet food.

Our hosts had been the definition of hospitable and thoughtful entertainers, and they had presented each couple with a gift basket overflowing with items that reflected things they loved. We'd received a cornucopia of surprises; out of our bag had spilled a book, DVD, puzzle, popcorn, word game, candy, fine restaurant certificate, bow tie, ice-cream dots … so many imaginative items that reflected our hosts' passions.

This gift basket had given us such pleasure that I'd decided to create a similar gift of thoughtful fun for Robin and Chester. I'd put in some pumpkin-spiced candy corn, a candle that made crackling sounds, some sports memorabilia, gel pens, even a smiley-face scrubbing sponge. I made sure that the bag survived our trip, and I put it by my purse so I wouldn't forget to take it. Then I relaxed with my wine.

Soon it was time to get dressed. I had texted Robin that I would probably wear a maxi dress so she would know what I was wearing and would feel comfortable in her style choice. Besides being comfortable and body-friendly, I thought that a maxi dress would convey to the young couple that their old aunt was somewhat fashion conscious.

We sent an *on our way* text and headed out, exactly at the time we had planned. I once again turned the wrong way and rushed to catch up to Pud at the elevator. The GPS lady guided us very well this time. Robin and Chester lived in a newer, modern apartment complex with trees and grass, and each unit was only several stories high.

I texted:

> We're here!!

She replied:

> Do you want to come up and see our apt??? ☺ ☺

I texted back:

> We'd love to. How about after dinner?

Robin and Chester impressed us by coming down to our car right on time. They had previously gained points with us by all their prompt responses to our texts about our plans.

Robin was a willowy brunette with long, perfectly groomed straight hair. She was a lovely mixture of beauty and intelligence. She wore a white blouse, dark-washed jeans, and booties, along with a statement necklace. Chester was taller than Robin, sturdy, with short hair and a handsome, open, and intelligent face. He wore a plaid shirt and jeans.

We jumped out and hugged them and then hopped in the car. I nervously coaxed the conversation.

"Hi!"

"Hi!"

"It's so good to see you!"

"Good to see you!"

"We have been looking forward to our night out!"

"We have too!"

Pud asked, "How's work?"

"Fine!"

"You like it here in Cincinnati?"

"Yes!"

The four of us struggled with small talk on the way to the restaurant. Robin and Chester always gave polite, friendly answers, but as we headed to our table, I reminded myself to focus on making this a fun, light evening.

We had selected the restaurant, Embers, because—according to the dining app—it was upscale, and the menu featured sushi, steak, and pasta entrées. We had an easy drive, and the GPS lady accurately located the restaurant. We would have found it without her because the sign with the name Embers was well lit by flaming torches. *Fire torches, really?* I grimaced, hoping that the fire wasn't a sign of a tacky ambience.

Once at our table, I was pleased to see linen cloths and napkins and a lit candle in a globe. The waiter conducted the usual ritual.

"Hello. My name is Jason, and I will be your server tonight. Welcome to Embers. Roger and Matt will be assisting me. We are known for our steaks and sauces, and we have an extensive wine cellar. Would you prefer tap, still, or sparkling water? Let me get your water, and then I will be back to take your beverage orders and tell you about tonight's specials." He handed us billboard-sized menus.

We quietly occupied ourselves with our menu assignments, and as I searched my brain for something to say, Chester mentioned, "My friend and I are starting to explore scotch and whiskey." Cue the dancing girls, raise the curtain, blaze the spotlights, and drop the confetti. Our polite, sedate visit suddenly transformed into a showstopping evening.

I perked right up. "What a coincidence. I am learning about scotch too. The boys and I set up a bar, and we are exploring spirits now that they're of age. We just bought a bottle of some kind of eighteen-year scotch, I can't remember exactly. If you order some, will you let me have a sip?"

After I spoke, I realized that letting your old aunt sip your scotch might be unappetizing. But Chester took it in stride. "Hey, if you're buying it, I'd be glad to share it."

"Do you have a favorite scotch yet?" Pud asked.

"My friend and I are researching single and double malt, the types of barrels, and the length of the aging process," Chester said with a precise and clipped tone. "I like the smoky highlights, and he prefers the smoother nuances."

"Robin, are you interested in scotch too?"

"No, thanks; I am learning about wine. I don't drink very much."

Pud asked her, "Do you like white or red? We like either one, so I'll pick something out, and you can try it, if that's okay with you."

"I think I like white, but is that okay to have with steak?"

"We drink wine we like and don't worry about the food. I know of a white California wine you will like."

Jason returned, poured our tap water, and announced he was ready to take our drink orders.

"Ladies?"

I ordered a hot and dirty martini.

"We are all going to have chardonnay reserve. And I think my nephew wants a drink too."

"Very well, sir." He turned to Chester.

"Johnnie Walker Blue. On ice."

I felt a mixture of pride and horror when I heard Chester order Johnnie Walker Blue. We had seen it in other restaurants for fifty dollars a shot, but tonight it was merely forty. *Money well spent*, Pud and I signaled with our eyes and a smile.

We didn't leave Robin behind; she enjoyed the chardonnay reserve. And we didn't skimp on the menu—calamari, oysters Rockefeller, ahi tuna, shrimp cocktail, surf and turf, scallops, potatoes Diana, rolls, bread, ciabatta, and brioche. If Robin or Chester so much as looked at an item that passed by, we ordered it for them. We wanted to surpass their expectations; we aimed for a Christmas dinner and Thanksgiving bounty experience.

The quantity of food was surpassed by the amount of conversation. We relished the tastes and reveled in the sharing and discussions.

"Robin, when do you start your clinical … what did you call them? Clinical *rotations*?" I asked.

"Yes, clinical rotations. The school assigns me to seven, and I get to pick three more. I am trying to decide if I want a research, hospital, or retail setting."

Chester said, "We all comprehend that Robin possesses the requisite intelligence and drive to accomplish any endeavor." Chester definitely had a formal and precise side to him.

"Yes, but they each have pluses and minuses. Retail means I would have to work weekends and holidays. I am not sure if hospital work would allow me the time to start a family, and I don't know if research would be exciting."

"Are you going to stay in Cincinnati after you graduate?"

"We are contemplating Texas, Colorado, or California," Chester declaimed.

Pud shared the stories about how he got each of his seven holes in one. He related some of his glory days from the racing world. I shared my recipe for baked beans and hot-and-spicy chili. We all laughed about Annie, Robin's sister, and her obsession with corgis and gerbils. We joked, and we forgot who were in their twenties and who were the old people.

We continued with our scotch tastings. Chester graciously let me have a sip of the exalted Blue, as well as samples of his other trials, Glenfiddich fifteen-year single malt and Johnnie Walker Black Label blended scotch. Johnnie Blue was the smoothest, but we enjoyed the smokiness of one and the fruity and spicy notes of another.

He continued to educate us in his deliberate way, whether he was describing craft beers, Tennessee versus Kentucky whiskey, or his latest podcast about board games that he and a friend produced. "This year, I want to develop an app to enable spirits drinkers to record their favorites and maintain a descriptive inventory. There are apps for wine cellars and beers but not one for liquor, according to my research."

We delighted in his stories about life at his job. I introduced the work topic.

"I told my kids that work was work, and they should be serious on the job and not goof off."

"Not so much at my job," rejoined Chester. "We spent

last Friday afternoon playing Stack Pictionary. It was just like Pictionary, but every time you added a drawing clue, you had to stick another marker on the end of your marker, so after a few turns, guys were trying to draw with a stack of markers two feet long. And my work basically shuts down the whole month of December."

"Where exactly do you work, Chester? I never took off the whole month of December," remarked Pud.

"It's a new start-up IT and media consulting firm, and December is a slow month for contracts, what with the holidays."

I also enjoyed seeing how Robin and Chester interacted with each other. They seem attuned to each other without being clingy. It was sweet how Robin turned her head to gaze up at Chester as he expounded on topics. And Chester made sure to include Robin as he spoke.

We won the award for the liveliest and loudest table in the restaurant, as we generally talked and laughed all at once. The restaurant treated us to complimentary desserts, cheesecake, lava cake, and gelato. Our repast concluded with port for the gents and Grand Marnier for Robin and me.

Feeling very satisfied, we drove back to their apartment. I grew teary-eyed seeing their first "nest." Robin assured us that Chester had worked hard to clean their place while she'd worked at the pharmacy where she was interning, which earned applause from us. We met their darling, cashmere-like cat, Smoke.

We were shown their dry-erase board hanging in the kitchen. Robin and Chester used colored markers to keep track of important dates, a grocery list, and a running total of the month's budget. They told us that they planned to save extra in October and November, since December would be a more expensive month. Now, Pud was the one who was teary-eyed with pride over their capable abilities to handle the adult world.

I no longer needed to remind myself to stay positive and encouraging. Pud and I were so impressed with how well they were doing that our compliments became an avalanche of genuine praise.

After many hugs, and calls of "proud of you," "love you," and "see you at Thanksgiving," we headed back to our hotel, very happy and grateful for an evening that had been so much more than just eating, drinking, or running up a big tab. It was an investment, and we were thankful for the opportunity to start an enhanced relationship with Robin and Chester. The restaurant, Embers, had sparked the flame of bonding.

Before we arrived back at our hotel, I received a text from my sister:

> Talked with R and C. They couldn't stop raving about what a wonderful time they had and how much fun you are. R said several times that you were fun. Thanks!

I appreciated the kind words, and I shared the text with Pud. I chuckled because little did my sister know! It was easy to be fun with scotch and wine added to the entertainment factor. Why did she sound so surprised that we could be fun?

We tucked ourselves into the big king-sized bed and eased into the cloud-like comfort of the crisp white sheets and plush duvet.

Pud patted my leg and sighed. "Everything turned out fine."

"Thanks to your great idea!" I fluffed, tugged, and harmonized the placement of the duvet and pillows. By the time I sank down near him, he was asleep. I rolled over on my back to think.

When I thought of Pud, I still felt we were disconnected. But, I reflected, we had discovered something exciting around the next corner—the next couple of corners, actually. Pud's idea had led to the first corner: our plan to get to know all the young cousins. We'd pressed on and organized the trip to Cincinnati. Around that corner, we'd found a lovely evening of food and festivities with Robin and Chester. What would we encounter together around the next corner?

5

Trick or Treat

When autumn officially started, we were blessed with calm and sunny days, and we pretended it was still summer, but by late October, the gusty and chilly wind and the departing sun convinced us that fall held center stage, and winter waited in the wings. The stage set and scenery changed. We had enjoyed a summerlong fanfare of purples, oranges, yellows, and rose colors that mellowed to sepia as fall deepened.

Our neighborhood followed the rhythm of the seasons. Christmas was the main decorating event with white lights outlining houses and trees.

In the spring, the mailboxes sported flower baskets. Flags flew on patriotic days, and haystacks, scarecrows, and pumpkins appeared in the fall.

I ventured to the basement to excavate the Halloween decorations. I had to lift and move several boxes before I found the black-and-orange box. I looked over my basement shelves with dismay. How had so much stuff accumulated? I resolved to start to go through things one of these days.

I peeked into a box of old costumes. When August had been three, we'd joined a new playgroup, and the leader had called me and invited us to their Halloween party. Pud had been away for work, so I'd thought that a party with new friends would be a fun time for August, especially since it was the first Halloween he could really enjoy. I carefully wrote down the time and directions.

We got to work designing the costume. August loved machines, so we came up with the idea of a robot outfit. We found a box, cut out arm holes and a head hole, and glued on all kinds of junk—wallpaper and buttons and pop bottle lids and lights. When August put the box on, he transformed into a high-functioning and complex machine. My new robot walked, beeped, knocked over its milk, and hit the dog with a badminton racket. It was very lifelike.

The night of the party, we left on time and drove into town to the church where it was being held. It was rainy and hard to see, but I was puzzled that I couldn't spot any other cars, and there didn't seem to be any lights on in the building. We waited and drove around the building again and waited some more. My son the robot was chattering about kids and candy. Finally, I called the head of the group and found out that the party had been the night before. One of use had goofed about the date. So I had to tell August there was no party, after all, and he looked so cute in his costume. I was more disappointed than he was.

We left, and we were thirsty, so we stopped at a convenience store. The store was loaded with Halloween decorations, the lighted kind that made scary sounds when you walked by them, and there were pumpkins and gourds and masks for sale, and the clerks had on Halloween costumes. I smiled.

We went back to the car and put on the robot outfit, and my little gizmo had a great time strutting around the store, beeping and flashing. August had been fascinated with the automated macabre decorations and dazzled by all the candy, and the clerks had made a fuss over him. For a three-year-old, this had turned out to be a swell Halloween party. I'd told him that it was too bad we'd missed the first party, but at least we'd made it to this party on time. I had been scrupulous about dates and times ever since.

I put away the masks and costumes and carried up the wreath of dried flower and leaves, and placed it on the front door. I stood my scarecrow couple by the jack-o'-lantern. August and his buddy had supplied the pumpkins and had created ghoulish scenes on them using downloaded patterns that were much more realistic and detailed than the toothy hacked grins of my childhood carvings. I stood back and studied the arrangement.

Halloween was not high on my list of holidays. It was fun for kids, but I thought grown-ups got too carried away. When the boys had been younger, I'd enjoyed and encouraged their Halloween projects. They'd designed elaborate haunted areas on our walkway to the porch. Creatures with masks and bodies made of old clothes had been hung on garden crooks and from the porch light.

August had made a picket fence from old wood and painted it white with many red-paint blood splatters. He'd created a fake cemetery and rigged a light and a recording of horrible, agonizing groans to an electric eye. Unsuspecting kids had been terrified as they'd innocently trudged past our juniper bushes and a creature from hell had suddenly appeared in the dark. Zimmer had operated the fog machine, which had further enhanced the creepiness.

Most years, Pud had missed Halloween because he had

been away on business, but one year he had been home. Zim had set up a microphone, and Pud had commandeered his own Halloween role. Pud had worn a scary mask as he'd sat on his lawn chair on our porch and commanded his netherworld. He'd crooned with a devil's voice over the microphone to all the pitiful, defenseless beings who dared to pass by our house, "Come up here. Come see me. I want to see you. Come up here, little boy. Are you brave?"

But now our sons were grown, and their interest in tombstones and haunted houses had ended. August's jack-o'-lantern and my autumn decorations would have to do. I still enjoyed Beggars' Night. I found the witch's cauldron that I used for the candy and filled it up. Pud perked up from the TV and came over and grabbed a few midget bars of candy.

"This is for Halloween?"

"Yes. I never know how much to buy. Some years we have a lot of kids, but with everyone on our street getting older and the crummy weather tonight, I may have bought too much."

"Oh, let me help! I'll have another one. When do the kids come?"

"Trick or treat is tonight from six to eight. The weather forecast looks lousy."

Pud turned back to the TV and studied the weather channel. He paused the weather map to show me the ominous green blob over our area.

"Yes, I can look out the window and see that it's raining, Pud." I softened my sarcasm by adding, "It's fun to have you around for Halloween! Do you mind passing out candy in the rain?"

Pud said, "I know! Why don't I put the cover on the golf cart, pull it out, and we can sit in the cart and do trick or treat?"

"Will we be warm enough out there?"

"With the cover on and zipped, we will be fine."

I added, "Let's park the cart at the bottom of the driveway, and the kids can grab the treats as they walk by on the sidewalk, and they won't have to walk all the way up to the front door in the cold rain."

"Good plan." We congratulated ourselves.

At a quarter to six, Pud and I were in winter coats, with a blanket on our knees, zipped inside the golf cart. Pud pulled the cart down to the sidewalk. He put the full bowl of candy down by his feet. We were fortified with two big mugs of wine.

"Did I ever tell you that one year, when you were gone at Halloween, I took Zim out trick-or-treating in the golf cart? We zoomed all over the neighborhood, and he scored a hefty bag of candy, but we came back after dark on the golf course. It ended up being a truly scary night because we couldn't see at all."

"Good job, uh, Mom," said Pud. "Was that the night he fell out of the cart and you ran over him? Didn't you tell me a story about that too?"

"No, he fell off the first summer we lived here. He was about six. We were riding back on the path, and he saw a cart up ahead with his friends, and in a flash, he jumped out to see them. He fell, and I rolled over his ankle. And another time I turned a corner too fast, and he fell out in the street. Thanks goodness he was totally fine each time. He was a tough kid. You missed a lot of excitement."

"And you're a bad driver. Just kidding."

At ten minutes after six, we had our first customers. Several couples came to our cart, holding umbrellas over a bunch of little Minions. They were adorable.

"What do you say?"

"Trick …"—mumble—"*treat!*"

Pud unzipped his side and thrust out the candy bowl.

"Just pick one piece," cautioned the parents.

"No, take all you want. You were brave to struggle out tonight."

"Yeah, it's a mess. You had a super idea to use the golf cart."

"Thanks. Take care! Happy Halloween!"

"I like doing trick or treat in the golf cart down here," I added to Pud.

"And we are staying pretty dry," he replied. He put the candy bowl back down by his feet and struggled to zip the wet cover. Suddenly, the golf cart rolled down the sidewalk, fast, faster, toward medium-sized devils and angels.

"Stop it! Watch out! Runaway cart!" I screamed.

Pud realized that the candy bowl had slipped onto the accelerator. He grabbed it, and we stopped sharply in front of the startled beggars.

"I guess candy really is bad for you," I told Pud.

"Here," he said to the kids. "Take all the candy you want. And don't sue us."

When we got back to our driveway, Pud said, "I'll go back in and get more wine. Looks like no one is coming down the street right now."

"Okay, thanks, hon! Just make sure I don't roll away again."

It was dark outside now, and the rain and wind blew harder. I was zipped in the golf cart. This would be the perfect scene in a horror Halloween movie; the older lady sitting by herself in a cart on a creepy, stormy night hears footsteps slowly approaching the cart and reaches out to greet her husband and instead is face to face with …

"Here you go. I opened a bottle of Prisoner. Why did you jump?"

We drank the wine, and then a group of teenagers came up to the cart. We recognized them. They were on the high school football team, and they were all dressed as curvy cheerleaders.

"Wow, this is really a treat," joked Pud as he hugged one of the "gals." "You can have all you want, but don't take too much if you want to watch your girlish figures."

They danced off. We sat quietly and drank our wine. I was just about to say, "It's so nice to have you here for Halloween," when Pud said, "Oh, um, Dick and, uh, Sam were talking about going to the Naples area to golf in December, the same time we will be in Marco Island. They wondered if I could maybe, uh, join them. I told them I didn't know."

"Marco Island? You want to what?"

"*They* thought of the idea; *I* didn't," muttered Pud.

"Hon," I said, trying to stay calm, "remember, this was our special trip to celebrate your retirement, and I'd like us to spend the time together. Plus, we haven't been on a vacation together for a long time."

"I know, I know," Pud said hurriedly. "I told them already I wouldn't go. I am just telling you about it."

"Well, I don't want to be sounding like a bossy mother; you are a grown-up, after all, but I would really like it if this was just our vacation."

"Yep, yep, I know, and they will probably go on another golf trip in February, so that may work better for me."

I didn't know what else to say, and I was saved from responding by a clutch of *Frozen* characters, a ninja, and an older kid with a hasty hobo costume. "Trick or treat!"

After the waifs left, we again sat silently for a few long minutes. For me, the golf cart had lost its coziness, and I felt awkward and unwanted.

"Uh, do you want a Snickers bar?" Pud mumbled quietly. When I didn't answer, he leaned over, kissed me, and squeezed my derriere. I rolled my eyes. I didn't know what to say. Part of me wanted to say, *Come on. You gave 110 percent to your career our whole married life, and now you are retired, and your new job is golf. I really want to spend time with you.* But the other part of me argued, *Pud loves golf; what difference do a few hours with his golf buddies make?* Well, right now, *I* wanted to be his number one, not golf. I was good at blustering to myself, but I didn't say any of this to Pud.

Did Pud really kiss me and give me the squeeze? Wow, that was a nice treat. I finally said, "I am looking forward to—" and Pud leaned in to kiss me again. *See, it does help to spend time together having fun.* Then I decided to stop analyzing and start enjoying. I turned closer to Pud and stroked his cheek. He kissed me more firmly and pulled me to his chest. We cuddled closer, and he nibbled my ear and gave me a firmer kiss on the lips.

My heart leaped, and I jumped. It wasn't love that propelled me, though. A *snap, tap, screech* and an evil chortle had pierced the quiet.

"Eeeek! What was that?" I gasped.

Pud jerked around.

Through the murky, rainy darkness, I could see a shape. It was a familiar shape, and it wasn't a Halloween monster. I gulped and sank back against Pud.

"August, is that you?"

"Did I scare you? I stopped by to help Tom—you know, from up the street—with his trick-or-treat duties. He had to watch his little sister, and I ate the candy and handed some out too. We're done, so I am going to stop by Rudolph's for their happy hour on my way back to Cleveland. Do you guys want to join me? Mom, you know how you like the scotch flight and bar bites."

Pud said, "I don't care."

I said, "Count us in, and here's a Snickers bar."

6

Never on Sunday

After Halloween night in the golf cart, I hadn't mentioned golf again to Pud. I did not like confrontation at all, and with the course closed for the season, it was easy for me to procrastinate and put off discussing my concerns with Pud. One of these days, I would tell him what was bothering me. One of these days, I would say that I wanted us to grow closer and savor retired life together. One of these days, I would be blunt and tell him, "Stop golfing and stay home, and we'll make love all afternoon." Well, that might be a little over the top.

On the other hand, I had to give Pud credit for his Project RSVP idea. Our kickoff trip to Cincinnati had succeeded on all counts. We had grown closer to Robin and Chester. The dinner had been something fun to do together, an icebreaker. Our kiss in the golf cart was evidence to me that the ice floe lodged between us had begun to move, albeit at glacial speed. Perhaps I needed to be patient and trusting, content with the blessings I had.

November, the curtain call for green vistas, sweater weather, and daylight after dinner, was upon us. The lawn had been mowed for the final time, the golf clubs cleaned, the cart put in the back of the garage, and the snowblower moved forward for easy access. The furnace had been checked and the lawn chairs stowed away. The first snow blew in, and we remembered to round up gloves, car window scrapers, and snow shovels only after the first inches fell. The Broadway spectacular that was the holidays hadn't unloaded its sets yet, so life was still calm.

I decided to pep up our bland Saturday morning. I had surfed the web for an hour, and Pud had changed the channel repeatedly in search of a golf tournament. August was home for the weekend, accompanied by his wash. I announced that I was making cinnamon rolls in the waffle iron.

This gourmet recipe called for a tube of large cinnamon rolls and a waffle iron. I heated the waffle iron, plopped in the tube of dough, squished it down, and waited. I tugged the fragrant, spicy waffle-ish shape from the iron and squeezed the frosting in all the warm little squares. There was no need to call anyone. The warm cinnamon aroma was guaranteed to lure my spouse and son.

We polished off the waffle roll and licked frosting off our fingers.

"Anybody have plans for this weekend? What should we do?" I asked.

"The Big Ten game is on this afternoon," offered Pud.

"How about the *Shark Tank* marathon?" I suggested.

"Dad, you could play the Formula 1 racing game with me," said August, "and let's make some more cinnamon rolls. I think there's caramel rolls in the fridge too. We could try those."

"Okay, but stop giving bites to the dog."

"Dad, come watch this hilarious video on YouTube about the honey badger."

In the midst of this revelry, Pud's cell phone rang. It was Susie, our niece on Pud's side of the family. She was in her thirties and married with a family. She bubbled and loved to talk, and after a lengthy dissertation, she revealed the reason for her call. She and her daughters were going to be in the area. I gleaned all this by listening to Pud's end of the conversation as I unloaded the dishwasher.

"Mom!" Pud yelled. "Oh, I didn't know you were right here. It's Susie, and, uh, um, are we doing anything tomorrow? She and, uh, the girls want to see us on the way to a gymnastics thing, uh, event competition."

"Oh, that would be nice. I think our whole day is free, so find out the specifics. Tell everyone hi."

With a few whispered promptings from me—"Ask her what time," "Where should we meet?" "Do they remember how to get here?"—we had our Sunday visit planned.

"Visiting Robin and Chester seems to have primed the pump," said Pud.

"What do you mean?"

"Well, we decided to visit all the young cousins on your side, and now Susie called. When was the last time we saw her?"

"Oh, gosh, when was it? Maybe it was a year ago summer for your brother's fortieth anniversary party?"

Pud was right. We had decided to focus on the young nieces and nephews and support the fledglings. Now we had the opportunity to encourage another branch of our family. Susie was a working mother with a busy husband and two active school-age kids, and I looked forward to sharing some smiles with her the next day. They aimed to arrive around eleven in the morning. All we had to do was pick a place for lunch.

There had been a time when a Sunday-morning visit would have been a problem. I had been raised a committed Sunday school attendee and churchgoer and had never missed a service. I'd sung in the choir and served in the youth groups. Although it had been harder for me to be faithful as a young adult, I had been back in the pew religiously when the boys had been young. But after August and Zim had entered school, our church attendance had dwindled. Once we'd skipped services, it had been easy to get out of the habit.

But the main reason I'd stopped attending was that I liked church when it was boring. The modern, contemporary babble turned me off. I wanted to sing verses 1, 2, and 4, hear a dry sermon, and go home. Instead, our worship service featured guitars and drums and a song leader. There were skits, dances, and personal testimonies.

I couldn't relate to the hullabaloo, but I told myself it wasn't because I was old and set in my ways. To me, the modern church was a thunder-and-lightning storm, always jarring me with unexpected blasts and jolts. The old way was a calm stream, and for an uneventful hour, my mind drifted along, paused by a bank under a tree to meditate, and enjoyed a sun-filled meadow around a bend where deer might graze or ducks might waddle to the shore in a line, like prayer petitions marching to God. That was what I wanted on Sunday morning—peace like a river, not a praise band.

I straightened up the kitchen after our cinnamon-roll festival. My family dispersed, and I could hear televisions and video games. Now that the kitchen sparkled again, I considered my options: clean the basement or a short walk with the dog. I reached for my boots, and instantly, a leaping, twirling, bright, bouncing creature plummeted her way to the door.

"Oakley, my beauty girl, what do you want to do, my sweet girlfriend?" I asked unnecessarily as we headed out the door together for a walk.

When we came back, August was at the stove surrounded by a frying pan, a pot, two big bowls, measuring cups and spoons, a ladle, and knives, and the refrigerator was open. Flour spilled on the counter, a beer can was open, and the cutting board was loaded with veggies.

"What are you doing?"

"I decided to make my famous beer cheddar soup."

"We just had breakfast. I just finished cleaning the kitchen."

"Well, Macy texted me, and she is coming over, and she said she'd love to try my soup."

"Macy?"

"The girl I am seeing."

I intended to sputter complaints but caught myself and managed a forced smile. "Okay, well, have fun with her, and please clean up the kitchen."

I evacuated to our bedroom at the opposite end of the house and curled up with Oakley and my e-reader. I read and dozed for an hour or so and realized I hadn't seen Pud in a while. "Pud! *Pud*!" I called.

August answered, "He's up at the club trying out the new golf simulator."

Golf never stopped, apparently. "The day is coming when I will have that talk," I told Oakley.

Sunday morning, I was enjoying my second cup of coffee when we got a text from Susie that she and the girls would be arriving soon.

"Do we have any, uh, gum for the little girl?" asked Pud.

Melissa was Susie's younger girl, and even though we only saw her once or twice a year, she expected to receive gum from Uncle Pud.

"I think I can find some gum. Say, why don't I make a little gift bag for each girl like we did for Robin and Chester?" I answered. Fortunately, I had some odds and ends in my gift supply box as well as some gum and candy, and we soon created two bags.

The doorbell rang; we hustled Oakley into her crate and eagerly opened the front door. Susie smiled and stepped in and hugged us warmly. We almost shut the door on the two little girls, who stood scared and shy on the front porch, afraid to move.

"Hi, hi, hi!" I called. "We are so happy to see you."

Susie reached for her girls, and they sidled two inches closer to her and huddled behind her leg.

"Oh, Susie, they are adorable and so big now."

"Come on in," we continued to cajole with our too-bright and enthusiastic voices.

The clump of Susie and a girl on each leg made it over the threshold and then stood mutely inside the door.

"Michelle and Melissa, you remember Uncle Pud and Aunt Charli? Let's tell them about our new fish and about breakfast on the way up and all about our trip to Florida and the funny thing that happened with the alligator, and, oh, look at their beautiful globe, and, oh, we haven't seen their dog yet."

"Yes, come on in, and we want to hear it all," I pleaded cheerfully.

The scrum lurched to our couch, and all three of them tentatively settled on half a cushion. The girls clutched Susie's arm like little cling-on window decorations.

"We have surprise bags for you!" Pud shouted joyfully.

Pud brought the gifts over to the coffee table and put the two small but bulging bags near the sweet girls. Their eyes lit up. They looked intently at the bags but didn't move from their mom.

Pud then said jovially, "I am going to tickle you!"

They dove behind Susie, and now we couldn't see them at all.

"That's okay. Let's have some hot chocolate and marshmallows while we plan our day. Oh, and we have Pop-Tarts too. Your mom was going to tell us about Florida." I tried to salvage the situation.

Susie, Pud, and I enjoyed our visit. She laughed that it was nice to relax on the couch after their busy morning.

"I got up and folded laundry and added another load. Then I packed the gymnastics bags, paid some bills online, and vacuumed before waking these sleepyheads. Oh, and I had a job interview last week. It's for a company that is only five minutes from our home. I would save over an hour in commute time each day."

"That will give you so much more time at home, won't it?" I replied. "I am sure every extra minute helps."

Susie reached into the treat bags and gave each girl a pack of gum. Melissa, the younger one, smiled and began to warm up.

"I have socks in my pants!" she exclaimed. "Socks in my pants, socks in my pants." And she did a little dance and patted her behind.

Pud looked shocked at this outburst, but we applauded and laughed as if we had front-row seats at a Vegas show. Then it was time for the girls to get their hair ready for gymnastics, and we planned our lunch. We presented several choices, and a grilled-cheese café won.

When we got to the eatery, the place was packed. Pud was concerned that they wouldn't have enough time to eat and get to their competition.

Susie wasn't fazed at all. "We'll be fine."

I admired her calm and pleasant demeanor. She had plenty on her plate, yet she stayed positive and relaxed. Susie had fun with her girls. I recalled that too often with our boys, Pud and I had worried and argued. I needed to conjure Susie and her gentle smile when I was stressed.

After a moderate wait, we were seated. The intriguing menu featured drawings and arrows and funny faces. It was an encyclopedia of grilled cheese sandwiches. We all talked at once.

"What are you thinking of getting?"

"American cheese with bacon, banana, and pretzels?"

"No, I want pepper jack on sourdough with salsa, pineapple, and coleslaw, but can I have a bite of yours?"

Pud and the girls settled on basic grilled cheese, pickles, and fries. Susie had the Beach-y Cheese-y, a grilled Cuban sandwich with kale coleslaw, and I braved the Tailgater, a hoagie with sliced bratwurst, cheddar, and corn chips. We soon had large platters placed in front of us, piled high with what seemed like loaves of bread, wheels of cheese, and a small produce stand.

Susie expertly cut up the girls' food into manageable bites. While they were busy pulling out the yucky parts of their sandwiches, Susie confided that Melissa, the younger one in the second grade, was having trouble with reading.

"The teacher said she's losing ground, but I think she's smart, and she's a whiz at math. And she's so funny and creative. I am meeting with her teacher next week, and I think they want to do formal testing."

"What do you think about all that?" I asked.

"Well, she went to reading camp all summer and is in an after-school book club, and then she reads to me for an hour each night, and they say she is still behind. She is fine in everything else, so we probably should find out more."

"Oh, poor you, Mom. Dealing with school issues can be overwhelming at times. With our two boys, we had some school snags ourselves. But you are so good with your kids; you are handling the challenges well."

Susie laughed quietly and smiled while deftly grabbing the ketchup bottle that both girls were grabbing.

Melissa, the one who was having reading issues, looked up at the wall, which was covered with a variety of signs and souvenirs. Her eyes gleamed. "Dairy Queen. They have a Dairy Queen. Can we get some?"

"No, silly, that sign is just a decoration here." Her older sister, Michelle, put Melissa in her place.

"She can't read, hmmm?" I smiled at Susie.

"Michelle, so tell us, what happens at a gymnastics meet? It sounds exciting."

Michelle shyly looked up.

Her mom prompted, "Tell Auntie Charli about your events."

"Balance beam. Vault."

We looked at her expectantly. "Wow! Good luck!"

"Thanks," said Susie. "Michelle is doing really well. It's a long day at a meet, though."

Too soon, the precious gang rounded up their hats and dropped mittens and hurried off to gymnastics.

"Good luck," we called. "Do you know where you are going? So good to see you."

"Thanks for lunch! Thanks for everything!"

Pud and I drove home, and Pud found the football game on the radio.

"You know what?" I began, but he was listening to the game, and I let him.

I had been going to tell him how much I'd enjoyed the visit. We'd given Susie and her dears lunch and little trinkets, but they had given us the gift of getting to know them better. Susie had shown me that children should be treated kindly and respected, not rushed or forced to talk. Had I been as patient with my boys when they had been young?

Robin and Chester had shown me better ways too. Young love and young marriage was a strong way to face life together. Had I been as patient and willing with Pud when we were younger? I was grateful for our plan of getting to know our younger relations.

A commercial blared. Pud turned down the radio and glanced over at me.

"What a nice time," he said. "But that food was weird."

It was Sunday, and we had been blessed by our time with Susie and her children. I'd hummed every verse of "Come Thou Fount of Every Blessing" as we'd headed home.

7

Surprise!

"Surprise!" When I'd turned fifty, Pud and Sibby had planned a surprise birthday party for me. They'd worked for months on the arrangements, but I'd had no clue about the festivities. Pud had told me that he and the boys were taking me to my favorite restaurant to celebrate, and that had seemed fine to me.

On our way to the restaurant, Zimmer had mentioned, "I hope you are not sad that you aren't with your whole family on your birthday."

"Why would you say that? I am happy to be with you."

August had punched Zim, and Pud had told him to fix his tie. No one had talked the rest of the way. When we'd walked into the place together, the hostess had led us to a different area than usual and … "Surprise!"

My neighbor had saved me from collapsing, propped me up, and handed me a glass of champagne. Pud and my sister had planned an elegant jubilee. There had been a specially printed menu with my favorite foods, all my dear family and friends, a pianist for entertainment, and a buttercream cake decorated as a bouquet of roses. My favorite card had been from Zim. He had made it and carefully printed "Happy Birthday! 50 years until 100."

That was the only thing about a big party; everyone knew exactly how old you were. Of course, now I would be happy to be fifty.

And surprise again! My cell phone rang, and it showed *Chester.*

"Hello!" I said cheerily, hoping nothing was wrong. This was the first time that Chester had ever called me.

"Auntie Charli, this is Chester! I am calling because I am having a surprise birthday for Robin and wanted to invite you and Uncle Pud." I tried to inject a happy response, but Chester continued with pride, "I rented the party room at our apartment building, and I ordered food, and we will have a bar, and friends from work, school, and church will be coming."

The date in early December was fine for us, so I eagerly accepted the invitation. A few minutes later, Chester texted back:

> Just reminding you that it's a surprise, so please don't say anything.

I ran to tell Pud. "Guess what! Chester just called, and we are invited to a surprise birthday party he is throwing for Robin. I am so excited."

No response. I thought Pud was in the bedroom, but he wasn't there. He wasn't in the kitchen, so I went out to the garage. I looked around and found him blowing snow. He couldn't hear me, so I went back inside.

I was thrilled to be invited. Our new plan to visit the young leaves on our family tree was bearing fruit. We really were bonding with Robin and Chester. We would meet their friends and have another fun weekend away together.

Pud came in, and before he took off his snowsuit, I told him about the surprise party.

"Okay, as soon as I get cleaned up, we'll work on the plans. I guess we can stay at the same hotel," he said.

"Thanks, and thanks for the snow blowing."

"There was only about an inch, but I decided to do it before we drove on it. I didn't want it to get icy."

"Isn't it supposed to warm up tomorrow?"

Pud was as dedicated to snow removal as he was to lawn mowing.

"Yes, for the next few days. Sam, Bob, and I think we can golf somewhere at the end of the week, though."

Pud and I were on the road to Cincinnati, ambient temperature: twenty-eight degrees Fahrenheit. We'd remembered to pack and bring everything this time and hadn't returned home for anything. As we drove, Pud kept me updated. He reported to me that there were horses running up a hill, there was a driver having a bad day, and he thought he saw a fox.

"Get her off the road. Take away her license."

We neared Columbus, and the traffic increased.

As we rode along, I reviewed our plans for the weekend, and I happened to think of our upcoming vacation. "Pud, you made the reservations for Marco Island, right? Pud?"

"What? I was looking for a rest area."

"Why don't we stop for lunch soon?" I suggested.

"Okay, tell me where."

I thought it over. I wanted us to have a good time. "Hey, you always told me how good that Mexican restaurant was. We don't have one at home, but you liked it when you traveled. What was it called?"

"Oh, uh, North of the Border."

"I wonder if there is one in Columbus. I'd like to try it out."

"Check with the GPS lady."

I typed and waited as the hourglass tumbled. "There is one, and it's at the big mall near the next exit. Do you want to stop?"

"Sure. I love it."

"And before I forget, you did make reservations for Marco, right?"

"Um, I'd better check when we get back home."

We found the restaurant, pulled into the parking lot, walked the long way around to the front door, and went to the bathroom. Soon we were seated in a booth with chips and salsa.

A good-looking waiter brought our menus and said he would be back soon.

"Why are Mexican menus always so big? There are thousands of tacos and burritos," I said.

"I know. I really like the fajitas here."

The waiter returned, and Pud asked, "What's your best margarita, the Cactus or the Cadillac?"

"I don't know; I only drink the cheap stuff."

I asked, "Which is better, the guacamole made tableside or the guac that comes with chips?"

"I don't know; I don't like guacamole."

I liked the waiter's looks, but he wasn't very helpful. We ordered a variety of cheesy, spicy food, and Pud chose a

Cadillac, and I picked the other margarita. We ate two and a half baskets of chips. We were quiet at lunch, but Pud was right; everything was delicious. I let Pud be; we would have fun together at the party.

I had texted Chester a few days earlier to see if he needed any supplies:

> Chester, I am sure you have things well in hand and I don't mean to interfere, but if it would help you out, we would be happy to bring some wine. 4-6 bottles or whatever you need.

He'd replied:

> I have beer and liquor, but wine would be good. 6 bottles.

I'd texted back:

> 6 bottles it is! And we would be glad to come early and help set up if you need us.

He'd texted:

> Sounds good. Thanks.

We decided to stop at the famous Jungle Jerry's to get the wine for the surprise party. Robin and Chester had told us about it when we'd had dinner with them. "Everyone who knows about the place says you can't describe it, it's so amazing," Robin had gushed.

They had said it was the biggest food emporium they

had ever seen. They'd said it had a plane, boat, and truck inside, along with an old airport waiting area. There had been thousands of varieties of everything imaginable—salsa, beer, wine, hot sauce, hot chocolate, pasta, cheese, olive oil. "It's unbelievable," they had gasped every time they'd come up for air.

Pud and I did know our way around gourmet food shops, and from outside, our first view of Jungle Jerry's disappointed us. The building appeared old and run down. It did have a monorail above the front door, though. Once inside, it truly lived up to all the hype.

"It's unbelievable," I said.

"It's unbelievable," Pud said.

We walked past the ski boat to the wine area. There were rows and aisles of every varietal, and we recognized many high-end California wines. I stopped to check the Rieslings and lost Pud. He found me a few minutes later, holding a bottle of Italian wine he had searched for online.

"It's unbelievable," I said.

"It's unbelievable," Pud said.

There were so many wines it was a challenge to select six bottles. We navigated to the checkout. I detoured to view the acres of spices, and Pud paused to see how many blue cheese selections there were.

"Unbelievable," we chorused. "People are right; you can't begin to describe this place."

Pud and I set off for the party. I wore my new navy pantsuit, and I was so excited about the party. If only I had known that by the end of the evening, I would be devastated. The night would be a success for everyone but me.

Pud and I arrived an hour early and helped Chester and his friends arrange the food and drinks. Chester had ordered personalized stemless wineglasses with *Happy*

Surprise Birthday, Robin! on them. We placed an intricately decorated cake—adorned with a theme park made from fondant on the top and sides of the immense pastry—on a special table. We set up a long table for the Chinese food that would be delivered. I hugged Chester several times; he had done a lovely job orchestrating the event.

All the guests arrived promptly. Sibby and her husband, George, were the only other older people. We mingled, and I was impressed that many of the young people were science graduates or studying the sciences. I met two doctors, a physical therapist, IT and software professionals, and several pharmacy students. Many of the students were graduating in June, so they were full of plans for job interviews and placements. We genuinely wished them good luck.

Chester left and picked up Robin and managed to get her to the party room by telling her that they had to pick up a copy of their new lease. The surprise part went off perfectly, and Robin was excited and thrilled. It was always a delight to shout, "Surprise!"

After the dinner and cake, Pud and I joined a group that was playing a lively game, WordUp!, using an app on a smartphone. It was a word game, like password, and the subject was "holiday." One person was "it" and held the phone up in front of his or her forehead, with the screen positioned so we could all see the word. Our job was to shout clues to get him or her to say the word. When whoever was "it" succeeded, the person bobbed his or her head, and a new word appeared. We quickly got into the spirit of yelling clues, and it was hilarious to see the head bobbing and shaking.

Annie, Robin's sister, took a turn and held up the phone in front of her forehead. The word was *Scrooge*. There were boisterous shouts of clues.

"Marley!" someone yelled, and Annie guessed, "Golden retriever."

"Dickens! Christmas ghost!" we screamed.

Annie hesitantly said, "Book?"

We shouted, "Cratchit!" and "Bah humbug!"

Annie cried triumphantly, "Scrooge!"

She bobbed her head, and up popped a new word: *wreath.*

Pud and I left the game and joined Sibby and George by the fireplace. We relaxed together and let the younger ones party without us.

Sibby said, "I am so glad you came!"

"We are too," I said. "We were so happy to be included. Chester planned a wonderful party."

"Woman, go get me some more wine," said George. He hugged me.

Sibby chided, "Go get it yourself, mister. Please get Charli and me some too."

"I'll come with you," said Pud.

Sibby and I tidied and repacked the opened birthday presents. Robin's girlfriends had given her lovely scarves and statement jewelry, and the guys had given wine or snack baskets. A few of Robin's high school girlfriends wandered over, and Sibby introduced me. We chatted with them about Christmas and school.

I looked to see where Pud had drifted. Where was he? He wasn't with the guys at the bar, and he wasn't playing the word game. I spotted him talking to someone over by the cake table. Another piece of cake, very tiny, sounded good to me. I strolled over. He and Annie were chatting. As I came closer, I overheard Pud, and he was using his intense voice.

"Why would you believe that? Don't listen to those liberals."

I couldn't hear Annie yet, but she was looking up at Pud. She was small, and he loomed over her.

"But that's not what happened … Police reports show … Media gets it wrong … mindless sheep …" Pud continued to hammer away.

Annie tried to say something. "People have rights—"

"Same thing as terrorists … too many taxes. That's what's wrong with this country."

Oh no, I thought. *He's on one of his rampages. I told him not to talk politics tonight.*

His black cloud obscured my sun. I waved, pointed, and semaphored Pud with elaborate hand signals. *Stop, easy, come here.* But he trumpeted on, and it seemed to me that the rest of the guests were giving him a wide berth. Was Annie upset?

"Terrible … welfare … border …"

I rocketed more gestures and intense eye gleams his way, but he didn't stop his braying. I was cringing. I knew what it was like to be pelted with the hailstorm of Pud's beliefs. At home, I ignored his outbursts and walked away or changed the subject, but Annie was trapped. Sadness, worry, and anxiety stripped my patina of party happiness.

Before we'd come, I'd told him and told him that our purpose with the young folk was to be positive and encouraging. Robin and Chester had invited us because we'd shown them we could be fun, not fuddy-duddies. Now he was wrecking it all. The kids wouldn't want to hang out with a droner. Those thoughts and more swirled in my head.

I marched over to Pud and Annie and firmly asked Pud to go get me a glass of wine. Annie smiled and went over to the couch to sit with her friends and watch the guys play video games on the nearby big screen.

I felt shaky and hollow; I was so horrified by Pud's

display. Poor Annie! All I could think of was that we had to leave. I barked at Pud that it was time to go. I walked rapidly ahead to the car. Pud tried to make feeble small talk, which I coldly ignored. I sat stiffly in my seat and glared out my window. I could barely breathe, I was so tense.

As we drove, I tried to keep quiet, but then I plunged into the swirling river of "How could you … I told you … important to be positive … Why do you always … I have had to listen to you rant for over thirty years … You need to … told you … told you … stop … can't take it … wrecked the party." About the only thing that I didn't touch on was why he golfed so much, but that was because I stifled my tirade when we entered the lobby.

This time in the hotel, we didn't snuggle together under the downy duvet. I was rigid at my edge of the bed, and I tossed and turned all night. My mind whirled with anguished questions. Would any of the nieces and nephews even want to go out with us now? What about our plan? Why couldn't Pud be more easygoing and not so blunt? Should I just stop the cousin project while we were ahead? I couldn't bear the thought of stopping our visits, but I wanted our time with the youngsters to be positive and not a dreaded encounter with oldster stereotypes. Should I take a break from Pud and leave? *What should I do?*

After arguing with myself all night, I calmed down. "Thank you, God, for this beautiful day!"

Maybe I overreacted, I reasoned. Pud was only lecturing Annie, not the whole room, and she knew Uncle Pud and what he could be like. I wished he wouldn't come on so strong, but he'd been lambasting people for over thirty years. And what about all my talk about perseverance? I decided to press on with Pud.

I rolled over and woke up Pud with a hug and a kiss.

"I'll let you take a mulligan. Every party needs a dash of conservative news analysis," I whispered.

He pulled me close. He rolled over and went back to sleep, and I caught up on my missed sleep too.

We met the birthday girl and her husband, along with Annie and my sister and her husband, for breakfast at a local pancake house. Pud and I were connoisseurs of greasy-spoon breakfast joints, so we were delighted to join the gang. The Sunshine Special at this place was a very large, fluffy pancake, oozing with cinnamon apples. We all shared that, along with omelets, waffles, and sausage gravy and biscuits as we reviewed the highlights of the party.

I whispered to Sibby, "I hope Annie wasn't upset by Pud and his comments."

She laughed. "No, she likes to debate. She and her brother were really getting into it the other night."

George added, "That's our Annie!"

All the more reason to get to know "our Annie" better, I promised myself. *Time to get that trip to Chicago planned.*

8

Big Egg

I was the big sister to my one sibling, my Sibby. We filled our respective family roles perfectly. I was the dutiful, quiet, older child who liked to read. Sibby was the baby of our little family, and we doted on her; she was adorable, pretty, spunky, and cute.

Our annual childhood Christmas photos in front of our tinseled tree highlighted our differences. I stood at attention with a tentative smile, in a plain robe, glasses on, and holding my favorite possession, most likely a book. Sibby posed with her hip cocked, practiced charming smile, and styled hair, holding a fifty-piece makeup set.

Whether it was early Christmas morning, watching TV, or dashing to the grocery, Sibby was always fashionable, and her personality was as put together as her appearance. Through the years, she'd gently helped me cultivate my look. On my own, I could comb my hair and wear nonclashing colors. She did her best to spruce me up. The previous year for my birthday, she'd given me a soft, pink-and-tan sweater with small cream-colored spangles woven in and a bold statement necklace that complimented the colors and style. I'd received so many compliments.

We both loved each other more than anyone else in the world, aside from our immediate families. She was petite, sparkly, and full of life. We had been through thick—me—and thin—her. We were sisters.

My mom, Sibby, and I had had a long tradition of lunching, getting together about once a week. Sometimes we'd met after church at a nearby breakfast spot or at the food court at the mall. One Sunday, Sibby and I'd agreed to meet Mom, but we'd forgotten where we had said we would meet. We'd gone to the breakfast place, and she'd gone to the mall. This had been before cell phones, so when it had finally dawned on us that there was a problem, we'd rushed to the other place. Of course, at the same time, Mom had dashed to the mall, thinking she had goofed. But most of the time, we'd had tranquil breakfast or lunch visits.

Every Thursday, I used to go to my mom's house in the morning and help her with her banking or taxes or the other routine matters of life. I'd tried to teach her how to use her cell phone (moderate success), how to pump self-serve gas (no success), and how to reset the clock on her microwave when there was a power surge (impossible).

My mom and I had grown closer through the years. I had been a sensitive kid, and she had been a strict mother, so we'd had our clashes, but I'd loved to organize, so we'd bonded over her chores.

After we'd finished our Thursday-morning tasks, I would take my mom to the grocery, and then we'd meet Sibby either at a soup-and-salad café or a Chinese restaurant. It had been the same routine every week. We'd set a time to meet—say,

12:15 p.m. My mom and I would arrive at 12:10 p.m. and settle at a table. By this time, there had been cell phones, so we'd wait for Sibby to call. Ten minutes later, she would ring with a breathless reason for her delay. It never had mattered. When she eventually rushed in, we would split egg rolls, moo goo gai pan, or orange-flavored chicken and laugh and talk nonstop.

When Mom had passed away, Sibby and I had pledged to continue meeting for lunch or breakfast several times a month. We hadn't seen each other since the surprise party breakfast, so I texted her:

> B fast or lunch?

Sibby replied:

> dog @ groomer early, then drop off papers @ CPA, then to mall 4 sympathy card & return cocktail dress, then hair appt. & need groceries for funeral meal so if u can meet from 10:45 to 11:25 at mall works 4 me.

I texted back:

> great, see you 10:45 at Big Egg

I was joyous. "Thank you, God, for the great day and the chance to see my Sibby!" I reminded Pud, "I am meeting Sibby for breakfast this morning, and then I will stop at the grocery on the way home."

"Have fun. Oakley and I will be fine, won't we, big girl?"

"Okay, well, there are buns and ham, so you can make a sandwich for lunch. Oh, and there is also some leftover pasta bolognese. So that should do you, right?"

It was snowy and icy, so I left early. I had to follow a school bus through the neighborhoods by our house, but I still made it to town by 10:40 a.m. I bundled up and scurried into the mall. I ignored the young man pitching me from the cell-phone kiosk, and I headed into the Big Egg. It wasn't very crowded, so I decided to get a table and wait for Sibby.

The hostess greeted me. "Haven't seen you in a while. Table for two?"

"Yes, please. My sister—"

"I know, will be coming soon. Good. I will get you a pot of coffee."

The hostess at the Big Egg had been the waitress that had served Mom and me years ago. Seeing her was a pleasant link to the past. It was 10:51 a.m. I fixed my coffee and waited for the phone to ring. A few minutes passed, and then my cell phone rang. It was my sister.

"I suppose you are already there."

"Yep. Got us a table and coffee."

"Sorry; I am running a few minutes late. I forgot the papers I was taking to Matt's office, and it took a while to catch the dog and get her in the car. But I'm on my way now. And I found a sympathy card at home, so we'll have a little more time."

"Fine. Drive carefully; see you soon."

Sibby had three children and had remarried several years earlier and added two stepchildren to our family. These were the five kids that Pud and I planned to visit this year. Her husband, George, was a foot taller than she was and obediently followed her wishes and commands.

I looked up and saw her struggle to open the door, drop her scarf, smile at the good-looking guy who picked it up for her, and then confidently stride in and look for me. She approached, beautiful and on trend with a black leather coat, statement necklace, skinny jeans, and tall black boots. Her hair was highlighted and in a perfect bob. By comparison, I had on a tan cable-knit sweater with a pull in it that I hoped didn't show too much, mom jeans, and old sheepskin-lined grandma boots. But I had put product in my hair, and I was wearing a bracelet that Sibby had given me.

"Hello, hello, hello!" We smiled and hugged.

"Sorry I am late. Good to see you, Charli!"

The waitress stopped by. "Do you need more coffee, and are you ready to order? Or do you need more time?"

"Coffee is fine, and yes, give us a few minutes, please," I said.

"It's kind of nasty out this morning, but we can't complain; we haven't had much snow yet. Oh, question for you. I have to go to a birthday lunch tomorrow. Do you remember those cool crackling candles? Where did you get them? Did you get them, or am I thinking about someone else?"

I told Sibby, "Oh yes, it was me, and I got them at that bed-and-bath store. They do make a nice gift."

"Good; I can stop there after I go to the CPAs."

The waitress came back. "Are you ready?"

"Oh, sorry," said Sibby. "We haven't even looked at the menu. We promise we will look right now, so come back in two minutes."

"Should we split something?" I asked. "Okay, bring me up to date on everyone."

"The kids are fine. Oh, and thanks again for visiting Robin and Chester. They are still raving about that dinner. And it was so sweet of you to come all the way to the surprise party. Did I tell you about Buddy?"

Buddy was her son. "No. Is he okay?"

The waitress was back.

"Oh, we have to come up with something," said Sibby.

"Do you want to share the Drowsy Egg Special, except avocado instead of sausage, and I like egg whites, and let's add kale and goat cheese."

"Sounds good to me. So what about Buddy?"

"Well, last week, he called us, and he needed his suit for a publicity photo for the team." Buddy played college basketball in Indiana. "He forgot it. He said his girlfriend could take his car and meet us halfway if we would bring the suit. Well, we were already planning to drive to Chicago to take Annie her gerbil food and help her buy groceries—she doesn't have her car at college, so we said we would—but that's two hours out of our way, and his girlfriend had to be on time, because we needed to get to Chicago by 4:00 p.m. to go with Lindsey to her ayurveda appointment; she didn't want to go the first time by herself."

Our food came, so we divided and shared it. "Oh, it looks so good," I said.

Just then, two ladies approached our table screeching my sister's name. She jumped up and hugged them and then introduced me to them.

"We are meeting to go over the final details for the medical society's Christmas bazaar and luncheon. It's coming soon—next week. Oh, you should buy a table; you would love the fashions," one of them said to Sibby.

Sibby agreed. "See you next week! Sounds like fun."

We settled back to our healthy breakfast.

"Whose funeral is it, and what are you making for the meal?" I asked.

"Oh, the funeral is a sad one. I am making an easy meal. Baked ham, those church potatoes, veggie, and salad, and I will either make a pie or some kind of fruit crisp."

"Oh, that's so nice of you, and it sounds really good! So who passed?"

"She was a grade school teacher at our school, and everyone loved her. You know that saying about 'what a ride'?"

"Not sure; tell me."

"Oh, it's something about skidding sideways into your grave, wild and crazy."

"Considering I am not wild and crazy now, I would probably just want to lie down on my lounge chair and drift off reading a book!"

"I hear you. But that's how this gal was, life of the party."

Suddenly, I had one of those dry-throat, coughing, sneezing, eye-watering attacks. "Sorry," I panted, and I continued to cough and hack. "Spice … throat … sorry."

While I was struggling, a man stopped at our table. Through my teary eyes, I made out a sharp blond haircut and neatly trimmed moustache, a cashmere coat, and a scarf.

"Hello. Haven't seen you in a while. How are you?" he said to Sibby.

As I continued to sniff and cough as quietly as I could, they chatted about knowing each other from the bank. He seemed to really like Sibby.

Sibby introduced me to him. I had barely recovered from my attack. He leaned over, held my shoulders, looked me in the eyes, concerned at my apparent frailty and decrepitude, and said, "Hello, dearie. You must be Sibby's mother."

I chuckled weakly. Sibby finished up the conversation with him as I continued to dab at my eyes. I waved feebly as he departed with a flourish.

"Oh, sorry about all that," said Sibby. "Okay, where were we? Oh, I was telling you about Buddy. So, like I said, we didn't have much time, because we had to get to Chicago for Annie and Lindsey, but it seemed like we could drive down to meet his girlfriend at the Wendy's at exit 186 and still make it. So we were a tad late leaving our house because George saw a big buck in the backyard—it really had a big rack; it actually was cool, and he wanted to take a picture of it—but he slipped and fell on the wet grass, so then he had to change before we left, but he got a good photo. I think it's on my phone; let me check."

The waitress stopped at our table. "Coffee? And can I get you anything else?"

"Yes, more coffee, please, right?"

I nodded at Sibby.

"And you can bring the check anytime."

"All together on one check?"

"Yes, that's fine," I said.

Sibby sprang in. "Let me get it. It's my turn."

"No, thanks, I want to get it. You got coffee for us the last time."

"It was just coffee. And it's been so long since we've been together—let me treat."

"Okay, thanks, but it's my turn next time for sure," I replied.

"How are you doing? I can't believe we haven't talked for a while. How are the boys? And how is Pud?"

"Oh, we are all great. School and work for the boys. Pud is at home more now that golf is over."

"So it's okay with him home and retired? We really haven't talked. Geez, when was the last time you told me about him?"

"To tell you the truth, I really didn't think he would spend so much time golfing all summer. He golfed like every day. I thought we would be spending more time together."

"Did he really golf every day? Wow, that's a lot."

"Yes, pretty much. And at least once a week, he and his buddies would try out a new course, so he would leave at

7:00 a.m. and not get back until after dinner. And I want him to have fun, but then what do I do? And we aren't close anymore. I don't know about you and George, but we haven't made—"

Sibby's cell phone rang. After a short conversation, she exclaimed, "Gotta scoot! That was my CPA. I'm late. Gee, the time went fast. Okay, I love you. Sorry I have to rush. Thanks for meeting me."

"Love you," I said, hugging her.

As she ran to her car, I called, "Sibby, you never finished telling me about Buddy!"

"I'll call you."

She did call me later that afternoon. I was at home, on my way to the basement to finally begin down there.

"Hi there. Can you come pick me up? I am at the grocery, all checked out, and I can't find my cars keys. I have looked everywhere. I walked the whole dang grocery again and checked on the floor and counters and asked at the deli and went to Customer Service and talked to Bob, that nice policeman, and I dumped my purse out and checked all my pockets. And I hate to bother you, but George isn't home, and I want to get this food home because I have to make that meal to take."

"Yep, I'll drive in, no problem. I needed to go to the post office, anyway."

I picked her up, and she continued her saga about Buddy.

"Well, it was a mess. His girlfriend never made it to the meeting place, because she drove Buddy's car, and he hadn't had the oil changed in close to a year, so it broke down, and she had to have it towed. And it didn't really matter, because when I called Buddy to figure out what to do, it turned out I'd brought the wrong suit, so we gave up and just went to Chicago.

"We got there late, but Annie didn't want to go get groceries, because her gerbil died, and she couldn't function. Plus she no longer needed the gerbil food. So we ended up taking Lindsey to her appointment."

Sibby went on to tell me about a confusing conversation she'd had with Robin. "I just can't hear anything on the phone anymore!" Then her cell phone rang, and it was George, so I drove her home and waved as she hopped out of the car, still chatting.

I smile fondly as I headed to the post office, thankful for my less-glamorous, boring, but calmer life. So what if I looked like my kid sister's mother, I wore "ugh" boots, and my husband was fixated on golf? I had enjoyed breakfast with Sibby. I had plenty of stories from breakfast to tell Pud at dinner that night. Beef stew should be bubbling in the Crock-Pot, assuming I had remembered to turn it on. I'd call him and ask him to open a bottle of wine.

"Another great day!"

9

Sunset

A calendar was a showcase of persistence. When Pud had worked in racing, he'd received a free calendar every year from a supplier that featured photos of classic cars. A month with a Packard 400 photo had given way to a Thunderbird, and then the page had turned to a Corvair or a Corvette and on through the year to a Ford Victoria. And then a shiny new calendar had been hung on the hook on the wall by the phone.

In the old days, before smartphones, we'd used these calendars to record all our appointments and events. I'd saved all these chronologies. They weren't as detailed as diaries or journals, just a jot or note: "Dentist," "Z's school conference," "Christmas break," "Grandma's B Day."

Each one of these events had taken time and energy. I'd constructed a full family life out of these happenings. At the time, these tasks had been more like the flotsam and jetsam that waves relentlessly pushed on or the widgets on a conveyor belt endlessly rolling down the line. I had mindlessly hurried through many of these assignments. I'd performed what I sometimes had seen as inconsequential tasks on my twenty-four-hour stage, and without fully realizing it, I'd assembled a life from these small bits. I had filled over twenty-five years—from the birth of my children to Pud's retirement—with chores.

Pud and I sat at our kitchen table with cell phones and paper calendar. We didn't get the calendar from the car vendor anymore, so this year, we used one from the visitors' bureau of the Lake Erie Islands, and it featured fish of the Great Lakes. It was time to plan our visit to Chicago to see my sister's daughter Annie and her stepdaughter, Lindsey, and husband, Erik.

We turned the pages of the calendar and tried to find a few open days that allowed us to stop at one of Buddy's basketball games in Indiana on our way to Chicago. We bypassed the end of the year, already filled with holiday events, and right after that, our long-awaited getaway to Marco Island. We opened the new calendar to the month of walleye and then checked perch. We stopped looking when we got to bass, as that was the start of the golf season. We decided that the best option was to fly from Florida to Chicago instead of straight home and hope that we could get to Indiana another time. I sent out text messages to Annie and Lindsey:

> We would love to come to Chicago and take you out to dinner and spend some time with you. How does Jan. 18 look? And please help us pick out an amazing restaurant. Hope all is well.

Once again, it was nice to hear the reply chirp almost immediately.

From Annie:

> Cool. Works for me :/

From Lindsey:

> Awesome. Yes!!! ☺ ☺

I showed my age by writing a book every time I messaged. I needed to adopt the culture of the youth tribe and write sparingly, with those emotion symbol things. But we were on our way with the plans for our second round of visits with the young cousins. I hummed "Happy" as I entered the dates on my phone.

I spent the evening researching restaurants in Chicago, while Pud made our hotel reservations. I was the modern-day general of Operation Overlord. I used all my tech resources. We decided to stay near the Magnificent Mile at the JW Classy by Hywet. I used the Internet map and my restaurant app to pinpoint three-dollar-sign and four-dollar-sign restaurants close to our hotel. I perused menus from places that sounded intriguing. I found plenty of tempting steak houses.

I texted Annie, Lindsey, and Erik the next afternoon with my first round of selections. I knew that Lindsey and Erik liked fine dining, so I figured they already knew of some gourmet restaurants.

> Hello! Hope you are staying warm. Following up on dinner on Jan. 18 I found: Stetson's, Baffo at Eataly, Aria, Sixteen. Please let me know if you like any of these choices or if you have another favorite.

> 6 pm? Looking forward to dinner. See you soon! Love, Uncle Pud and Auntie Charli

An hour later, Lindsey replied:

> Hi! I am oddly enough reading an article about Baffo in the Tribune right now! As far as Sixteen—Erik and I have eaten there in the past … It's very pricey and the food is extremely unique but great view! Baffo looks like a great place we all can enjoy. Plus—Eataly is also a fun place to just explore.

More messages followed:

> Hi! Have you thought about TRU? Their head chef is from Ohio and it's supposed to be a super nice contemporary American style. You should look it up.
>
> Or RPM. Bavettes Bar, Boeuf! Totally could be making decisions worse lol!

I replied:

> Thanks! Will look them up now. It's fun to be a foodie!
> Haha! I checked Sixteen. But they only offer prix fixe. Not sure if that's good for our group.

I read Pud the texts and looked up the prix fixe menu. I didn't know if he liked prix fixe or even knew what it was.

Lindsey texted:

> We are huge foodies as well☺ We know that at TRU the chef will pick tables who are truly enjoying the food and give them a tour of the kitchen

I texted back:

> Oh that would be us for sure! Checking it out right now.

Lindsey again:

> Awesome I'll text Annie today and pick her brain.

After a few minutes, I texted back:

> TRU is closed on Sunday. Next time! RPM Steak looks good too

Lindsey texted back:

> RPM steak is supposed to be phenomenal

I replied:

> Only an early reservation is available. Should I grab it?

Lindsey replied:

> Let's keep looking. You can look forever at Chicago restaurants, lol!

I certainly had enjoyed my exchange with Lindsey. She seemed warm and open and zesty. Our dinner date was off to a good start.

"So, we are all set, right?" I said to Pud. "We fly to Florida for ten days and then to Chicago, have dinner, and spend the night."

Silence.

"We're good to go for Florida and Chicago, right?"

"I said yes the first time."

"Oh, sorry, I didn't hear you. And thanks so much for doing this. We had such a good time with Robin and Chester, and I am really looking forward to spending a nice evening with Annie, Lindsey, and Erik."

Like sands through the hourglass, so passed our days, and soon enough, we wheeled our suitcases to the airline check-in counter. Pud had earned millions of hotel and mileage points during his decades of travel for work. He liked to remind me that even though he had been away from home, he had gained low-cost vacations for us. I had to think about that. I'd earned mom points too, staying home with two busy boys, hadn't I?

For our Florida trip, we not only used free points for travel and our hotel, but Pud himself had earned our spending money. His job had turned up when we'd surveyed our basement. Part of the floor in a back corner had been covered with jugs and pans and bags and purses full of change, pounds and piles of coins we had taken from his parents' house after they'd passed. Pud planned to count it all when he got around to it after retirement. Retirement had come. The task looked daunting.

Pud bravely carried up each jug and container and spread the contents on the kitchen table. He looked through the mountain of dimes and quarters first. He examined each coin and kept the silver ones or specially marked pieces. Regular dimes and quarters went into bags for the bank. He had lines of coins, bags, and containers all over the floor and table.

He checked every penny, looking for wheat-back pennies, or "wheaties." Pud had me look up their value online. Pennies from 1909 to 1956 had been minted with two sheaves of wheat on the back. A wheatie was worth only a few cents more than a penny, but it was fun to discover them and pluck them from the pile of pennies.

I know the difference between *literally* and *figuratively*, and both applied to Pud. His thumb and index finger figuratively and then literally became quite sore from picking up so many coins. He worked diligently for over a week, hours each day. He was a master of persistence. Coin by coin, the bank bags grew heavier.

Finally, it was time to go to the bank. We made an appointment at the branch located in our grocery store, and the day of the big event, we each grabbed a grocery cart and pushed in a load of coins.

The bank employees—"girls," Pud and I called them—made a big fuss over Pud and his treasure. "It's King … what was his name?"

"Midas," I said. Women really did like Pud.

"How did you find so many coins, and how did you get them here?" They bubbled at Pud as they figured out how to tackle the project. The girls were strong and carried the bags into the back room to the counting machine. We all guessed how much the grand total would be.

The bank employees exclaimed, "$563 … $641 … $660 …"

I estimated $450, not wanting to be disappointed.

Pud settled on, "I'm guessing $688, but I don't really know; it could be more or less."

It had turned out that we had almost $1,300 for our trip to Florida, plus over $15 in wheat pennies at home. Pud had clarified that he had approximately $700 in quarters and $300 in pennies. The last $300 had been nickels, dimes, and some half dollars. I'd praised Pud for a job well done.

Now the big day had arrived, and we were on the plane to Marco Island. Tray tables were in the locked position, and seats were upright. Electronic devices were in airplane mode. Seat belts were fastened, and engines started. I had learned how to handle the oxygen mask. The flight attendants seated themselves and prepared for takeoff, and we rose and banked over Lake Erie. Pud and I sat in aisle seats across from each other. I spent the time reading a magazine on my tablet, and Pud worked on a sudoku puzzle in the flight magazine and then gabbed with his seatmate.

Most of their conversation centered on the economy and the job market, so I didn't pay much attention, but then talk turned to our destination, Marco Island and Naples. The gentleman asked if Pud was a golfer. Pud enthusiastically said that he was indeed. The man told Pud about his favorite courses down in Florida.

Pud replied, "I wish I were golfing this trip, but I'm not."

His seatmate agreed, “I know; golf is like a religion.”

I wasn’t sure what the *religion* reference meant exactly, but golf certainly wasn’t a religion I believed in.

I stewed the rest of the flight. “I wish I were golfing” clanged in my head. But it was the start of our vacation, and I didn’t want to spoil it right at the kickoff. When we’d planned this trip, we had wanted it to be a dream come true to launch our retirement. Would it be just another dreary stretch for me, alone with Pud?

We landed in Fort Myers and stopped and had lunch at a salad bar restaurant. Then we picked up some basic groceries and checked in at our timeshare on Marco Island. We had originally planned to stay on the beach at a Hywet Hotels property, but Pud had kept forgetting to make reservations. By the time he’d remembered, the hotel had been booked, but he’d managed to get us into a nearby timeshare.

The timeshare property was small and rather spare looking, and it was located a block from the beach. As we walked to our unit, we passed a sunny pool area. Folks were lounging with cocktails.

“Oh, let’s go unpack and then head right back down here,” I suggested.

“Okay, but I don’t want to be in the sun too long,” said Pud.

We walked on and passed a pool area called the Grotto that appeared to be created to be completely shaded.

“There you go,” I said to Pud. “That’s a good idea, though; I assume it can get pretty warm here. I might even want some shade.”

Our accommodations proved to be grander than my first impressions of the place. I was drawn to the spacious balcony with tables and lounge chairs arranged toward the panoramic vista of the Gulf of Mexico.

"This is more like it," I called to Pud. "Here's our hangout! It's spectacular!"

"Oh, good for you, but I like it in here with the big TV."

We unpacked, and Pud arranged the wine we'd brought on the kitchen counter.

"Do you want to go down to the pool?" I asked.

"Oh, not really right now."

"Okay. Well, I would be happy having a glass of wine on the balcony. How does that sound?"

"I'll pour us a glass, and you go on out. I'll watch a show and be out in a little bit."

I tried to smile, and I went out to the balcony. I pulled a lounge chair to the sunny side of the balcony, as it was getting cooler in the afternoon. I told myself I would stay happy no matter what. My view of the beach and sea improved my outlook. Colorful cabanas and flags contrasted with the cream-colored beach and sky-blue water.

A buzzing sound grew louder and louder.

Pud opened the sliding door. "What is that?"

"I don't know. I hear it too. Is it some type of machinery—a Weed Eater?"

"Oh, look, I see it now. It's a blimp!" said Pud.

We watched it motor over the beach, pulling a sign advertising a Mexican restaurant and bar.

"Now that you're out here, get your wine and keep me company. We have a great view of the beach."

"Okay."

We watched pelicans dive into the water and people dig for something in the sand and parents and children walking and skipping at the water's edge.

"I have been looking, and I think we can cross the road and walk on the beach to that bar over there and eat right by the water. Want to try it?" I asked.

"Okay. I'll have to figure out what shoes I can wear on the beach. I hate getting sand on my feet."

We carefully stepped on the beach and slowly made our way to the bar I had spotted. We sat at the counter and bantered with the bartender. It was easier to talk when we had a straight man. We enjoyed our Sensational Sunset rum drinks, which turned out to be well named. We had a front-row seat to a dramatic orange-and-red sun sliding into the gulf.

The second day we were there, we decided to walk the beach at the right time to see the sunset. It was a clear day with a few low clouds on the horizon, and we hoped for a colorful closing ceremony.

"I am going down to the pool to read in the sun. What time should I come back so we can get on the beach in time for the sunset?" I asked Pud.

Silence.

"What time should we head out to see the sunset?"

"I don't know."

"Should we go at five?"

"That seems too early. Let's go at five fifteen."

"Really? I thought it was getting dark by then."

"I'll look it up on the Internet."

We settled on 5:05 p.m. We cautiously walked through the sand to a point on the beach where other sunset fans had gathered. Minute by minute, the yellows turned to orange and then coral, rose, and even purple swag for the sun ball to shimmer through.

We tried to take a selfie with the sun's masterpiece. Another couple offered to take our photo. The man took my phone and lined up the shot. "Hey, stand closer. You two know each other, right?"

Pud surprised me. He swept me off my feet and posed us in a dramatic embrace and kiss. The man laughed and took the photo. We matched the ardor of the sunset, and our selfie rivaled *Gone with the Wind*'s panoramic passion.

The sun was poised to ooze down into the water.

Pud exclaimed, "The sun is going down! We will have to walk back in the dark!"

"No, we won't," I said, rather puzzled. "It won't be *dark* dark for fifteen to twenty minutes. The light lingers after the sun sets."

Pud shook his head negatively, and we tentatively navigated the sand and headed back to our timeshare. Pud surprised me again. He put his arm around my waist and whispered, "It's getting dark enough." He kissed my hair.

What? What just happened? We walked a little farther, and he stopped by a palm tree and pulled me to him. The sun was almost down. He squeezed my shoulders and ran his fingers up and down my back. He cupped my ample seat and pulled me much closer. Then he pulled me closer still. I kissed him questioningly, and he answered with a firm kiss. He kissed my lips and then leaned against the palm tree and kissed me again, even slower. He began to nibble my ear and then my neck, ear and neck. We were body to body, and I was dizzy. The ocean surf surged and roared, and this time the scene was out of *From Here to Eternity*.

I saw a flash. "Pud," I gasped.

He shifted and turned my head the other way.

"Pud, I think—"

His tongue moved and probed.

"Pud!"

A string of white lights flashed on.

"Hello! Would you like to be seated?"

Pud jumped. It was a waiter. We were right by the bar we had visited last night. Apparently, the bar lit up when the sun went down.

"Ah, no, thanks, we'll be on our way," Pud replied.

We tittered and composed ourselves. *Wow, I guess vacations and sunsets are aphrodisiacs,* I thought. The waiter had interrupted our mood, but we strolled back, hand in hand, flopped on our couch, turned on the TV, and watched a basketball game.

Like the tide, moods and feelings ebbed and flowed. Sunrise found us enjoying orange juice and Pop-Tarts in our living room, clicking between the business channel and the opening of the stock market and the weather channel.

After an hour of silence that was a bit more bearable for me given Pud's recent warming trend, Pud said, "I think we might, uh, want to get a winter, you know, place here and come down for half the year."

"What? *What?*" I dropped my pastry.

"Yeah, uh, yeah. Oh, look, the market is opening up." Pud dodged my question.

"What were you saying? Move here?"

"Well, Bill and Sam come down every winter. Bill and his wife have a condo, and Sam stays with his in-laws. I could golf with them, and you could read and relax by the pool. Get away from the snow and have fun."

What? What had Pud hit me with? He might as well have actually hit me. I felt as if he had pushed me out of a tree and knocked the wind out of me. My thoughts swirled.

"Uh, that would be a no for me," I finally muttered.

"Oh."

No way was I going to live down here so Pud could golf with his buddies all winter. We hadn't talked about any kind of move at all before this. Was this whole trip just a ploy by Pud to try to convince me to move near his golf buddies? All he thought about was golf.

Pud looked stonily at the television. I didn't know what

else to say. I got up abruptly. I huffed out to the balcony and threw myself down on the lounge chair. I angrily sprang back up and paced to the railing and held it tightly. Then I pounded it, and my tears flowed. I stood stiffly for a few minutes and then swallowed hard and fought to calm myself. I never cried. I breathed and then slowly sat down again on the lounge.

What is happening? Where is my something wonderful? Is golf the only thing around the next corner?

Instead of looking ahead optimistically like I usually did, I turned back and stepped onto the path of sad thoughts. I turned away from joy and focused on my wounds. On my path of heartbreak, I passed many of the hurts I had accumulated through the years. I had buried and hidden these sorrows under a rock, or I had thrown them into the underbrush. But they were still there, waiting to be uncovered. As I walked again down this hopeless path, I unearthed those aches and gently touched the tender places.

I walked back to the balcony and gazed into the distance. I dug up a pain and remembered one weekend years earlier. Pud had been home, and he'd hardly talked to the boys and me except to complain and reprimand. All weekend, he'd harped at us. Then the phone had rung at some point, and it had been a friend of Pud's. When Pud had spoken to his friend, he had been a new person. He'd sounded so warm and welcoming. I had been devastated. Why didn't he sound the same way with his boys?

Enough! I firmly and abruptly stopped the bad thoughts. I stretched and pushed back my hair. My lips tipped in a small smile as a bittersweet memory came to mind, a tale of wine. I joked with friends that wine had saved our marriage.

In the early years of our marriage, Pud had gulped his dinner, put down his knife and fork, pushed back his chair, and headed back to the TV. The boys and I would be starting to eat, and he would be finished. We would continue with our meal, and then I would clean up the kitchen by myself. Even if the two of us had been out for an evening at a restaurant, Pud had bolted his food and then sat impatiently while I'd finished.

Wine had changed everything. Pud had toured some Napa Valley vineyards when the race crew had been in California. That had been the turning point. Pud had started introducing me to new wines when we went out and stocking wines at home so we could enjoy it at meals. When Pud relaxed and sipped wine, he was jovial, mellower, and more inclined to linger at the table.

Before wine had come to my rescue, I would prepare for dinner with Pud. I would save up bits of conversation I hoped would be interesting to him, like I was saving kindling to ignite the conversational fire. I'd toss out something cute one of the boys had said or something that a neighbor had told me and would hope that tinder would start a blaze of sharing. Sipping wine had made it so much easier and cozier to interact with Pud.

I was jerked out of my thinking by the sound of the sliding door. Pud came out and brought me my orange juice.

"Thanks, hon," I said, deciding to smile and forget about our earlier altercation about golf.

"Uh, thought you might be getting thirsty. We can, um, sit here and watch the gulf. Look, there's a pelican diving."

Later in the afternoon, after some time at the shady pool, we came back to the balcony and sipped wine, held hands, and savored the deepening hues of the sunset. The dusk moved like stately Bach organ chords progressing across the horizon. The comfort and warmth of being with Pud also swept over me, and my spirits lifted, but like the light that lingered after the sun had set, the traces of sadness still persisted.

10

Dry Aged

We woke the next morning to the bongo sound of our smartphone's alarm. We planned to catch an early flight for our dinner with the Chicago cousins. It didn't take long to pack and check out, and soon we headed to the airport in Fort Myers. After several cool days, we left on a day that was forecast to be in the upper seventies. Oh, well. Good-bye, sun, and hello, Windy City.

Everything continued to go smoothly, and we had the TSA Pre check-in, which allowed us to keep our shoes on. Our flight left on time. Ever since our New York snafu a few years earlier, I'd appreciated on-time flights. Pud and I had planned to fly to New York City to see our younger son, Zim, perform at Saint Patrick's Cathedral. He had been a member of a renowned Cleveland youth choir. We'd booked the first flight of the morning so we would be sure to make it to the concert.

Snow had fallen lightly on our way to the airport. When we arrived at the airport, it was snowing harder, and our flight was delayed, but we were told to stay by the gate.

After forty-five minutes, they announced that there was a short break in the weather, and we were to board immediately. Relieved, we scrambled on and heard a rushed version of all the safety announcements, and the plane pulled back. We taxied to the deicing area. We sat there and sat there; Pud told me that was a bad sign. He was right. The pilot informed us that the weather prevented us from taking off, the crew had been on duty too long, and the flight was canceled. I cried, thinking that we were in danger of missing our son's performance.

Pud launched into stern businessman mode and rushed to the airline desk. He scheduled us on a late-morning flight to LaGuardia. We texted our change in plans to our son and friends and waited like hawks at the gate, our unwavering gaze designed to keep everyone working to ensure our flight would go as scheduled. It did not; the snow got even worse.

We grumbled, complained, snapped at each other. Then we tramped to lunch. After a subpar meal, we decided to look for seats with a power outlet so we could recharge our phones. We found the last two available seats in the terminal, and resigned and dejected, we planted ourselves in them.

And then a Zen-like moment overcame us. We grew calm, and the world moved more slowly. We stopped fretting and enjoyed the simple pleasure of a place to sit together while our precious phones charged. All was well, and we relaxed and thought, *It is what it is.* We texted and let everyone that needed to know that we were still stuck, and then we enjoyed ourselves.

I invented a game called Finding Pud's Second Wife. I rated each woman who walked by, trying to pick the perfect mate for Pud. One was too fat; one was too old; one looked too cranky. He thought I was nuts, but it made him smile.

Even though I was transcending our troubles, I was still a bit weepy at the thought of missing our son's concert. Pud girded up his loins yet again and made one last attempt. He managed to get us on a late-afternoon flight to Newark, New Jersey. We boarded, we deiced, we waited and waited, we held our breath and prayed, and then we roared down the runway and headed east. We were on our way. En route, we plotted that if we made like O. J. Simpson in his airport commercial days, combined with a few Jack Bauer moves, we could still make the concert in time.

We rushed off the plane, barreled through crowds, and arrived breathlessly at the baggage area. Our karma continued because our suitcases were the first bags to roll around. We grabbed them and slammed out to the taxi stand. We dashed to Manhattan and made it to the church on time. We'd waved to our son, eased into a pew, and sighed with quiet joy as we heard the angelic voices ring throughout the venerable cathedral.

That crazy travel day had changed us. We had developed our patience muscles and amped up our *c'est la vie* attitude. We were still type A, but we were less impatient when faced with travel snags. We were not quite to the level of drugged-out hippies, and we were still uptight in many aspects of our lives, but we had experienced life on a different plane.

Today, so far, we hadn't needed to meditate, as our flight to Chicago was going as planned. The only untoward event had been when Pud had tried to dive into a restroom on the way to our gate and had clipped a lady with his rolling suitcase. It turned out that she ended up sitting right by him on the plane. Pud gave a friendly apology, and they both had a little laugh over it.

We accepted our napkin and cup of soda from the flight attendant and then talked about the weekend plans with the young cousins.

"Okay, um, yes, so we will check in to our hotel first, right?" said Pud.

"Yep. We get there early evening, so we may just want to eat at the hotel." We were staying downtown near the Magnificent Mile in a top-tier Hywet. "Maybe we'll even have time to walk up Michigan Avenue. Otherwise, we can do that tomorrow during the day before dinner. And it'd be nice if we could get to that big art museum."

"Or watch, um, golf on TV."

"Hmmmm," I replied.

"Hey, we're, uh, used to that warm Florida weather now. It may be too cold for us to walk around," Pud tried to explain.

In addition to seeing our young cousins, I also looked forward to the big-city experience of Chicago. I hadn't been to Chicago since Robin had turned ten. My sister had orchestrated a special trip for the girls—Robin, Annie, and our mom and me; we'd experienced the ultimate birthday extravaganza, featuring a high tea at the American Girl flagship store.

"Uh, okay," Pud continued. "The kids are coming to our hotel, and we are meeting in the lobby at six thirty, and we can, uh, um, have a drink, and then we are walking to the restaurant. Or maybe a taxi?"

"Far as I know, that's the plan."

"Sounds good. And there are six of us?" asked Pud.

"Right." I paused to give my trash to the flight attendant. *Maybe I should traipse down to the restroom now that the seat-belt sign has been turned off.*

"Yep, there's Annie and her roommate, Alice." I decided

to give Pud their dossiers. "Annie is a junior and is majoring in advertising. I don't know about her friend Alice. Lindsey is finishing her MBA, and Erik is a nurse in the ICU. Sounds like everyone is doing well."

"What did you say about Lisa and … what's his name? Bob?"

"No, it's *Lindsey* and *Erik*. They are both doing well. You can learn more about them at dinner; you won't remember it all now," I said.

I decided to scurry to the bathroom before I had to answer any more questions from Pud.

Our trip to the Windy City continued to be a breeze. As soon as we landed, I texted all the cousins that we had made it and received smiley-face replies.

Then Lindsey texted:

> Hey! Are you guys looking at bars?

I replied:

> Sure—do you have some good ideas?

Lindsey texted back:

> Rebar Trump Tower overlooking river.

I replied:

> Wonderful idea, meet at 5 pm before dinner?

Pud and I took a taxi from the airport and arrived at the splashiest hotel we had ever seen, stayed at, or imagined. The lobby was all marble and chandeliers, with a striking, modern bar. We checked in and were upgraded to an executive suite. I thought, *Oh, that sounds nice.* Turned out, that was like saying Versailles was *nice.*

Our suite was glorious. Every room was oversized, starting with the large living room with a plush couch and huge TV and granite-topped bar. We counted 1.5 bathrooms; the "1" bathroom was as big as our first home with a tub the size of a backyard pool. There was a TV embedded in the bathroom mirror. A large tile shower was another beautiful feature, along with a gorgeous granite counter and makeup area. The fixtures were polished nickel, and they gleamed; I wondered if they replaced the hardware after each guest. The ".5" bathroom featured fine furnishings too, and it was about the size of our dining room at home. The bedroom had a restful seating area in addition to the usual cloudy cushion of a magic-carpet-ride bed, and there was another giant TV.

"We are Cinderella and the Prince and the Pauper!" I exclaimed to Pud.

We bellied up to our honors bar and spent the rest of the evening making cocktails with the cute elf-sized bottles. I mixed a Jack Daniel's with pineapple juice and called it a Hula Jack, and then I experimented with vodka, pinot noir from the bottle beautifully displayed on the bar, with a splash of grapefruit juice for Pud, and christened that a Sunset Surf. I told Pud I didn't realize I was so talented!

We watched our two immense TVs at the same time, and then I took a swim in the bath pool and watched the TV in the bathroom mirror. It took a while to get the water the perfect temperature; first it was too hot and then too cold, and then I added a smidge more hot, and in the midst of doing that, I found some heavenly scented bath salts and added that to my brew of bathtub bliss.

I soaked for a few minutes and then called out, "Oh, cabana boy?"

Pud hollered, "Did you say something?"

"Yes, oh, cabana boy," I trilled in an enticing voice.

Pud came to the door. "What? I can't hear you."

"Come here, please, cabana boy," I muttered in a regular tone and not the sexy voice I had tried before.

"Cabana what?"

"Oh, just come in here. I wanted to show you the tub. Look at the mirror. There's a TV in it. Do you want to join me in the tub? The water's fine."

"Uh, no, I just want to relax."

"Okay, well, can you bring me my drink? Bring yours too. Top them off, and at least you can keep me company for a little bit."

Heavy sigh, but off he went to fetch my drink. There was plenty of room for him to perch on the marble that rimmed the tub. I added a skosh more hot water.

"Well, here we are," said Pud.

"We are, and it's perfect. Why don't you wash my back?"

Pud hesitated and then obliged and gently rubbed my back with the warm, fragrant water. After a few minutes, he kissed me on top of the head. Then he kissed me on the nape of my neck, lingered on my shoulder, and smoldered his way to my collarbone.

"Do you think I should get a tattoo above my breast?"

"*No!*"

"Oh, I thought it would be seductive."

"No, hmmm," Pud murmured as he nibbled my earlobe, a magical sensation for me.

Pud bumped something on the tub and stopped. "Oh, here's some lotion. My legs are, uh, dry. I am going to try this."

"Oh, it smells good. Try some on me, please." He spread the cream on my face and neck, and the balm was fragrant and soothing, essence of roses and lavender with a spicy over note of ginger.

"Ahhhh," I whispered as huskily as I could.

I was in an aqua haven, ready for romance with a strong, caring husband. I leaned my head back and sighed. My sighs turned to screams. My eyes were on fire.

"Oh my gosh! Towel! Water! Washcloth," I panicked, throwing my head underwater and then rubbing ferociously at my eyes. I kept dunking my head and wiping my eyes, and finally I could peek out of a slit.

"Something very stinging must have been in that lotion," I said. "Sorry for all the commotion, but it was killing me! What kind of lotion was that?"

I grabbed the small tube and realized it said *shampoo*, not *lotion*.

"Look, Pud. It's shampoo. Not lotion."

"I wondered why it was so hard to rub into my legs. I guess I couldn't see without my glasses."

"Oh geez. I am getting out now," I huffed.

I consoled myself with the luxurious terry-cloth robe the hotel provided, and then I curled up in bed. I was blinded, but not by love. Pud went back to the living room to watch SportsCenter.

We slept pretty well, interrupted by the sounds of jets taking off—which, in the morning light as we looked out the window, turned out to be the public transportation system. We made a halfhearted attempt to cuddle and get the romance fired up again, but Pud dropped his pill, and I had to get out of bed to help him find it on the black-and-white tile floor. By that time, we were hungry for breakfast and settled for a hug.

We had access to the concierge floor for breakfast, so we set off. Pud turned left, and I turned right, and then I hurried back as he held the elevator for me. We found the place and piled our plates with cage-free chicken scrambled eggs, applewood-smoked bacon, and house-made yogurt. Over croissants and the complimentary newspaper, we planned our day and decided that we would go on a morning walk. We would combine sightseeing with some exercise—not too much, though—before the gourmet evening. We grabbed our coats, headed down to the magnificent lobby, and asked the doorman the way to the Magnificent Mile.

We bolted off, and after a few blocks, we realized we were going west, not east, so we corrected our course. Then a snowy and drizzly mess began to fall. Pud didn't have his hat and gloves. They weren't even in the room; they were back in Ohio. His hands were all right, as he had long sleeves and pockets for warmth, but his balding head needed some love. Up ahead, we saw a drugstore, and we went in and picked out a sock hat. Pud looked cute in it, and he put his arm around me.

We soon came to the art museum and then turned north up Michigan Avenue.

We strolled for an hour and stopped for coffee and sweet rolls. Then we bought a deep-dish pizza to sample some genuine Chicago cuisine and brought it back to our palace. We enjoyed the cheesy, doughy wonderfulness. We relaxed on our couch and napped a bit—resting our eyeballs, as Pud called it. We dressed for dinner, hailed a cab, and headed to Rebar at Trump Tower for our big evening with the Second City young cousins.

The entire evening was a success. When recounting the night, I always launched the story at the finale. The end of the evening found us in a refrigerated room that contained a mammoth pile of pink salt blocks created from 250,000-year-old Himalayan salt. Arranged on stainless steel shelves around the room were chunks of meat and steak cuts, such as filet, rib eye, and sirloin. They were dark red, and some were almost black in color. We touched a black one, and it was hard and firm. This was the dry-aging room of the number-one steak house in Chicago.

The manager of the steak house had invited the six of us to see the room because we had heartily embraced the steak house experience from wine, appetizers, and steaks to side dishes and desserts. The tour of meat was the culmination of our gastronomic evening.

We'd begun our visit at Rebar. Pud and I had settled in to view the Chicago skyline from a comfortable sofa, and Annie, Alice, Lindsey, and Erik had joined us. They had relaxed in comfortable armchairs. We chose our beverages—cocktails for Pud and me, sparkling water for Annie and Alice, and red wine for the other two. We invited each twosome to select an appetizer. From the time we entered Rebar until we slid into taxis at the end of the evening, we talked and laughed nonstop. Lindsey, Erik, Annie, and her friend Alice were delightful companions.

First, we wanted to hear each young person's current headlines. We asked Annie and Alice to start. They were roommates and juniors in college. Annie was just over five feet tall with an interesting, dramatic look and a skewering sense of humor. She was majoring in graphic design, not advertising as I had thought. Alice was also petite, the picture of the sweet coed, and was studying literature. They both were pleasant although on the quiet side. But these careful facades hid two women who were adventurous and aimed to live life to the fullest. They surprised us with their plans.

"This summer, we are doing something cool," Annie told us. "We are going to work together at a zip line camp in Wyoming."

Alice explained, "Last summer, my boyfriend and I visited Wyoming and seized the chance to skydive and hike the mountains. We plunged eighty feet into a glacial lake. We decided to go back and experience some more of the wildness, and Annie decided to come too."

"Cheers! Bravo!"

We all raised our glasses and wished them well on their next round of adventures. Annie also shared that she planned to go to Iceland at the end of the summer.

"You know Iceland is green, right?" asked Lindsey.

The appetizers came, and we passed them and took a few minutes to munch. The pancetta flatbread that Annie and Alice ordered turned out to be the favorite, beating out the fried chicken sliders and lobster spring rolls.

Then we focused the spotlight on Lindsey and Erik, who had married the year before in a storybook reality-show wedding. Lindsey was model-like with her strong features, long blonde hair, and sculptured figure. Erik could have been a model too, or the good-guy boyfriend on a sitcom. They shared their news.

Lindsey began, "I found my dream job. I was hired by an investment company, and I start my training to be a financial advisor on Monday."

"Hear, hear!" we cheered.

Erik then told us his big news. He was starting medical school in the fall.

I was heartened by how varied our group was and also by how close we felt. We were two young, bold friends searching for action and adventure, a young married couple with more traditional career aspirations, and an older couple who had done some of each and were now content to sit in the stands and cheer the younger generation.

Pud auctioned off the remaining appetizers among the group, and we prepared to taxi to the restaurant. Soon we had arrived at our dining experience and were seated at a cozy table large enough to make eating and handling the plates comfortable but small enough for easy conversation.

Our waiter, James, was friendly and very knowledgeable and shared his information in a confident and engaging manner.

Pud said to him, "So this is the number-one steak house in Chicago? Why is it the best?"

James had a good but unexpected answer. "It depends what you mean by *best*. If you want a juicy, traditional filet, this is not your place. But if you want a place that aims to create the most flavorful, savory piece of meat possible, then you will enjoy your evening here. We are number one because we have focused for years on producing the best dry-aged steak. If you look at your menu, you will see descriptions of each type of meat. We have twenty-eight-day to fifty-five-day steaks. Dry-aged beef is an acquired taste, so if this is your first experience here, you may want to start with the twenty-eight- or forty-day meat."

After the preliminaries were completed, we settled into a comfortable evening of dining and conversation. We sampled such appetizers as dry-aged steak tartare and an amazing bacon chunk on a skewer with maple syrup dipping sauce. We decided to order a variety of steaks, and we shared steaks aged twenty-eight, forty, and fifty-five days. The interactions and banter continued to flow, and I was pleased that all the young people seemed to really like and enjoy each other, as they had only been together as our family for a few years.

Pud was on his best behavior and conversed quietly and calmly with each one. I relaxed and enjoyed the pleasure of seeing us all together. I focused on being supportive and encouraging, although I did step out a bit and gave one piece of advice.

The topic was communicating at work. Lindsey explained that she was attempting to be more assertive at work and wanted to be a better communicator in her new job. Annie and Alice agreed that they would like to be bolder, more confident speakers, as well.

I told them, "Actually, each one of you is very mature and in control of your speaking skills. I am impressed. But here's one guideline that a professor shared with my class way back when I was in college. No one was participating in class discussion, so our professor encouraged us by explaining his number system. Each one of you has a number. One of you might have a low number—say eight. So it only takes you eight times to speak in public before you are confident and assured. Another one of you may have 225, so you have to talk 225 times before you are capable at public speaking. The point is, you each have a number, and every time you express yourself in a group, you get closer to becoming an accomplished speaker."

Alice had laughed. "What if my number is two million?"

"It doesn't matter. Keep on speaking, and you will eventually hit your number and be at ease with speaking. I think I am still working on my number, but I am sure each of you is getting close."

Erik had joked, "Okay, I am going to talk nonstop the rest of the evening. That should boost my number."

After a dessert of cake pops and fruit presented on a little leafy tree, we had been invited to visit the dry-aging room. We then ended the evening with hugs.

"We hope you all feel loved and supported," Pud told them.

"Oh, I almost forgot. We brought you a little something." I handed each cousin a yellow sponge shaped like a smiley face. "It's a smile because we were so happy to see you!"

We hugged again and then headed to our separate taxis.

In our taxi, I leaned against Pud and reviewed the evening. Now we had visited with Robin and Chester, Annie, and Lindsey and Erik. We were so proud of all of them.

Robin was the daughter I'd thought I'd always wanted. If I had been given a child order form, I would have checked *smart, pretty, responsible, friendly, has a backbone, likes school*, and *likes to read.* And Robin would have been delivered to me.

But now I saw that Annie was the daughter who would have been out of my comfort zone but really fun to have around. She was witty, cute, eccentric, and modern. She was a pill that would have been delightfully good medicine for me.

And Lindsey was spectacular and in a different galaxy from me altogether with her striking blonde looks and very polished and competent manner. She would have been an amazing daughter too, and she would have taught me grace and elegance.

I focused on the girls because I already had the two best boy children in the world, even though Chester and Erik were great guys too. I was very pleased that we were connecting with the young people. But were Pud and I connecting with each other?

One last thought hit me from out of the blue as we pulled up to our Versailles. The young cousins saw Pud as a friendly and interesting guy. Lindsey had talked to him seriously for quite a while at dinner. Maybe I should look at him through their eyes. I leaned over to kiss Pud, but he was jerking at his wallet and stressing about paying the cab driver, and I missed and kissed his elbow. I hoped he realized I was thanking him for a lovely evening.

11

Journey to the Basement

If I rated our recent trips like a review on a shopping website, I would give our trip a 4.5 out of 5 stars.

> Fantastic Trip—Would Do It Again
>
> I really researched this vacation before I went, and I compared it to many other trips, and I am so glad we went on this trip. It was great! The beach and scenery in Florida were better than I expected. Chicago is a top city, and you won't be disappointed with the restaurants and cultural experiences. My one complaint is that my husband was moody part of the time and would have liked a golfing junket better. If you buy this trip, I recommend that you invite young people to go with you.

Home suite home! My new mission was to inject some of the Chicago hotel suite dazzle into our comfy but humdrum home. Pud and I were back from our Florida and Chicago adventures. Northeast Ohio was a snow globe, so we were hibernating. I sat at the kitchen counter and ate my morning greek yogurt. Pud made a fried egg sandwich and shared some bites with Oakley. He checked his social-media page, and I read my news sites.

"Thank you, God, for another great day!" I said as I scraped the last of the yogurt from the bottom of the container.

"What? Oh, I know what you said. What are you doing today?"

"I decided that my number-one priority must be the basement. I want to go through everything down there before spring."

"Have fun," Pud said as he opened a video about a kitten scaring a Great Dane.

"Well, I really want to get it done, and I told myself that I would plow through the boxes and bins and clean out at least one shelf a day. After I survive that, I want to redecorate. How can I capture that Chicago vibe here at home?"

"I am going to go snow blow; a few more inches came down. And then I am going to the club to have lunch with the guys."

"Oh, thanks, hon. Have a good lunch."

I headed down to the Island of Lost Memories. I approached the four big metal storage shelves. Boxes, containers, and shopping bags were crammed and stacked to the ceiling. Christmas and other seasonal decorations were jumbled in a nearby alcove.

I lugged four large plastic containers to the floor. I

opened one and rooted through containers of old theater programs, baseball hats, and odd small appliances. I was ruthless and disposed of most of that bin. I peeked into the next plastic tub. My perseverance energy was flagging when I discovered my old summer marching-band uniform in a department store box at the bottom of a bin of old yearbooks and photo albums. I stopped to look through the treasures from my glory days.

Life in the public school music program began in the fifth grade when you chose your instrument, took lessons, and joined the other honkers in an ensemble that sounded like the boys' band in *The Music Man.* My girlfriend and I had signed up, and all we'd known was that girls played the clarinet or the flute. I'd wanted to play the piccolo. I'd yearned for the Sousa spotlight, but the band director said I had to start on flute before piccolo. We both became flutists, and we both stuck with band through grade school and middle school. Our reward came in high school.

In high school, the marching band played at football games, community parades, and band contests in the summer and fall. In the winter, the orchestra provided the pit for the big school musical, and in the spring, we prepared for the all-city music festival. Friends and music were my salvation in adolescence.

Marching band was the highlight of my high school life. There was nothing like riding back from a football game in a crowded bus, kids piled into the backseats. We screamed old-fashioned fight songs and had tickle fights, fell in love, and savored the elixir of friendship and comradeship that joining a group provided.

I hadn't played the flute since graduating from high school, and my summer uniform had been packed away since that last parade over forty years earlier, but there were several things that had always stayed with me from my band days. I hadn't known it was called *persistence* at the time, but I had been introduced to it in band. Airy puffs had become sounds, and clearer, dulcet tones had turned into scales and songs, and a bunch of kids like me had become a precise marching unit. I'd made great friends and learned in the years to come that marching-band kids were going to be good people.

In fact, when I'd first met Pud, I had been attracted to him because he was a conservative, he played bridge, and he had been a trumpet player in his high school band. I should have asked if he were a golfer, though. From my band career, I'd also learned that life was richer when you joined a quality group that was dedicated to a purpose. In the basement I showed Oakley our opening band salute for old time's sake. "Kick down 2, 3, 4, UPPPP 2, 3, 4."

I'd continued participating in groups after high school. When I was younger, I'd volunteered for various church groups, youth fellowship, guild girls, women's society, and diaconates. When I'd faded from church life, I'd gone on to help with neighborhood and community events, Red Cross, Salvation Army, and school functions. I now served on the board of two nonprofit organizations; one was a group for able-bodied and disabled gymnasts, and the other was a multigenerational civic chorus.

Regardless of the various causes and groups, the one thing that had remained constant was that I often served as secretary. I liked to write, and I didn't mind tackling meeting minutes. Persistence and organization were good skills for a board secretary. Determination enabled me to sit through long meetings spiced with strong opinions and personalities. I enjoyed the service and friendship of these positive groups even though none of these organizations provided a ride in the back of the bus with a pile of buddies.

I reluctantly tossed my marching-band memorabilia, including my "FHS All Hail to the Green and Gold" T-shirt, into a trash bag. I would finish this box, scope out the next few boxes, and then call it a day.

I moved to a different shelf and grabbed a decrepit suitcase that I had brought from my parents' house when we'd closed and sold their home. I opened the lid and found some old shirt boxes and plastic bags. I took out a box, broke the old rubber band that held it together, and looked inside. I was dumbfounded. Photo albums were piled in the box. They had leather covers and black pages. The photos were secured with white photo corners.

I opened one of the books and gazed at a photo of a pretty girl about ten years old, dressed in a sailor pinafore. There was a name written along with a date in white ink: Grace, 1898. Grace was my dad's mother, my grandmother. I carefully turned the aged pages. There were more photos of Grace and those who I assumed were other family and friends.

I put that album down and continued to peer into the suitcase. There were several albums in another box and plastic bags of loose photos. I carefully put down the suitcase and noticed that there was another battered suitcase on the shelf. I opened that one and discovered small boxes. The boxes contained slides. I remembered that my dad had loved his thirty-five-millimeter camera. I peered at a few slides lying in the bottom of the suitcase and checked the labels on the boxes: "Baby Charlotte," "Trip to Arizona," "Christmas 1964." My childhood history was stored in these canary-yellow Kodachrome boxes. There were about two hundred boxes of slides, and they seemed to be in good shape as best I could tell.

I reached back into the first suitcase and opened one of the plastic bags. It was full of photos. I looked at the top photo, which I recognized was my dad as a young boy. He was dressed in a tie and knickers, seated on a wooly pony. That photo was dated 1931.

I carefully placed the photos in the boxes and carefully put the lids back, as they were dusty and brittle. I stacked the suitcases back on the storage shelf. I reached for a box on the shelf above, and I lost control of it as I heaved it to the ground. It was crammed with old vases and terra-cotta pots. That's why it was so heavy.

I glanced at the contents. The terra-cotta pots reminded me of my mom. She had placed pots of red geraniums outside her porch each summer. As I thought about my mom, I reconsidered the photos. Now that I had found them, I couldn't leave them, ignored in the basement like they were junk. What should I do with them? I would have to think this over.

I realized Pud was calling me. "I'm back from, uh, lunch, lunch with the guys."

"I'm downstairs. I'll be up in a minute."

I tidied up what I had completed in the basement and carried two trash bags up to the cans in the garage. I walked into the kitchen, and Pud was peering at his computer.

"I have been paying, uh, ahead. On the car payment. Uh, each month. So I figured we are making about three extra payments in a year. So we will be done eight months early." Pud liked numbers.

"Great," I said. "Good job, hon. Do you want a pop or water?"

I handed Pud a pop. He closed the bank page and opened his social-media page.

"Did you see that the, uh, um, the president made a soldier change his wedding time so he could continue his golf round?"

"What? Change his round?" I replied.

"Yes, the soldier and his, uh, wife, girlfriend, were getting married, married on the course, but the president was playing. So they had to change their ceremony at the last minute and let the president play though. That's as bad as when he, uh, golfed right after that press conference."

"Sounds like something any of you golfers would do. Golf is the only thing that matters," I said impatiently. That ended that topic.

Throughout the week as I did my chores, I thought about all those photos I'd discovered in the basement. I wanted to do something meaningful with them to preserve them and enjoy them. My sister would want to see them. Should we divide them up? Should I give her a box? Maybe I could frame some of them, but there were so many. I was lucky to have found them. Thank goodness I hadn't thrown those boxes away while cleaning out my parents' home. What should I do with this legacy?

On Saturday, I had time to venture down to the basement. I pulled down the photo suitcases again. I had an idea. August was home this weekend. I called to him and asked him to please come down. Five minutes later, I yelled to August again and asked him to come downstairs right now. Five minutes after that, I texted him:

> PLEASE COME TO BASEMENT I HAVE A QUESTION FOR YOU.

Five minutes after I texted, I tramped back upstairs to the second floor and found my beloved son under his desk, scrambling through his box of spare computer parts. His black computer box balanced on his bed with the compartments open and wires sticking out.

"Did you hear me calling you? Can you please come downstairs with me? I have something to show you, and I need your technical advice."

"No," he mumbled.

"*No?* You won't come downstairs?"

"No, I didn't hear you, and yes, I will come. Give me a minute. I am looking for the NVIDIA 7600 processing card that has the water-cooling component to switch out with my two 3400 video cards that will increase my power by 50 percent without even overclocking."

"Hmmm. Okay, thanks. I appreciate it. See you in the basement."

I walked back downstairs. When I got to the kitchen, the dishwasher was singing its song to signal it was done, so I stopped to empty it. After I put the dishes away, I decided to look in the fridge to see what we had for dinner. There was some old salad in the bin, so I wrinkled my nose and snatched that and looked for any other weird items to take out to the trash. I went out to the garage to throw that refuse away and found Pud rearranging the deck chairs on the *Titanic*. Actually, he was moving the stored patio furniture out into the driveway.

"What are you doing?" I asked.

"Um, I thought I should clean out the snow chunks that have melted and fallen off the cars, so I am moving this stuff"—he used a different word—"so I can pull the cars out on the driveway and clean the garage floor."

"Oh, thanks. That's a good idea." I grabbed a chair and helped him carry it.

I heard Oakley crying at the door, so I decided to let her out so she could run around for a little bit while Pud and I were working. Pud asked me to get him some paper towels, so I headed back into the kitchen. When I got in, I heard August shouting my name.

"I have been in the basement for ten minutes. Where are you?"

"Oh, geez. Sorry, I got swept away," I called to him. I tossed the paper towels to Pud and rushed back downstairs.

"Hi, August. Sorry; I was helping Dad. Thanks for being patient. Look what I found." I showed him the old cases. "There are boxes of slides and years of photos and photo albums. Many of them are really old. Look."

August peered into one of them. "I can't look at this dusty stuff with my allergies. And these are stored in the absolute worst way possible. You need to get archival storage boxes for them so they don't degrade any further."

"Okay, good to know. That's why I wanted to show all this to you. You are the tech/media master."

"Yes, yes, I am. How can I assist you, madam?" he replied in one of his funny accents.

"Well, now that I have found all these again, these are all so valuable to me. What should I do with them? You said I could store them in … what did you call that storage? But should I organize them? Should I frame them? Should I put them in better albums? What should I do?"

"Whoa! Okay, first of all, if you want to save all of them, we need to get you archival storage boxes. You want museum-quality, acid-free document storage."

"Okay, can I find those online? Look at this one; it's your grandfather on his wedding day!"

"That's cool. Now once we have them stored safely, what I recommend is that you scan everything."

"Scan? What's that?"

"You scan them into a digital format."

"Digital format?"

"Yep, on your computer, Mom."

"I can get these on my computer and look at them?"

"Yes, and you can send them to people or make DVDs with them. They will be just like your digital photos you take with your smartphone."

"Wow. But I would have to pay someone to do this?"

"You could pay, but I can get you all set up here at home if you want to do it yourself."

"You would help me? And you think I can do it? Would that be the best thing to do, scan them into my computer?"

"No matter how carefully you handle and store your photos, time and age will eventually cause them to fade and deteriorate. By scanning them into a digital format, you will preserve and protect one of your most irreplaceable possessions." Sometimes August sounded like an infomercial.

August added, "Let me check to see what we can get. I think photos are scanned into 300 or 600 dpi JPEG files. We should get you top-quality, eighty-year archival DVDs. Plus, when you digitize the photos, you could also do some neat things with photo software."

"Oh, honey, thank you so much for checking. And can I scan in the slides too, not just the photos? Oh, and I could make some kind of copies, right? I bet Aunt Sibby would want copies of these. It might be neat to do this myself, if you think I can."

"Yep, you will be the media queen. Okay, I will check for you. Oh, and while we are down here, let's talk again about refinishing the basement."

We had discussed for fifteen years whether or not we should refinish the basement. While I could see some pluses, I always ended up balking at the price. But August had a new approach to the project.

"I was thinking that we could just finish one area and use it as an entertainment room. Come here." He walked me to the other side of the basement, away my from my storage quagmire.

"We could paint this wall and floor, mount a giant-screen TV on the wall, and set up speakers. Get theater seating. It will be fantastic. You wouldn't have to do the whole basement, just this part, so it would hold down the cost. And we would all love it."

"Hmmm, interesting concept," I replied. "Show me more about what you mean."

Well, we had a blast. We created August's concept. We took an old tarp and hung it from the I beam to have a visual for where the wall would be. Then we took blue gaffer tape and outlined an eighty-inch TV on the wall with six-foot speakers. We arranged bins to replicate a couch.

"Well, you do have a cool idea, but let me get the storage area cleaned out first before we tackle a new project," I said after we had studied the layout. "The basement shelf area would look glorious if I bought all new matching storage containers, don't you think?"

"No, it would look glorious if the basement were finished with a giant TV and awesome entertainment area."

"Ha!" I pretended to punch him. "Let's go up and play with our booze and talk about it."

"Okay, but first I want to finish my computer stuff. I am adding RAM DDR3 1600 MHz. I just got a new motherboard that will support eight sticks. And I will look up what you need to scan too."

August and I were always in search of the perfect margarita recipe. We liked to play with our booze and try out cocktail recipes. We met later in the afternoon. We mixed Patrón, Grand Marnier, and pineapple juice instead of sour mix. I sipped our new concoction. August chose to start out with Patrón on the rocks.

"Well, if you want to do the photo thing, I found everything you need. Really good stuff too."

"Oh yes, I would love to save all these photos. I did look online, and it seems like it's about fifty cents a photo to have a service scan them. Plus I would have to mail them, and that makes me nervous about losing all my memories, so yes, I am psyched to give it a try. How's your Patrón? I think the pineapple tastes pretty good."

"Patrón is wonderful. Okay, I found the Epson V600 photo scanner."

"It can do photos and slides?"

"Yes, it can do it all, and it has all the pixels you need. You can scan documents too," he answered. "And then you will need an external hard drive to save all the photos, because they take a lot of space, and your laptop won't handle all of them. So I found a really nice one like what we use at work."

"Oh, I am so glad you know all about this. Okay, a scanner and hard drive. I never would have thought of a hard drive. Is that it?"

"Yep, well, let's get some DVDs and cases, because you said you wanted to burn some of the photos. That should do it. The scanner is $250, and the hard drive is about $180. I think we can Primo it so you can get going right away."

"Wow, sounds great. Thank you, thank you. I think I will make another margarita, a baby one this time, to celebrate. Maybe try some cranberry juice this time."

"Okay, lush," said August. "So I will order everything for you, right? Oh, and while I was looking, I saw some really good deals on seventy-five- and eighty-inch TVs if you want to do that downstairs project."

"Um, probably need to think more about that," I said. "But I am thrilled about this photo project."

I looked forward to learning how to use all my new devices. I couldn't wait to get to work and make the photos come alive again.

Little did I know all the joy I would soon find around the corner of my photo-scanning project.

"Thank you, God," I told myself quietly. "Life is good. And I do like the cranberry juice better in my margarita."

12

Light the Corner of My Mind

Sibby texted me:

> Can't remember name of bar we used to go to in the '80s.

I immediately replied:

> Billy's

She replied:

> Yes! Knew you'd remember. Fun times.

If it was the early 1980s, fun times were a given, and Billy's had been classic 1980s, with a movie-set dance floor and disco bar. Sibby and I had first bravely ventured there after we had seen an ad for half-priced beer and a free disco lesson on Tuesday nights. We wanted to meet guys, but on Tuesdays, we only ever met other girls who also wanted to take dance lessons and meet guys. Friday nights were the money nights.

I went with a gang after work on Fridays, and Sibby usually showed up with her friends. Billy's was always packed with young corporate women with big shoulder pads or fitness buffs with neon minis and leg warmers. Lots of guys on the prowl were there in tight shirts, gold chains, or turtlenecks, warm-up jackets and Air Jordans. You could always count on somebody in my group crying during the course of the evening. Friday night at Billy's was exhilarating but could be a night of highs and lows.

The high feeling began when you arrived, found your friends, and claimed a place at the bar. That hopeful buzz continued as you scanned the crowd and made eye contact with a decent-looking guy. If you linked up with him and danced, it was a great night. If he ditched you for someone in a slinkier dress, it was a night of tears. Sibby and I had survived Billy's for about a year before we'd met our future husbands.

I texted:

> Why are you thinking of Billy's?

She replied:

> Who is Billy?

Then she added:

> Oh I understand. We drove by where it used to be today, and I couldn't remember the name.

I decided to look Billy's up online. I couldn't find anything about the incubator of my heyday, so I surfed and found an interesting link about a young man who had been taking a photo of himself every day for the past five years. As I was into photos now, I decided to read more.

"What have you learned from this endeavor?" he was asked.

I assumed he was captivated by how he had changed over time. I was wrong.

"I was surprised that I really hadn't changed very much over the years. I still had a shaggy haircut, glasses, beard, and wore plaid shirts. I wondered if I should even continue the project."

I guessed that he'd decided to quit. Wrong again.

"I decided to keep going because I liked the sense of purpose that taking a daily photo gave me. Every day, I knew I had accomplished at least this one thing."

Here's what I had to say to him: "Honey, that's why God invented laundry. There have been plenty of days where I would have gotten nothing done, zero off the to-do list, if it hadn't been for laundry. Throw a load of towels in the washer and voilà! I've accomplished something."

I finished the story and then wondered if Pud had been surprised at how many routine tasks were involved in maintaining a home. I had to admit that since retiring, and in spite of his golf priority, he had become a capable assistant housewife. Running the household had been 99 percent my responsibility, but now that Pud had stopped working, he pitched in with the chores.

One day the month before, we'd orchestrated one of our monthly shopping routines. For this errand run, we'd eaten lunch at Country Barrel and then cruised to the warehouse club to stock up on pop, water, paper products, and other sundries. It had been a fun way to manage these chores.

As we'd driven to home, the back of the SUV loaded with supplies, Pud had said, "Well, it's amazing how much we've, uh, gotten done this week. Changed the oil in the car. Paid the bills. Dry cleaning. Met with the financial guy. Went to the warehouse club. I am sure we did lots more too."

"You said it," I'd replied. And then I'd continued with a rare showing of my feelings. "You know, when you were away on trips, you would call home, and you would ask, 'So how was your day?' or 'What have you been doing?' and I would start to tell you. I'd say, 'Oh, I took the boys to the library, shopped for groceries, finished three loads of laundry, attended a church meeting, and helped my mom.' I could tell that you weren't listening to me, and I could hear you turn up the TV and listen to the weather report while I talked. Even though it didn't seem like much or very exciting when I reported it to you, the day-to-day chores did require energy and planning. Do you get it now?"

"Uh, I guess, yeah, it does take time," Pud had replied after a long pause.

I hadn't pursued it any further, but at least I had told him about something that had bothered me. I didn't like to get into it with Pud—or with anyone, really—partly because there were enough problems and tough situations in life without dishing out more bad news but mainly because I was a chicken about getting into sticky discussions. But I had succeeded in telling Pud about how I felt, and we had both lived through it. And I realized that we were growing closer by sharing the ordinary, routine moments of life.

August texted:

> I ordered the photo scanner, external hard drive, and dvd disks and jewel cases.

My new treasures all came two days later thanks to Internet shopping.

The next weekend, August helped me set it all up. I decided not to commandeer the kitchen table, as we so often did for projects. Instead, I decided to set up my own office. There was a quiet space in the loft on the second floor above our great room that we didn't use. I asked August to carry up a composite-board table from the basement. I didn't have a desk chair, but August had a spectacular idea and recommended that I use a large blue exercise ball that was cast off in a corner of the basement. "It will be ergonomic and comfortable for you."

I wasn't sure, but it turned out he was right. It was supportive to sit on and seemed like it would be handy for me to roll around and reach all my important office paraphernalia. I retrieved an old filing cabinet from the basement and a small green shelf. I now had room for my printer, paper, envelopes, notepads, pens, Sharpie markers, stapler, ink, and of course, the fabulous photo scanner, laptop, and hard drive.

I was in business. I rolled around my space arranging all my goodies. I had an official office and work space. A benefit of being in the loft was that I could hear and see most of the house and be accessible to my family but still somewhat separate from the hubbub.

I proudly showed it all to August. "Yep, it's good to have your own dedicated space. Okay, I will get the scanner and hard drive set up for you and show you how to use it. We can probably get you going tomorrow. What's for dinner?"

"Well, I guess I will mosey down to the kitchen and see what we want to eat."

We had leftover ham for four days straight. I figured we could make two of our favorite Bomb Shelter recipes to go with it, and if Pud opened a bottle of wine, we would have all the food groups, and it would make the meal seem fancier.

I called these recipes Bomb Shelter—or BS—recipes because I made them with cans and staple products that I could theoretically store in a bomb shelter and live on for ten years. Our two favorites were Bomb Shelter Beans and Bomb Shelter Macaroni. I found all the ingredients in the pantry and got to work. It was comical; my family and I enjoyed fine dining, but everyone was thrilled that night with the canned Bomb Shelter dinner.

"Oh, it's so good. I always eat too much of this stuff," moaned Pud.

"Thanks," I said. "And kudos to you; you picked out the perfect wine to pair with this dinner."

"Ha! Can't go wrong with Joseph Phelps."

I encouraged August to finish what was left in the bowls, and then I loaded the dishwasher.

"Thanks, Mom. I'll have you set up tomorrow for sure. Tonight, I will get my workstation and cloud set up, and I also have a match, and then I will work on your gear."

"Thanks, hon. It's really great how much you know about this."

Pud and I decided to watch college basketball on the TV in the bedroom and finish the Phelps cabernet. We arranged the pillows just right, snuggled in together, and clinked our wineglasses.

"To a perfect weekend at home together."

I sipped the big, fruity cab and waited for Pud to turn on

the TV. He reached across me and brushed my breasts. *Is he feeling frisky? Has he changed his mind about TV?* I sighed and relaxed into his chest more to indicate I was all right with anything he had planned. He pawed around my stomach with one hand and gripped my derriere with the other hand.

What's going on? Has Pud read about something new for the boudoir? I wiggled and kissed the back of his elbow as he grabbed under my legs and moved them brusquely to the side. *My big guy is getting a little rough. I'll go with it.* I rubbed his back briskly. I licked his ear. He put his head under the covers. *Oh my!* I patted his bottom.

"I love you," I murmured.

"Damn," he said. "Where's that stupid remote? I can't find it. It's supposed to be on the bedside table, and it's not there, and I thought maybe you had dropped it."

"Oh," I mumbled, feeling a little disappointed. I sank back onto my pillows and took a big breath. "Okay, let's look for it."

"Those darn boys probably moved it. They don't care about anything."

"It has to be here."

We both jumped out of bed and shook the covers and then checked every surface in the room. I even looked in my purse in case I had gotten absentminded and put the remote there. We finally found it under the bed.

"Maybe the dog got it," I said. "We're good to go now."

"Now I have a cramp in my leg from all that," complained Pud. "I'm going to have to walk around to get rid of it."

"Oh, that's too bad," I said, trying to be concerned.

I grabbed my e-reader and decided to get back to my book about a young lady who grew up in a house of hoarders. *Always good to learn about exotic lifestyles.* That and a good wine would have to do.

After breakfast, I gently reminded August about the photo project.

"I can help you after lunch; I am waiting for my software to download," he said.

I used the rest of the morning to round up the boxes and suitcases of slides and photos from the basement.

I heaved it all to my new office, perched on my exercise ball, and surveyed my project with pride. I was glad I had a large table so I could sort through all the images. I made a rough estimate and figured there were six photo albums, plus several hundred loose photographs and studio portraits in each suitcase. There seemed to be over two thousand slides.

"Wow, this is going to be a big project. But I have to digitize them; otherwise, they're going to waste just sitting in a suitcase."

Fortunately, it looked like many of the photos were labeled. I read: "Coney Island—July 4, 1916"; "Kitty and me in a field"; John and canoe, August 1918."

I called to my son. "These are amazing. Photos from the early 1900s. Oh my gosh, come see."

In addition to the albums created by each grandmother, there were many formal photographs taken at studios. I found my grandmother Grace's eighth-grade graduation photos. She wore a white shirtwaist with a white skirt and a broad ribbon at her waist. Her long hair streamed down her back. She reclined on a lounge, holding a rolled diploma. Next I found Grandmother Bertha's brother, Great-Uncle Heinrich, with a stiff collar, cravat, and Edwardian-style formal suit, showing a serious but pleasant countenance. They could have starred in *Downton Abbey*.

August joined me. "This looks like it will be a cool project." He leafed through some of the photos. "Some of these are old! And who took all the slides?"

"My dad took them. He was so proud of his camera. I remember it took him forever to focus it, but now I appreciate having so many good slides and memories."

"You do have the mother lode here," said August. "Okay, let's see if we can get this all going." He loaded all the software, set up the scanner, plugged it in, and attached the hard drive to my laptop.

"I hope I can learn this. Go slowly, and let me do it so I remember. Should I organize all these photos and put them in chronological order?"

"No, just scan them in, and you can organize them on your laptop. Here, I will set up some folders for you."

He showed me the process, and I tried to pay attention to all the steps: load photos, click, preview, select, and then scan. After a few fumbles, I could do it. I was thrilled to see the sharp, clear images show up on my desktop.

"I did it all by myself! Thanks for teaching me!"

"No problem," said August. "This is my life."

"Look how awesome the photos look! The ones we just scanned are over a hundred years old!" I exclaimed.

"Well, black-and-white photography was actually well developed—oh, pardon the pun—by the 1900s. Chemicals and materials have continued to improve, but the basics were well known by that time. Well, I think you are good to go. Good luck."

"Okay, but let's check to make sure they are really saved." I didn't want to lose the photos I had scanned.

"Here," my son said as he showed me, "if we close everything and then open your photo file again, look—there they all are, all saved. Oh, and you may decide that you want a more powerful computer with quad core and a lot more memory and storage, so I can look into building one for you."

After thanking August again, I grabbed a handful of

photos from the suitcase and loaded four onto the scanning bed just to practice. *Click, buzz, whir,* and then there were four photos of my young grandmother and grandfather apparently at someone's farm. One photo showed them on a wagon holding the reins of a mule, and the others had them posing with chickens, a cow, and some other folks who were either friends or relatives. I clicked to save them. I clicked Save again to make sure they were really saved.

"This is so cool," I murmured to myself. "I wish my parents were here to experience this. They would have loved to see these so big and sharp." Just then, an idea formed, an idea that would be a great surprise for everyone. I stretched and considered my plan. *Yes, I could do it!*

I reached for a clump of studio shots and initiated the scanning process. Nothing scanned into the computer. I panicked, but I realized I had goofed and placed them so they faced up instead of down on the scanner. I simply placed them correctly and scanned again. I repeated the scanning steps to embed the instructions in my poor brain. I stopped after a few practice runs and worked on putting the photos in some type of order.

August walked by and asked, "Are you having any problems? Why did you stop scanning?"

"Everything is fine. I think I am going to be able to handle all this tech. I decided to put the photos in better order before I scan them in."

"You don't really have to do that. You can scan them and then look at the thumbnails, and I could get you a facial recognition software—"

"I see what you're saying," I interrupted, "but I have a special project in mind, so I want to look at the photos mindfully."

"I should have ordered you the $1,700 scanner; with that

one, you load fifty slides at a time. Oh, and if you aren't ready to get a bigger 4K TV, how about a new sound system?"

I smiled and arranged a pile of photos on my table desk and scanned them with my own eyeballs. After viewing most of them, I decided to sort them in subsets based on each grandma's chronology.

I recalled that my paternal grandmother, Grace, had been born in New York City and lived her childhood and young adult life on the East Coast. Her husband, Cyrus, had grown up in New Jersey. My maternal grandmother, Bertha, had been born near Cleveland, Ohio, and her husband, John, had moved to Ohio from Pennsylvania. I reached for Grandma Bertha's suitcase and explored the contents.

It's kind of neat, I thought. Here I was growing better acquainted with the younger generation, the freshest leaves on my family tree. At the same time, thanks to the photos, I was meeting the generations before me, the roots and trunk of my history. I stood in the middle between the past and the future. I had the opportunity to learn from both. And that would change my life for the better.

13

Firenze

A gentle spring morning gracefully dawned. Cheerful daffodils and diligent robins sparked in the early morning light, and sparrows bobbed in the puddles that glistened from the refreshing, early-morning shower. A blue jay screeched grumpily to a trio of squirrels skipping through the branches playing tag. Was that a rainbow I saw? Did I hear the tinkle of angelic chimes?

I was kidding about the weather; four days in a row of icy rain and mushy snow; dark, evil clouds; and fierce winds were enough. I shut down my feeble attempt to cajole myself out of the weather blues. According to the calendar, the vernal equinox was propelling the sun closer to our polar abode. My greeting of "Thank you, God, for this beautiful day, but could it be a tad warmer?" went unacknowledged.

Peering out the sliding door as I let the dog out revealed no singing birds, dancing flowers, Disney chipmunks, and certainly no sunshine. I did see a loose trash can that had escaped and was rattling down the road. Oakley came straight back to the door to be let in, and I tried to swipe at her muddy paws as she zoomed back into the kitchen.

I puttered behind her, wiping up the crumbs that August had left from his breakfast as he had hurried off to work earlier. He wouldn't be back for a week, so my counter would stay clean. While my coffee brewed, I settled in the family room to watch the morning news and read my tablet. Pud soon appeared, fresh from his shower, clutching colored markers in both hands.

"Good morning," he said. He saw me looking at the markers and explained with a small grin, "Oh, um, well, I have an idea about color-coding our receipts to help us budget and also to get ready for tax time. I can use one color for medical bills, one color for donations, another one for entertainment, and so on."

"Really? Okay, well, not sure if we need all that, but go for it," I said.

He set up shop on the kitchen table. When I came back in to get a coffee refill, I stopped, patted him on the shoulder, gave him a peck on the cheek, and looked at what he was doing. He was sorting bills.

"Is that the entertainment pile? Wow, we were busy," I said.

"Yep. Here, let's, uh, look at what we've done since summer ended."

I reached for the stack of papers and knocked some on the floor. Pud rolled his eyes as he picked them up and took over.

He read, "These are the payments for the all-member and member-and-guest tournaments. What happened in September? What is this one?" Pud squinted at a date on a blurry receipt. "Why did we go to a steak place in Cleveland?"

"Oh, let me think. We went out to eat with ... I know. We took Dan and Mark out to dinner to thank them for the landscaping and to get to know them better, remember?"

Looking at bills always made me anxious. I decided to change the subject. "Oh, and when we took Dan and Mark out to eat, that's when you had the great idea to take Robin and Chester to dinner, and then we decided to keep the dinner idea going with all the young cousins."

"I was sorting out this other wad of bills. I didn't hear you."

"I was saying when we treated Dan and Mark to that nice dinner, it gave you the great idea to visit Robin and Chester, and that led to our other young cousin trips."

Pud's phone dinged with an e-mail notice. He reflexively reached for his device and checked his e-mail. "Oh, look what Sam sent me. He was telling me about these golf shoes that he really liked. He sent me the link. Look at these. What do you think?"

"Oh." *Geez, golf again.* "Oh, they look fine."

"I might check these out. I need new golf shoes. Did I tell you the funny story? Sam was having his wife trim his hair, and every time she touched the clippers to his head, he screamed that it hurt."

I partially listened as I continued with my own thoughts. "Oh, and then Chester invited us back to Cincinnati for the surprise party for Robin. We had such a good time at our first dinner with them, and then it was so nice to be invited back."

"Turned out she was, uh, using the clippers upside down."

"Oh, those clippers can bite, I guess. It really turned out well with Robin and Chester, didn't it? And then our next trip was to Chicago to see Annie, Lindsey, and Erik. That was a blast," I continued.

"To tell the truth, I think Chicago was even more fun than our dinner in Cincinnati," said Pud.

I bristled a bit about that. "Well, the restaurant was superb, but Robin and Chester were so sweet and friendly. Anyways, I am so glad we have been doing this. What's been your favorite food?"

Pud said, "Well, I thought I was going to like that dry-aged steak the best, but it had a different flavor. The steak appetizer was really good, what was that called? I think Erik liked it too."

"Oh, geez, that was … I think it was the steak tartare. I liked that, and I think all of us girls really liked the creamed spinach."

"Oh, I liked that too, and I don't even like spinach," Pud agreed. "Uh, so who do we have left to schedule?"

"Well, we need to see Buddy, but he seems to be pretty busy. I have texted him several times, but I haven't heard from him. We should at least find time to go to one of his basketball games. And that leaves Byron. We haven't contacted him at all, so we need to do that."

"Isn't he away somewhere?" asked Pud.

"Oh yeah, he's enrolled in that grad program at Boston. That's pretty far away. We need to get to know him better, for sure."

"Oakley, I don't have any food for you," said Pud. "The last trip we took was to Marco Island and Chicago in January, but now we don't have anything planned. You know, let's try to plan a dinner while we have time before golf starts."

"Plan a dinner? Go out?"

"That would be the idea. Like, you know, maybe people from my old work group. Harlan and Jewel have talked about seeing us. So has Donald. And Kenna texted me about getting together."

"Oh, that could be good. What are you thinking? Should we go out with all of them? Maybe get your whole group together—so Harlan, Jewel, Donald … who else?"

Just like our other chat that had gotten the whole ball rolling for the young-cousin visits, Pud had once again come up with a great idea. He seemed to spin these ideas from the ozone, but I was glad he did. We stopped color-coding bills and got right to work on our dinner idea.

We talked over restaurant options and picked Firenze's Vineyards. We looked at the month ahead and selected a date. Then I checked the Firenze website to see about reservations. I reserved a table, created an event in my smartphone calendar, and sent e-mail invitations to Pud's former work gang with one click. We organized the event in less than ten minutes. How had we gotten things done before the Internet?

Almost immediately, we heard the e-mail reply ding, and Pud checked his incoming mail. We had positive replies from three couples in the group.

"We are amazing," I said modestly as we connected for a high five. "That's almost half the group. This is going to work out."

Firenze's was much more amazing than we were. A local family had taken their farmland and created an Italian tableau outside of an old industrial town in northern Ohio. It had taken them only five years to change their fields into Firenze. They cultivated vineyards that produced varieties of red and white wines, which they bottled and purveyed in their bistro. A replica of a big Italian country farmhouse, the bistro featured hearty food, wine tastings, and a festive ambience. The restaurant also had a large outdoor patio area overlooking a picturesque pond.

Across the pond was a lovely and authentic pavilion and

piazza for weddings and other celebrations. Nearby sat the Grape House, which showcased a winemaking observatory. Walking paths led to villas for private group dining and for guests to spend the night. The grounds were exquisite; it was like being in a theme park. "Celebrate Life!" was their motto.

We had fun planning and anticipating our work-group dinner. The night of the event, Pud and I arrived early at Firenze. Before our friends came, we checked the table arrangements; we put a little favor at each place, the famous bright-yellow cleaning sponge with a smiley face. I wrote "So happy to see you!! ☺" on each one.

Pud hadn't seen many of his associates since he'd retired. The group gathered on time, and after a flurry of hugs and happy greetings, we all found our places, women at one end of the long rectangular table and men at the other end. Everyone was able to attend, so we had fourteen at the table.

Pud and I stayed fairly calm and amicable, at least for us. We made sure wine was on the table when our friends arrived, several bottles of the house-made wines, a bold red and a milder pinot noir, a rosé, and a sweet white and a dry white. Everyone drank and compared the grapes.

Pud offered a toast. "Thank you all for coming tonight. My happiest years at work were spent with this group. It's so good to see all of you again. Cheers!"

Pud and I got a little miffed with each other when we were all considering appetizers. Pud announced, "I have selected some appetizers for the whole table."

I interrupted him, "Oh, let's have everyone select what they want, and we can all share."

Pud hissed, "No, that will be a mess. I want to make sure we get things everyone will like."

After a few more of our glares and emphatic hand

gestures, the waiter overheard us and came to our rescue. He said he would bring the most popular appetizers for the table to share.

Soon we had plenty of starters. We all agreed that the white pizza, mushroom ravioli, and bruschetta trio were winners. Pud's former boss, Marv, wanted mussels, so I was gutsy and said I would be glad to try some with him. Then I decided I needed the smoked-gouda pierogi, so I talked Marv's wife, Jo, into trying some with me.

The waiter continued to take charge, which worked out well. He announced the evening's specials and then discussed entrée choices with each couple. He also did a superb job keeping the wineglasses full. Pud and I were back to having a good time.

I knew Pud would order the house-made bolognese. I debated many items but ended up choosing the stuffed ravioli with tuscan kale and ricotta, tomato cream sauce, grape tomato, zucchini, and squash. My meal was delicious; how did they squish all those veggies into those little pasta pillows? I didn't really see what anyone else ordered, but I heard talk of tuscan beef short ribs and monkfish osso bucco.

The guys talked about racing, and the ladies talked about children and grandchildren and major life events, such as weddings and births. Pud was back in his element. He kept saying how much he missed the action at the track each weekend. To me, race tires were black and round, but Pud and his colleagues analyzed every aspect of those rubber doughnuts, the size, shape, weight, material composites used, and temperatures at the track. All this data was vital to the race teams, and Pud knew and had advised every driver and owner and had met many celebrities in his years in racing.

Most of us punctuated our stories by sharing photos on our smartphones. We scrolled through Jewel's grandson's first birthday and her daughter's wedding in Las Vegas, and Jo showed us her son's wedding in San Diego. I shared photos of Zim scuba diving and snorkeling at the Great Barrier Reef.

Mae had the best photos, though—shots of their new, darling golden retriever puppy. The roly-poly puppy's name was Indy, after the Indianapolis Motor Speedway. Even the guys wanted to see the cute puppy pictures.

After the parade of photos, I trotted out my number-one conversational icebreaker. My topic was a surefire discussion starter at parties and luncheons, and it even worked for me in the dentist's chair. Most of the ladies were younger than I was, but there were several who were approaching those big birthday numbers.

I opened the conversation with a general comment. "I am finally getting brave, and I am cleaning out my basement."

"Oh, God bless you. I need to do that."

"It would take me a million years to do that."

"I hate to throw things away."

The seal was broken. When I was with an older crowd, the cleaning conversation percolated with the trials of downsizing. With this group of gals, organizing the kids' toys became the key word. "How do you store LEGOs? Stuffed animals? Game pieces?" We shared pointers on how to organize memorabilia, collectibles, and plain old stuff that accumulated.

I settled in for a heart-to-heart with Jewel, who was closer to me in age challenges.

"You know what I do?" she said. "I have so many precious cards that the kids have sent me through the years. I have saved them all."

"Oh, how sweet," I cooed.

"Well, I couldn't throw them away, so I have been sending them back to each child. If it's their birthday, I pick out a birthday card they sent me, cross out their name, and write a new message. That way, we share the love again, and I don't suffer the wrench of throwing the card away."

"Oh, I imagine they really like receiving a card that you specially saved," I replied.

"I hope so. Once I accidentally sent a card that crowed, 'It's a baby girl.' Not sure how that went over!"

Jo joined us. She firmly declared, "Kids don't want our stuff. When my mother passed, I gave her large collection of Hummel figures to a local charity that we both supported."

I thought I was the queen of organization, but it seemed to be a movement. There was likely a Facebook group called Your Kids Don't Want Your Stuff. I left the ladies and headed back to Pud's end of the table to see what the men were up to.

Pud was in the middle of one of his famous jokes. "'We should review our finances. And since we're getting married, I have another question,' the old man said to his elderly bride. 'Yes, dear, what is it?' said the old lady in a concerned voice. 'Er, I was wondering how, uh, often do you plan to have sex?'"

Pud paused and looked at his expectant group. He continued, "The old lady spoke without hesitation. 'Infrequently!' The old guy stopped to think."

Pud smiled and took a big breath. "The old man then asked, 'Would that be one word or two?'"

Pud looked around. The guys looked puzzled.

"I don't get it."

"Me either."

"You have to think about it," said Pud. "'Infrequently.' 'Is that *one* word or *two*?'"

For a few more seconds, there were still bewildered expressions. Then Harlan and Brett howled. "In. Frequently!"

Everyone laughed and explained the punch line again.

Even though we all insisted we were full, we splurged on the house specialty—double chocolate fudge lava cake that took twenty minutes to make. The gents finished the night with port, some of the ladies had coffee drinks, and I enjoyed a Grand Marnier. I made sure I went around the table and sat with each couple for a few minutes. The evening ended with more hugs and talk of a summer get-together at Firenze on the patio.

On the drive home, Pud and I reviewed the evening and compared notes. I told him what the ladies had said, and he gave me the news from the men's end of the table.

I said, "It sounded like everyone was fine; no problems or crises with motor sports, and everyone seemed to have a good time."

"Yep. It was good to see everyone."

"It was great to hear you telling jokes again," I said. "When you heard what's going on at work, I bet you began to miss it. Everyone truly seemed glad to see you again."

"I guess," said Pud.

"Planning these types of dinners is really fun for us to do together, isn't it?" I commented.

"Uh-huh. What dinner should we do next? Might as well keep on."

"Oh, wow, you want to keep on with our dinners? Let's take August out to dinner. And whenever Zim gets back home, we can take him out too. I don't care what you say; we can get them to go out with us."

"Okay, whatever you want. At least we'll enjoy it."

We rode past strip malls and carpet and tile stores, and I reflected that I did feel closer to Pud. In the darkness, driving by plain block buildings, I was riding with my prince through his kingdom.

14

Trapped

While we wrangled with August to wedge a dinner date in his calendar, Pud and I were still in the mood to take someone out for a special meal, so we invited Oakley to join the RSVP Project program. She was an engaging member of the family and deserved a nice meal too. She loved to accompany us on errands. Whenever we grabbed the car keys, we endured her ecstatic jumps, prances, and twirls as she threw herself into the backseat.

Oakley especially adored going to the bank. When we pulled up to the bank drive-through, Oakley would watch the tube intently as Pud put in the paperwork. You could tell exactly what Oakley was thinking. *Dad, you have to stare at the tube to make sure it works. Stare at it with laser focus. Stare. Now.* When the pod came back, Oakley would bound to the front seat as Pud pulled out the slips and the dog biscuit treat from the bank. Two joyous chomps of the biscuit completed Oakley's pleasure.

For Oakley's special meal, we invited her to a fast-food drive-through. Her fine-dining experience required less planning, and we relied on Oakley to provide the positive encouragement part of the meal. When we pulled in line to order, she delighted in the smells and was amazed when we treated her to her own box of chicken nuggets. Hands and paws down, she was our most enthusiastic guest. We notched another successful relationship-building event!

When we got home, I texted August again:

> Let's eat at Pier M. You can bring a friend.
> Next Saturday?

He replied on his lunch break:

> K Love the place.

I followed up:

> Great! Saturday at 7. For 4?

He replied:

> Yes.

"Pud," I called out happily, "August can come to dinner next Saturday. We picked Pier M."

Pud and Oakley came in the back door.

"Oh, I didn't know where you were." I told him about August and dinner.

"Sounds good, but he'll probably cancel."

"I'll make the reservations. Also, I am going to the grocery; do you want anything?"

"No. Anything's fine."

"Okay, I am going to check the pantry and fridge before I go."

I took pride in a well-run household, and in recent years, I'd become interested in just-in-time (JIT) inventory. I'd read that JIT was an inventory strategy companies used to increase efficiency and decrease waste by receiving goods only as they were needed in the production process. That made sense to me, so I'd decided to apply those ideas to my own kitchen and household.

I enjoyed surveying my larder, going to the grocery, getting supplies and ingredients for the week, and then using them all up in a timely and healthy manner. I challenged myself to stop throwing away food, and I improved my creative use of fruits, vegetables, and leftovers.

I made a game of inventory. My goal was to have good meals, not a weird mixture of leftovers. A dinner of sauerkraut, fruitcake, and baked beans didn't count. Each meal had to be appealing, balanced, and use the resources that I had in the fridge or cupboard at the time. Another rule of my JIT system was that I was only allowed to keep one extra box in inventory, not ten. My goal really was just-in-time inventory.

I'd scored big the week before when I'd served cold shrimp cocktail and a vegetable platter one night and then used all the leftover shrimp and veggies for a sizzling pasta shrimp diablo the next night. Bread was the hardest thing for me to keep fresh in inventory. Invariably, one or two dried-up old-maid buns remained in the bottom of the bread bin each week.

My inventory management enabled me to keep my home life running smoothly, improved our bottom line, and reduced my stress. No more running out on a cold, snowy night to get milk or dog food or struggling with a dark closet because we'd forgotten to stock lightbulbs.

Was I over the top about tidiness and inventory? I didn't think so. I knew a gal who wouldn't let her husband lay a magazine down in the living room. There was a place for everything, and the casual tossing of reading matter was not allowed.

Not me. I let mail linger on the kitchen table for days. I helped my family members find their keys, and I let them leave batteries, dry cleaning coupons, stray socks, and screwdrivers on the coffee table. I also focused on balancing my orderliness with a little wildness; I could make a martini, and I tried to be fun after dark, as long as it wasn't too late.

I finished my review of our food inventory and made my list. I still wrote out my grocery list. I found my purse and keys and debated about wearing a jacket. I shouted good-bye to Pud and left. As I turned to drive out of our neighborhood, I felt to see if the grocery list was in my pocket. Nope, and I didn't see it in my purse either. *Rats.* I turned around and drove back.

Once again, the hands of the clock whizzed by at top speed, a blur as in a vintage movie. Soon it was Saturday night, and Pud and I were driving to Pier M.

"August is still coming?" asked Pud gruffly.

"Yes. My persistence paid off. You know, I have been thinking about persistence and determination lately."

"What? Those are big words you are using."

"Think about how useful it is to be a focused and steady worker. Think about when we raked leaves." Every year, we raked our leaves to the street the night before the designated

Leaf Day, when the township came by with a sucker-upper machine.

"When you look at how many leaves there are, it seems overwhelming. We think we will never get it done. But we have a system. You blow the leaves into a fluttering pile while I rake the odds and ends. Then we entice the leaves onto a tarp and carry the tarp o' leaves to the street and dump them. We move piles and piles and more piles in an afternoon, and it all gets done. Not all at once, and it's not a snap, but most of the leaves are corralled at the curb when we are done."

Silence.

"Sometimes I wish that each leaf were a dollar bill!" I added. "And think how you persist when you blow the snow. Right?"

"It seems like it."

"And think about all the chores and tasks we share now that you are retired. We press on. Don't you think it's bringing us closer together?"

"Turn on the GPS and put in 'Pier W.'"

Silence. Well, it did seem to me that we were growing together, bit by bit. *Bit by bit? Is that the key?* Maybe we hadn't connected in earlier years because we hadn't been together much to share the day-to-day fun and challenges. Funny how spending more time together now showed me how far apart we had been.

With a little coaching from the GPS lady, we made it to Pier M fifteen minutes early. The restaurant, an iconic structure, was east of Cleveland on Lake Erie. I'd always thought it resembled a Frank Lloyd Wright design, but on the website, the place was described as a unique building designed to resemble the hull of a luxury liner cruising along Lake Erie.

"I hope August isn't late," said Pud.

"I am sure he'll be fine. Did I tell you he's bringing a friend? It will be fun to meet her. And please stay positive and happy. Oh, there's his car."

We met up with August and his friend, a tall, attractive strawberry blonde who greeted us with a charming smile.

"Mom and Dad, this is Claire."

We all hugged.

"Wow, great to see you, August, and I am so glad you could come, Claire. Nice evening—we didn't even have to wear coats or jackets. We could almost eat on the patio!" I called as we walked into the restaurant.

Pud approached the host and requested a window table. Soon we were all seated in a modern dining room with a breathtaking view of the sunset over the Cleveland skyline. We hefted our oversized menus and encouraged our young guests to order plenty of their favorite cocktails and starters.

We could have dined solely on the small plates. After much deliberation, we chose calamari fritta served with gremolata, Sriracha aioli, sweet-spicy tamarind dip, gulf shrimp and baked hearth bread, shrimp cocktail, and, for me, Prince Edward Island mussels.

Pud selected wine, which was fine with me, and August kept changing his mind but decided on Booker's Kentucky bourbon, and Claire, at my urging, ordered the vodka cucumber lemonade.

The first order of business completed, we jumped right into getting acquainted with Claire. She seemed confident and poised.

"I am a marketing specialist for the Cleveland Cavaliers."

Pud and I gasped; he was thrilled. The Walleyes were Cleveland's NBA basketball team.

"Well, I want to hear more about the team," said Pud. "Seems like they have struggled this year."

August said, "I thought I told you about Claire."

Claire calmly replied, "Well, you know this is a rebuilding year, and it's a young team, but we are seeing some positive steps forward now. And there have been injuries too."

Our wine and cocktails came, so we raised our glasses. "To life and to the Walleyes!"

"Claire, please tell us more about your job. What do you actually do?" I asked.

"I primarily handle the special events during the game."

August added, "You know, the national anthem singers, the contests during the game, she keeps it all running."

Claire turned to Pud. "Mr. McAntic, whenever we get new associates or new interns, it really does take a while for us to gel and accomplish our quotas and goals, so I can understand that it is going to take time to get these roster changes sorted out."

"Teamwork is really important, isn't it?" I commented.

Pud said, "I want to see us in the playoffs sometime, that's for sure."

Two servers delivered our small plates, and we all passed and shared the starters. We ended up ordering more calamari because Pud and August liked it so much.

Pud asked August, "So, how's work? When are you going to get a raise?"

"Geez, Dad. Work is fine."

Claire came to the rescue. "How is the instant messaging wall project going?" August explained that he was helping a client develop an electronic message board for a large-scale conference.

I resolved to monitor the interactions between Pud and August the rest of the evening. The two of them could be prickly together, and I wanted to keep any friction to a minimum this evening.

Our waiter returned, and we listened to a recitation of the entrée specials.

"Live it up," I said.

Pud ordered salmon, August picked the Alaskan king crab legs, and Claire and I discussed the sea bass special and the bouillabaisse and decided to get both of them and then share.

With our meals settled, we relaxed and enjoyed the lake view.

August asked, "Is that the lakefront airport? Is that the runway over there by the stadium?"

"Oh, yes, I see it," said Pud. "I spent many weekends there throughout the years."

Claire looked at Pud with interest. "Oh, did you fly planes?"

"No, but what I did was even more fun and exciting. I worked at the Cleveland Grand Prix every summer; it was one of the races in the circuit for about twenty-five years. It was always the hottest weekend of the summer here, but it was an exciting road course, and it drew big crowds."

"I came as a baby," added August.

"Yes, one day at qualifying, I carried you around in a backpack. We checked used tires together back at the paddock, and we collected autographs on your onesie."

Two women at an adjacent table who were about forty years old and full figured were gathering their jackets and purses to leave. As they scooted out of their booth and passed by, the heavier one in a polyester suit dropped her scarf.

"Excuse me, miss, but you, uh, dropped this," called Pud.

"Oh, thanks," said Ms. Polyester. "I keep dropping things. I guess I am getting old. Thanks for telling me. We are in town on business, and I am glad I didn't lose it."

"You aren't old. You aren't old at all; you look great. Welcome to our, uh, fair city, and what are you doing here?" Pud responded.

The other woman said, "We are here at the medical center for a genome project conference."

"That sounds interesting. It's nice to, uh, meet young people like you who are doing so well."

"Oh, thanks," they both replied. "We felt so tired and bedraggled after a long day at meetings, so we decided to come out for a nice dinner."

"Well, you both look great. Did you enjoy your dinner here?" Pud said.

I chimed in, "Pud, let them go. Good luck."

The two went on their way, and I decided to take advantage of the interruption to head to the restroom. I had just walked into the bathroom stall and locked the door when I heard some women walk into the main sink area.

"Oh, that old couple was so cute."

"They were so nice, and they thought we were good looking!"

"I know; they said it a couple of times."

Oh my, are those the same two ladies that we had just talked to at our table?

"I guess we did look pretty snappy tonight, all things considered."

Yes, it is! I'd better hide quietly in my stall until they leave. It would be awkward to come out while they were talking.

"Do you think they were with their children or grandchildren?"

Ouch! Grandchildren! I'm not that old. Well, I am *that old, but I don't want to look that old.*

"Actually, the old guy was kinda cute. His wife was a little bossy."

Ouch again. Bossy? Really? It's hard to keep quiet in this stall! Hurry up and go!

"You know, they are right; we are pretty and smart. Let's go with our original plan and head to one of the bars by our hotel and have fun."

"You betcha. We are effing fabulous. I am glad we talked to them. Let me work on my makeup."

They kept bubbling and primping and having a delightful time while I was stuck in the stall. Pud was probably wondering what was going on with me. I decided I should text him. Carefully, I sent him:

> Still in bathroom. Those 2 ladies are here, and long story, I can't leave until they do.

Finally, they were ready for their big night, and they left, saying, "Cleveland men, watch out! Here we come."

Geez, I guess Pud and I really are getting into the encouragement business. Now we're encouraging strangers. I hope the rest of their night goes well!

I slowly opened my door and peered to see that the coast was clear. Then I slunk back to our table. Pud and August were bickering about whether or not people should be more patriotic. Fearing another Pud manifesto coming on, I steered the conversation into calmer waters and suggested we think about dessert. No one was keen on sweets.

"We are having a competition at work," said Claire. "The person that loses the most weight wins $500. We each received an armband tracker to monitor our weight, calories, and exercise."

"Wow. How are you doing? You look great."

Claire said, "I am exercising more. I like to run on the treadmill. I can plug the armband into my computer, and it's motivating to see the miles add up. We even have walking meetings at work. We walk around the arena."

"Wow again. I bet you could walk pretty far going around and around that big place."

I noticed that August had his arm around Claire. He said, "Well, it's a work night for us, so I guess we'll be on our way. Thanks, Mom and Dad. We loved it here. This place is amazing."

Claire added, "Thank you so much, Mr. and Mrs. McAntic. I enjoyed meeting both of you. I really liked hearing the racing stories."

"Our pleasure!"

We didn't wait long for the valet to bring our car, and it was still mild outside. Soon we were on our way, but we didn't get too far, because the bridge over the Cuyahoga River was raised for a freighter. There was nothing to do but wait. Inconveniences like this made Pud impatient, but he sighed and said, "By the time we tried to drive around, we might as well wait for the bridge to open."

It was such a pretty spring evening, and I was feeling rosy and optimistic after our dinner with August and his friend. Maybe there was something we could do while we waited. I felt mischievous. I snuggled over to Pud as best I could with the big center console between us.

"Don't you think drawbridges are romantic?" I murmured, and I nibbled his neck and ear.

"I think this, uh, one is actually a lift bridge, but they are romantic too," Pud said quietly.

He lightly rubbed my back. We kissed. His kisses grew longer and slower and deeper. I cuddled in even closer and moved my hands down to his thighs. His fingers began to caress sensitive places of my anatomy. I kissed him on the collarbone, breathed heavier, and may have moaned. I fantasized about us jumping into the backseat like we had at the parking lot of that Mexican restaurant when we had been engaged and unable to wait to get home. That time, we'd both sprawled and groped and …

Honk! Honk!

"Oh, I guess the road is open now."

Pud pushed me away and stomped on the accelerator. He hated it when people honked at him. I tentatively patted his arm and then sat quietly, not really sure what to say and not wanting to break the mood.

Pud and I did seem to be bonding over our special dinners with the young cousins and with our friends. We were genuinely having fun together. We worked well together planning the dinners, and we enjoyed each event. The more we shared together, the more comfortable I felt with Pud. We were flexing our relationship muscles, and they were growing stronger. We'd introduced the dinners to help the young cousins, but the dinners were actually helping us.

But was it enough to close the chasm between living for golf and loving me? Were Pud and I truly building a bridge over the river of cool politeness? I didn't feel as lonely anymore, but spring was budding. The days were growing warmer and longer. Golf season was looming.

15

Swing

I was a faithful flosser. I cleaned my teeth every night after dinner. But sometimes, like this morning, I flossed after breakfast. I had a nagging piece of steel-cut oatmeal that needed to be searched and destroyed. As I tugged, I looked in the mirror. *What should I do today? Thank you, God, for this beautiful day.*

I finished with my teeth, but I continued to look in the mirror. *Do I look old? How do others see me? Maybe Pud would like me better if I were younger looking and snappier?*

I was about five and a half feet tall. In the mirror, I saw my sturdy nose, full lips, and green eyes. *Am I pretty?* Then I looked closer. In all honesty, I was getting chunkier. My neck looked crinkly. My curly hair was gray. *No, it's not gray; it's platinum.* I could use a haircut and style, and I vowed to walk the dog more this summer.

I slapped on some body lotion and put eye cream on my bags for good measure. I filed a rough nail and put on jeans and a T-shirt. Then I headed down to my albatross, the basement. I could clean one more area down there before the outside spring cleanup chores beckoned. My reward for an hour of work would be to get back to my photo-scanning project.

I chose to go through the four red-and-green boxes that held the Christmas decorations. I opened the first box and found handmade decorations that my boys had brought home from school or Sunday school every year. I rewrapped the ornaments with glittered photos of my toddlers as well as their shaky handprints cut and pasted into lopsided wreath shapes. Lumpy clay snowmen, painted unusual colors, and cracked cookie-dough baubles I carefully protected with bubble wrap. I reread the imploring letters to Santa with hastily drawn pictures of sleighs and elves and found a plastic folder for their safekeeping. I spent a few happy minutes studying the loveliest Christmas decorations in the world. I would never part with these gifts from my boys. *Someday, these are going to the nursing home with me to hang on the little tree in my room.*

I labeled the box "Boys' Christmas Treasures—KEEP" with a marker and put it back on the shelf. Next up to review was my box of collectible glass crystal ornaments, a new edition each year. I had a special little gold tree that I hung them on, proudly displayed in the foyer each December. I wondered if I had put them away correctly this past Christmas. I decided to get each one out to make sure that the 2002 special edition was indeed in the 2002 box.

I moved the storage box to a table. I carefully opened each box, removed the ornament, and placed it on the table. I checked the date on the ornament and checked that it was in the correct box.

Was that Pud calling me? I didn't catch what he was

saying, and I didn't want to leave my ornaments helter-skelter, but, yes, I definitely heard him yelling my name again. I went partway up the basement stairs.

"Yes, Pud, what do you want?"

"I have been calling and calling. I need help getting something on the computer."

"Really? Now?"

"Yes, now. I can't, uh, can't get this damn computer to work."

"Okay, just a sec; let me make sure everything is okay down here." I put the ornaments back in the storage box so they would stay safe until I could get back to them.

I trudged up the stairs, perturbed about being interrupted midproject, but I needed to go to the bathroom anyways, and hopefully this thing with Pud wouldn't take too long.

"I plan to go to the, uh, driving range, and before I do, I want to look up some videos that uh, uh, oh, why can't I think of his name? Uh, that guy who lives on hole six that won the senior championship last year—no, it wasn't him ..."

"Okay, what do you need help with?" I interrupted.

"Somebody told me that there are videos that would help me with my swing. I want to see them before I go up and practice, but I don't know how to get on tube."

"Tube? What's that?"

"Oh, for crying out loud, that computer thing with all the videos. August looks at it all the time. You know what it is."

"Videos ... tube ... oh, YouTube!" I shouted triumphantly. "Okay, I think we can find that."

"So what should I type?"

"Youtube.com."

Pud entered *Utube.com*. "Damn, nothing's happening," he said.

"Oh, let me see. You have to use the word."

Pud tried again. Soon a colorful and busy site opened up.

"Now what? I don't want to see all these parrot videos."

"I saved those. There's a really cute one of a green parrot singing 'If You're Happy and You Know It.' It's my favorite. Do you want to see it? It's really adorable."

"*No! No! No! I want golf!*"

"Easy. Okay, go to *search*."

"I don't see anything that says *search*."

"It's up at the top. See, right there where the magnifying glass is? Put in, hmmm, what do you think? *Golf swing*?"

"Why do they do dumb stuff like that with magnifying glasses?" Pud typed *How do I develop a professional golf swing.*

"I think that will be too long a search phrase. Try something shorter."

"I know what to do," Pud told me emphatically.

I told myself to stay patient. Pud knew everything about spreadsheets on a computer, but social media baffled him. After a few more clicks and tries, we found millions of golf videos. Pud selected one.

Even though it was very hard for me to leave my ornament project in partial disarray, these swing videos looked interesting. I stuck around.

Pud watched the first one and then said, "How the hell do you, uh, stop this video?"

I paused it for him.

"I need to get a golf club and try this exercise with a real club," he said.

"You are not swinging a club in the house. Here, let's use something else. How about a yardstick? I want to try it too."

The first video instructor had an English accent and instructed us to yank our left shoulders under our chins as we swung our club—or yardstick. I thought we looked pretty good—maybe a little too much hip sway, though. Through the years, I had soaked up golf from being around Pud and glimpsing the TV golf tournaments. I was like a secondhand smoker, only with golf. I could recognize a good golf swing when I saw it.

Pud swung in the kitchen, and I swung in the foyer. The dog bounded between us, very excited about this new game. I had never had the patience or desire to golf for hours on a course, but it was fun to practice with Pud. Maybe we could start a new sport and house golf together?

The next video golf instructor wanted us to focus on our belt buckles. He had an Australian accent. In this exercise, we were to assume a golf stance with our yardstick and then turn our belt buckles to the left. I liked this routine too.

"Pud, I think this one will work. It keeps our hips and legs turning as one unit."

I observed that Pud was still moving his hips and knees too much, but I didn't say anything. We practiced a few times. Pud hit the fridge with his yardstick, so I was glad he didn't have a seven iron.

"Stick to the thirty-six-inch wood," I joked.

Pud didn't get my fantastic humor, so we went on to the third video. This golf guy had a South African accent, in my opinion, not that I know every accent in the world. I liked this drill the best of all. We had to stand facing forward with both arms held straight out at our sides like a cross. Then we had to take our right hand and reach over and clap our left hand. Pud moved to the second-floor landing to do this after he hit me in the back.

"This one seems to help too, doesn't it? You looked aligned and solid."

"But I don't want to clap when I golf," Pud said. "Hey, are you getting interested in golf?"

"Not a chance for me, but I have to say I do like learning these things. Learning, not doing them for five hours on a hot summer afternoon. Also, there are no lakes or sand traps here in the living room."

"Okay, thanks. I am going to head up now. Sam and I are going to meet at the range." As he walked out, he yelled back before the door swung shut, "Did I tell you that we are golfing here tomorrow and then the next day at Wyndham and then this weekend is the Opening Day tournament?"

No, you didn't tell me, I thought as he zoomed off in his golf cart. My heart sank. Golf season was here.

I put the yardsticks away and wandered to the crystal ornament organization site in the basement. *I am down. Down in the basement and down in the dumps.* Pud's golf plans made me feel so sad and alone. I had a queasy feeling in the pit of my stomach. It was just like when I had been in the third grade; my family had moved, and I'd faced a new school. My first day, I'd taken my lunch tray to a table of girls, and the entire table had jumped up as I'd sat down and moved to another table. I'd felt rejected and awkward and miserable.

Another long season of golf, and I have to face months and months alone. I didn't do anything about it last year, and now here we go again. I can't stand it. What should I do?

I forced myself to get back to work. I picked an ornament, checked the date, and then searched for the correct box. Oakley kept me company, lying on her side, legs out and snoring. All the golf exercises had wiped her out. The process soothed me. By the time I was done and the ornaments were neatly boxed up, I could reflect more calmly.

It wasn't so much that I didn't want him to do something he enjoyed or that I didn't want him to be with his friends or even that I couldn't live without him; he and I had been separated for at least half of our married life due to all his travels, and I had done many things socially without him. So what was my problem now? Just a few minutes ago, Pud and I had shared a pleasant time with the golf videos.

The videos, the computer. Yes, that was it; Pud could handle spreadsheets and numbers and equations that had one correct answer, but could he handle feelings? Feelings weren't like numbers; they were fuzzy. Did I feel so blue and shaky because Pud just assumed all his plans were set in stone like his black-and-white numbers? Pud didn't ask me about times or dates or care about what I thought; he told me as the door was swinging shut behind him.

"Okay," I said to Oakley. "His attitude is at the heart of what's bothering me. It's not so much that he golfs; it's that he doesn't think about me at all. Well, Oakley, what do you think? My mind can understand Pud, but my heart still hurts."

The dog came wagging over and licked my hand.

"I don't want this summer to be like last summer. I don't want to be sad all summer," I told her. "What should I do? I could ask him to cut back, but to tell you the truth, I wouldn't want him telling me when I could meet my sister for breakfast or when I could go out to lunch. But I always try to schedule those dates when it doesn't interfere with our life. Oh, I don't want to get into all this with him. I don't like confrontation at all. I want it to all to work out without any hard feelings."

I sighed and scratched Oakley's ears. I was done with the internal wondering and wandering. Time to turn that frown upside down; time to press on. *What can I do? Should I throw Pud's clubs in the lake? Hypnotize him so he hates golf? I don't want to take up golf, but maybe I could get a job at the clubhouse so I could see him there every day?* I chuckled, and my mood improved.

I went upstairs and fed the dog. Time to get back to my photo-scanning project. The dog and I headed upstairs. I carried a cup of coffee and a bottle of water. Oakley brought her green, squeaky-baby toy. As I settled myself on my blue exercise ball, I heard my phone alert me to an incoming message. It was from Pud.

> Finished at the range golfing now see you
> by 5

I replied:

> Ty see you at happy hour, ly

This would give me over two hours to work on my photos. I studied what my next step should be. I had already completed a general organization of the photos. I had two large photo piles—one for my mom's side of the family and one for my dad's side. I also had a good-sized container crammed with boxes of slides from 1950 to 1980. The yellow packs had been labeled in my dad's precise technical writing, so that enabled me to arrange them chronologically—"Marriage," "Honeymoon," "Newlyweds," "Baby Me," "Baby Sibby," "Childhood," "Teenagers."

"Well, Oakley, what should I name this project? How about Suitcase Scans?"

I was an astronaut in my command center, ready to blast off on my special project. For the first phase of my project, I aimed to convert all the slides and photos into digital images. Then I would work on phase two, which was to be my exciting surprise.

I hoped I remembered what August had taught me about how to run the scanner and how to save the photos on my computer and external hard drive. *I have an external hard drive!* It had been a few weeks since I had first learned to scan, but now I was committed to going full speed ahead. I reviewed my notes that outlined all the steps of the scanning process.

I opened the correct folder on my computer and then physically opened the big lid of my scanner. I put four slides in the frame thing that held them and shut the lid. On the scanner software, I clicked Preview. Nothing happened. I opened the lid and repositioned my slides and pressed the Start button a little harder. Still nothing.

Shucks. I was ready to text August and plead for help when I decided to check the plug. *Aha!* All I needed to do was plug in the scanner. I pressed Start and Preview again and was relieved to hear some charming buzzes and whirs, and I saw a light move.

In a few seconds, four images appeared on my computer. I was scared when I saw them, as two of them were upside down, but then I remembered that my son had shown me how to rotate them, so I clicked on that tool and double-checked my written instructions.

Good! My bride-and-groom parents were now standing on their feet and not their heads. I clicked again to finish the process and was relieved to again hear the whirs and buzzes. Silence and the images showed up as JPEG images in my computer folder. I read my notes again and decided that all was well. I saved everything three times. Then I clicked Save once more to be sure. Then I opened up the folder to see if the photos were still there, and I punched Save again.

"Just think, Oakley sweetie darling, whoever took these photos of my folks on their wedding day surely didn't know that one day sixty years later these pictures would be viewed on a gleaming computer."

All went well from that point, and I had no glitches at all. It was thrilling to see the slides pop up as large colored images on my screen. I hummed "You Are My Sunshine" and scanned relentlessly for almost two hours without stopping. My mom as a bride, with her mother, with her bridesmaids, with my dad cutting their wedding cake, all passed before me. I decided that I would finish the wedding slides and then get ready for Pud to come home.

I found a box to put the scanned slides in and set aside the Kodachrome boxes of honeymoon slides that I wanted to work on next. It would take me weeks to scan all the slides and then all the photos. This project was certainly going to be another lesson in persistence, but the thought of the special surprise I was creating, plus the enjoyment of looking at photos of long-gone relatives, would keep me going. Suitcase Scans was off to a good start in spite of my primitive tech skills.

August called me on his way home from work.

"Hi, Mom. I am done with my day, and I am going to stop at the computer store and get more water-cooling equipment."

"Okay. Will you be home for dinner? And how was your day?"

"It was a long one. I'll tell you about it. No, I am not coming tonight; I plan to go to my place and work on my server and then crash."

We continued to chat as I tidied up my desk, and the dog and I headed back to the kitchen. I picked a bottle of sauvignon blanc for Pud to open, and I decided to serve blue cheese and trail bologna for our happy hour when Pud finished golfing. As August told me about his day, I put out snacks and commented "Hmmm" and "Uh-huh" and "Good job."

Then I told August, "Thanks again for helping me with the scanning. I did all the wedding slides today, and I really love this process. I feel like Rumpelstiltskin; I am spinning these old forgotten slides into gold that we can all enjoy. I found crummy old suitcases full of slides and photos, and now I am restoring these treasures. I am so glad you taught me how to do this."

"No problem. I still think I should get you a scanner with an automated loader. And who or what is Rumpel … Rumpo … whatever?"

I laughed and decided to open the wine myself. It would be fun to sip a glass as I visited with August. I put the cheese plate, snacks, wine, and a glass for Pud on the coffee table and settled on the couch to enjoy a happy hour phone chat with my boy.

16

Indiana Calls Us

Oakley frolicked, turned in circles, and careened back and forth from the door to me, and I knew Pud must be home.

"Hi, hon. How was the golf? And you're just in time for wine and cheese." I blew him an air kiss.

"Great. It wasn't all that cold. I shot eighty-four, Sam had, uh … what did he have? I will tell you after I go to the bathroom. *Oakley, get down!*"

Pud returned shortly. "Thanks, Mom, for the cheese. Uh, looks good," he said as he nibbled a piece.

"Here. Sit down. I opened the wine too. I was talking to August and decided to start happy hour."

Pud poured himself a glass of sauvignon. "Oh, so I was telling you that Sam shot, uh, eighty—not bad for, uh, him, and Bob had eighty-six. So I made a skin."

"Oh, good job," I replied.

"I had two bogies, four birdies, and the rest pars. I made

a great shot on eleven; I hit the green from 120 yards. But on eighteen, I risked it and tried to hit across the lake, and I landed in the sand trap."

"Hmmm," I replied pleasantly.

Too much information, I thought to myself. To me, the correct answer to "How was your golf?" was a one-word answer, such as "Fine," "Better," or "Lousy." But only a very cranky shrew of a wife would enforce that requirement on her golfing husband, so I tried to listen to all the golf mumbo jumbo.

In the early days when I'd inquired, Pud would give me the description of the whole game from stroke one to stroke eighty, and sometimes he would detail the stroke-by-stroke report of the entire foursome. Although it had been deadly to listen to, part of me had been impressed that he could actually remember every play of the round. After over thirty years, I had succeeded in limiting the summary to the condensed version that he gave me tonight.

We settled in with our wine and cheese.

Pud said, "We should try to get to one of Buddy's basketball games. His season is almost over."

"Okay, sure," I said. "What does his schedule look like?"

Pud fumbled with his phone and then told me, "There is a home game this Saturday, and we are free. Check your calendar to make sure."

"Um, okay, looks like that would work," I said. "Let's stop in Columbus on our way down for lunch; that's always fun." There was no answer, so I sipped my wine and waited.

"Hey, I know," said Pud. "We've been wanting to see Susie again. Let's stop in Columbus on our way down and see if she can meet us for lunch."

I didn't miss a beat. "Oh, that sounds fine. Good idea. Do you want to call her, and I will text Buddy and let him know that we are coming to the game?"

Long silence. Sometimes talking with Pud was like using a See 'n Say toy.

"Sounds good," said Pud. "I will call her after dinner."

"And while we are planning things, we should see if we can schedule Byron for dinner. He's the last young cousin on our list, but he's in school way up in Boston. I don't know if we have time to go, because your golf season is starting," I explained.

"We can go whenever; ask him," Pud mumbled. "Do you want some more wine?"

I sent off two texts.

To Buddy:

> Hi this is Uncle Pud and Auntie Charli. We are coming to your game on Sat would love to take you to dinner after the game or brunch on Sunday? Ly

To Byron:

> Hi, this is Pud and Auntie Charli. We would love to visit you and take you to dinner and learn more about your grad studies. Any dates sound good? Thanks ☺

We continued on with our evening. Pud called Susie, and agreeable and easy as always, she was able to meet us for lunch on Saturday. By ten o'clock at night, it was time for me to close up shop. I let out the dog, emptied the dishwasher, and let the dog in and tucked her in her crate. I remembered there was a load of towels in the dryer, so I folded those and put them away. I emptied the bathroom and kitchen trash into the garbage can, as the next day was trash day. I turned down the thermostat and told Pud I was going to go read in bed.

"I'll be in soon," he called.

I put on my face cream, grabbed my e-reader, and settled into bed. Then I realized I didn't have my phone. I got back up, searched in all the suspect places, and found it on top of the dryer. I must have put it there when I was folding the towels. As I plugged it in to charge at my bedside table, I was surprised that there weren't any messages from Buddy or Byron.

Oh, well. I will try again tomorrow.

I clicked on my e-reader and resumed the memoir I was reading about two men building their dream home on a Caribbean island. It was soothing to read about their pursuit of a languid lifestyle as they courageously faced their travails with island time and the quest for the perfect chargers for their dining room table. After two chapters in a cozy bed, I nodded off. Pud came in and cuddled close.

I whispered, "I just fell asleep," and then I fell asleep again.

Bright and early, after seeing Pud off to his golf and starting my day with two cups of coffee and a greek yogurt, I still hadn't heard from either of the young guy cousins, so I texted them both. I received a prompt reply from Byron:

> Thx! 2 busy w school 2 plan. C U when I get back????

Oh, well; I could understand. I remembered Sibby saying that Byron was in a prestigious program, and it was only a year long and accelerated. By the time Pud got back from golf—four bogies, two birdies, and twelve pars later—I still hadn't heard from Buddy. Was our young cousin-visiting plan unraveling? At least we would see Buddy at the game.

Saturday morning came, and we were on our way to Columbus and then Buddy's college basketball game in Indiana. As usual, we had to return to our house after we had left. We had forgotten the GPS and my clothes hanging on the bedroom door, so Pud took the opportunity to go to the bathroom. And once again, Pud looked longingly at the golfers as we passed the clubhouse.

"Looks like that's Sam's car, so he's here," he said.

"Hmmmm."

On the way to Columbus, Pud complained about the trucks that were going so slowly in the passing lane, yelled about the orange barrels blocking a lane with no workers in sight, and asked me if we had received the property tax bill. We checked the ambient temperature, and it was fifty-three degrees.

I decided to text Sibby. I figured she was going to the game too.

> On our way to Buddy's game. Trying to arrange a dinner with him. Haven't heard back. Do you know what is going on?

She called me immediately. "Hello, hello. You are on your way? That's so nice of you to go."

"Oh, we want to see him play, and it's a good weekend to drive over. Do you remember Susie? We are stopping to see her for lunch in Columbus."

"Oh, good for you. Don't you like to stop at the big shopping area right off the highway?"

"Yes, that's the plan. We are meeting her at that Chinese place we like. Hey, I wanted to ask you something. So, about our fine-dining plan with your kids, you know how we did with Robin and Chester and the Chicago gang? I haven't been able to get in touch with Buddy. I know he's busy, but I was wondering if you knew anything."

"Oh, well, yeah. Well, I can't really say."

"What?"

Just then, Pud yelled, "Am I supposed to get off at this exit? Help me!"

Sibby said, "I heard that; talk to you later."

Mildly exasperated with Pud and puzzled with Sibby, I clicked off my phone and told Pud to take the next exit. We turned left at the light and made our way into the huge shopping area and found a place to park a good hike from the restaurant.

Susie was standing and waving outside the door without her kids. She looked cute with skinny jeans and a big scarf with teal and peach springy colors. We had a nice meal—bang bang chicken and sushi—and got caught up with the family news.

"Jim bought a new motorcycle, so now we have that new toy to deal with," Susie told us. As usual, she handled all her family happenings with tact and poise.

"Ha!" I chuckled. "Susie, we wanted to hear about your trips. You've been to Atlantis and Cancun. Lucky you. Which did you like best?"

"Oh, they were both wonderful. Atlantis was a great place to go with the girls. Michelle had a gymnastics tournament there, so that was exciting. Cancun was probably the nicest place we have ever been. You knew we went with my brother, Mark, and his wife, right? The resort was amazing. And we were there when the turtle eggs hatched."

"Oh, tell us more about your resort."

"Well," Susie said, "it had rooms with a swim-up feature as well as a swim-up bar. And it was all-inclusive drinks and food. Oh, and this is so funny. One day, we were planning where to eat for dinner, and I said, 'Wait, we didn't eat lunch today, so let's go to the big buffet,' and everyone looked at me strangely and said, 'Yes, we had lunch today; you had chicken.' I guess I had too many margaritas for lunch, and I totally blanked out about it. But, yes, you should go."

Soon it was time for us to head to Indiana for the game. We hugged Susie good-bye and gave her some gum to give to her girls.

As we drove on, Pud pointed out a large flock of birds and a road that led to a small town where he'd played in a basketball tournament as a boy.

My phone rang. It was Sibby.

"Are you on speakerphone?" she asked. When I told her no, she continued, "Well, I am sworn to secrecy, but I don't like to keep secrets from you, so can you absolutely keep a secret?"

"I will try my best," I told her seriously. "As you know, I have kept a few secrets locked in the vault."

"Okay, and try not to let Pud hear."

"Okay!"

"Well, Buddy is getting engaged this weekend! He is asking Maddy to marry him! He is going to ask her tomorrow. He wanted us to bring all kinds of things. We have silk rose petals and candles and luminaria and Japanese floating lanterns and a trellis and a spotlight and music. George and I are heading to Indiana soon."

"Oh, what wonderful news!" I managed to squeak in the middle of Sibby's excited description.

"Yes! Well, they are meant for each other. Maddy is so good for him."

"Congrats! Well, I am trying not to say too much so I don't give it away. How do you feel about all this? This is your baby boy we are talking about," I said.

"Well, yes, I feel a twinge, but I really am happy that he is marrying a darling gal."

"Okay, well, I'll let you go, and mum's the word. Love you!"

"Love you! And thanks for not spilling the beans; he really wants this to be a surprise, so he doesn't want anyone knowing."

I clicked off the phone, and Pud said, "So Buddy's, uh, getting engaged?"

"Yes; I don't know why she wanted me to keep it a secret from you. I was going to tell you."

"Well, we expected this to happen. Right?"

"Absolutely. It's still nice, though. Buddy's such a good guy, and now we have another wedding in the family!"

My phone lit up. Sibby was calling me back.

"Hello. Are you still driving? Can you still talk? I talked to Buddy, and he said it is okay for you guys to know about the engagement, and anyways, he is asking Maddy before dinner at this quaint restaurant, and then we are all going to surprise Maddy and eat and celebrate together. So he said you are invited."

"What? Wow! You said it's tomorrow? That sounds wonderful! We will be there, and thank you so much!"

Pud interrupted to ask what was happening, and I told him that we were invited to the engagement dinner.

"Okay," Sibby said. "Are you still there? Well, I am not sure if George and I will make it to the basketball game, because we have to finish making the luminaria, and now Buddy wants mason jars with flowers for all the centerpieces, and we have to get a box of chocolate-covered strawberries—he's going to fasten the ring box to that, I guess—and he told me to come up with some type of favor for everyone. Buddy suggested little basketballs with 'Buddy and Maddy <3' but I don't know about that—"

I had my phone on speaker now so Pud could hear it all. He rolled his eyes, and I laughed.

"Anyhoo, we haven't even left Akron yet, so we may not get to Indiana until late tonight, and I hope I don't forget anything."

"Well, good luck with everything," I said. "We will see you tomorrow, I guess. We are definitely going to the game. Oh, and text me the address and times for the dinner tomorrow."

"I will, and don't say anything about the engagement tonight at the game in case Maddy hears you."

"Gotcha! Love you!"

"Oh my, this is really something," said Pud.

"I know. We didn't expect to be going to a big event tomorrow night. Gee, I hope we have something to wear; we didn't bring much since this was going to be a quick trip to the game."

Pud replied, "We will figure something out. Oh, and the odometer just changed to 33344.4."

"No wonder we haven't been able to get in touch with Buddy to schedule our dinner. He's had a lot on his mind. Getting engaged!"

No comment from Pud.

"I am so glad we are a part of this, and I can't wait to hear about the wedding plans."

No comment from Pud. So I relaxed and looked out the window.

About ten minutes later, Pud said, "What's happening tomorrow? A dinner? Something about Buddy?"

We arrived at Buddy's basketball game forty-five minutes early, got our popcorn, and settled in to cheer for the black and red. Buddy was athletic, a point guard, and his team was always at the top of their Division II conference. They won easily, and it was great to watch him play. He hit several long three-point shots. Pud made conversation with some of the older guys sitting around us on the bleachers, mainly so he could brag about being Buddy's uncle, which I thought was sweet.

After the game, we gave Buddy a big hug for another great win and an extra hug for the special weekend event that was coming up. "Love you, good game," we called as we left him so he could greet his other fans and friends.

We stayed outside the small college town at a Hywet Suites. We checked in and rode up the elevator with another gentleman. He had on an Ohio State T-shirt. Pud said, "*O H*," and the man smiled and said, "*I O*," as he left the elevator. I carefully read the sign showing the directions to the rooms and still turned the wrong way off the elevator.

I texted Sibby to see if she was staying at the same place and if she and George had made it to Indiana yet.

She texted:

> No just left. Car is packed to the gills.

I texted:

> If you can, send me address info for engagement place.

She replied:

> I will if I can find it, but its called Mapleside Farms.

I texted:

> Ok, I can get it ly and safe travels.

Pud and I tucked into the white ironed sheets and downy duvet. He scrolled the channels and settled on a *Law and Order* rerun. I grabbed my tablet, checked my e-mail and social media, and then looked up Mapleside Farms. I found it right away and clicked on the link to the website. "Mapleside Farms: apple orchard, farm stand, bar & American comfort-food restaurant in a quaint country setting."

I clicked more on the website and saw that there was a three-hundred-acre working apple orchard and a fifty-mile view of the countryside. There were pages of photos of the restaurants, scenic lookouts, and various weddings and parties. It looked lovely, and I handed the tablet to Pud, but he didn't have his glasses, so he couldn't see anything.

When his show went to a commercial, Pud said, "So tell me what is going on tomorrow."

"I will if you give me a back rub while I tell you."

"Oh, I can do better than, uh, that," he said. "Let me get the lights off. Where are all the damn light switches in this place?"

"Oh, just come here, big guy!"

"Okay, but let me make sure that the deadbolt on the door is set."

Pud checked the door and managed to grope his way back to bed. He didn't fall over the coffee table or knock into the desk.

He slowly bent and eased himself under the covers. "Oh, my back," he groaned.

"Brace yourself, Bridget," I said.

Maybe it was time for me to turn off my tablet. I placed it on the nightstand and arranged my nightie. Pud tried to turn over, and his elbow caught me on my head, but that didn't affect my developing ardor.

Pud rolled closer and threw himself on top of me. My left arm was pinned under me, but I ignored the pins and needles and concentrated on other sensations.

"I love you," whispered Pud.

I murmured agreement, and we embraced in a long, sweet, slow kiss. Longer, fuller, closer, deeper … we joined together.

"Your skin is so soft and warm. I want to stay with you forever." Pud caressed me.

The bed didn't break, my arm didn't cramp, and the phone didn't ring.

Afterward, as we lay close together, I said, "Do you remember, at our wedding reception, an older couple told us to put a dollar in a jar by the bed every time we had relations? And that way we would save money for a big anniversary trip someday?"

"I guess."

"We didn't do it, but how much money do you think we would have saved?"

"Hmmm … I don't know, but we could start to save dollars now."

After a few more quiet moments passed, I laughed. "Pud, do you think all those coins we found in your folks' house that you counted last winter was their anniversary money? Maybe we used their dollars that they saved after every romantic time to pay for our special trip to Marco Island!"

I hooked up with Sibby in the morning, and we rushed to a big-box store to get more vital supplies: crepe paper, streamers, tape, and balloons to decorate the dining area for the dinner celebration. Sibby thanked me for helping. "Oh, I didn't do much; you did an amazing job getting all these special things. You are always so good with decorating."

"Well, I enjoy it," said Sibby. "And Buddy is such a romantic. He planned it all. And I am so glad you guys could come. It's so nice to have family here for this."

"Oh, we are so delighted to be here," I replied. "You know, now that Pud is retired, we are so much more available. When he traveled, we could never come to things; he was always away. It's a blessing to be here."

We ate lunch with George and Sibby, and they decided to go for a long walk in the afternoon. We passed on the walking, as it sounded too far for us. We headed back to our hotel to lounge on the bed and watch the weather and *NCIS* reruns. This time on the ride up in the elevator, Pud talked to a man and his wife and learned that they had farmed tobacco in Virginia and were visiting their children.

We dozed on the bed. "You know, one of these days, we really should start some kind of exercise program," I told Pud.

"I guess, but I think we are too old for that."

"Well, getting up from this bed is hard, but once I get my legs going, it's a little better."

We met Sibby and George at Mapleside and helped them carry all the party paraphernalia. Buddy came a few minutes later, looking handsome in an oxford shirt and pressed jeans. He gave us a few directions, and we arranged the set with lanterns, trellis, luminaria, and rose petals. It was all so thoughtful and charming.

"Buddy, thank you for letting us share this special day. We love you and Maddy and are so happy for you."

"Thanks, Auntie Charli. Thanks for helping. I want this to be a beautiful evening for Maddy."

"It will be. This is one of those days that you will always remember. So how are you getting her here?"

"I told her we were invited here for a surprise birthday party for my basketball coach."

Buddy gave his mom a list of directions, including when to cue the music and light the candles, and then he left to get Maddy. Pud, George, and I waited in the upstairs private dining room for the other guests to come. Soon we had a crowd of excited family friends. Sibby finished her last-minute tasks and then, in her friendly, charming way, mingled and introduced everyone.

There was a good turnout from both sides, and Pud and I were so happy to meet Maddy's parents, grandparents, aunt, and siblings. Of course, we had our usual trouble remembering everyone's names, but at least we were able to decipher who was on Maddy's team and who was on Buddy's.

And then it was time to hide on the upstairs deck, and we paced and peered down, looking for the couple with nervous anticipation. The lights were turned off as we hid in the dusk, nervously shushing each other. The engagement show was about to begin. There were a few nervous, tired old jokes: "What if she says no?" The staff at the restaurant had taken over the directing jobs so Sibby didn't have to light candles or start the music, and she was standing by me, clutching my arm. The engagement area was stunning. Nature provided a romantic backdrop of deeps reds and oranges as the last light gilded the rolling hillside. The trellis was crowned with flowers; the candles and luminaria cast a gentle glow.

We all froze when we heard quiet talking followed by a surprised gasp and "Oh!" from Maddy. Buddy and Maddy walked arm in arm to the trellis. She leaned into his shoulder and clutched his waist. He guided her to the trellis, appeared to say a few words, and then dropped to one knee. The tissues we had been clutching were put to good use.

Holding her hand, he quietly spoke his proposal and then jerked the ring box open. We could see her laugh with joy and smile with love, and they hugged, and he gave her a small peck. Then they laughed and hugged again, and this time their kiss was much closer and longer. They remained in each other's arms and turned to face the caress of the sunset and the benediction of heaven.

17

Walk

Pud had clocked in early at the clubhouse to golf, and I had wiped the counters, dusted the furniture, and then vacuumed the main floor. The sun streamed in, and I joined with the flora and fauna to hum, "Oh, What a Beautiful Morning." I planned to tidy the buffet drawers and clean out the freezer, but the day was already one of the top five beautiful early-summer mornings, and Oakley and I voted for a walk instead.

"One more cup of coffee on the patio after I finish the kitchen chores, and then we'll go," I told Oakley. I expected even the dog to know my schedule and plans.

While my coffee cooled and before I settled into my lounge, I puttered in the backyard, deadheading the petunias. It was time to trim back the irises. And even though I didn't want to face it head-on, it was also time to talk to Pud about the golf situation.

On the one hand, I missed him. I was now spending

just about every day by myself. And I got it that I could be making plans with others, but I liked to relax in my house and yard and be with the dog. And if the boys stopped by or texted with a question, I was there for them. I was content at home; I wanted Pud to be content at home with me.

But, on the other hand, if I liked to golf, I would certainly want to be on the golf course on a perfect day like this. Although it was still morning, it was in the low seventies, blue sky and sunny, with a pleasant breeze that was typical for our location. I was unhappy that Pud was gone so much, but basically I was going around and around with no solution. "Oh, well, I will figure something out. Something will happen to show me what to do."

As I settled down with my coffee, I had to admit that Pud and I were talking more. And after our passion in Indiana, I did feel closer and warmer, no longer like I was living in a hotel where I passed him occasionally in the lobby. The catalyst for many of our chats was the visits to the young cousins. We either relived a visit or planned a new one. Sharing these chats led to more memories and connections.

Just the night before, we'd shared wine and relived the trip to Indiana and the momentous engagement party. After the proposal, Buddy and Maddy had flown upstairs to join us all. Maddy had cried when she'd seen her parents and family. She had been swept up in a flurry of hugs and kisses. Buddy and Maddy had posed for photos, and she'd kept that left hand front and center in all the group poses. Pud and I were in some of the shots; my eyes were shut, as usual. I hoped those photos didn't make it onto the kids' social-media accounts.

We all had wanted to hear about the wedding plans. There hadn't been many details yet, of course, but we'd savored the headlines. "Soon, probably in the fall!" The evening of love had ended when Buddy had asked us to all to join hands as he led us in a prayer of thanks and blessing.

I enjoyed reminiscing about the engagement with Pud. He raised the bottle of wine to me.

"I don't remember much, I know, but did you and I do all this engagement stuff?" asked Pud.

"Just a little more wine. And no, remember, you and I were getting ready to go to a holiday party, and I said to you, 'Have you ever thought that you would like to have a party, like a once-in-a-lifetime party?' I basically asked you to get married because I was worried you'd be too scared to ask."

Pud sat there.

"But we had fun when we were first married," I continued. "Remember, we used to meet Garry and Lauretta and Hal and Joan on Friday nights at Larry's for the crab-leg special? My work was the closest, so I would get there, grab a booth, and order a pitcher of beer, and then you would all come. We finished off pounds of crab legs and gallons of beer."

"It was Wednesday night," said Pud.

"It was Wednesday night? What was Wednesday night?"

"The crab special was on Wednesday night. We should go sometime. I wonder if Larry's still has that special."

Pud had poured us more wine. "This Meritage isn't bad. I need to send in the estimated tax payments this week. Remind me."

Then he'd turned on one of his cable news shows. But it had been a start; we really were talking more, and I was enjoying our time together.

The morning was even prettier by the time I finished my coffee. Oakley had run off to the next-door neighbor's. She had a crush on their little pittie-mix dog. They had a fenced-in yard, and Oakley and her friend would run the perimeter of the fence together, each on their own side.

"Oakley, come on, let's get ready," I called.

She came bounding over, big, hanging ears flopping and mouth open in a happy grin, tongue lolling out the side.

She had spent the weekend in the kennel while we were in Indiana, so she was happy to be home and ready for a walk. I had to chuckle. When I'd picked her up, the kennel caregiver, as she styled herself, had handed me my bill and also a paper that turned out to be Oakley's boarding report card.

Under personality, she was "friendly with people & dogs," "easygoing," and "goofy." She was not "picky," "reserved," or "independent." Good job; Oakley and I thought it was okay to be goofy. It also listed "I was a great eater" and "I always pottied outside." This was an outstanding report card for our house.

I went to the bathroom, grabbed some plastic bags, and found my tennis shoes. The bags and shoes turned on Oakley's extreme joy switch, and she turned and leaped and twirled and then rushed to the door and sat down, panting and squealing, big brown eyes gleaming until I opened the door.

Oakley had been professionally trained. When we'd rescued her, I had decided that I wanted a perfectly behaved dog for once in my life. She'd gone to boarding school for two weeks and come back a well-mannered—if still goofy—dog. It was a joy to have an obedient pal who still tolerated baby talk.

We headed up the hill. Oakley didn't even need a leash when she walked. She had a routine that she always completed at the beginning of our outing. She would run as fast as she could up the hill about fifty feet. Then she would turn around and zoom back to me, blazing fast. She was like a race car warming up her tires. Then she would settle in and walk by me.

Part of the walk, I kept her at heel, but when we got to an open grassy area, I told her, "Free," and let her frolic and sniff. When she was free, she never went too far ahead, and she always came back when I called. If she saw another dog, she sat and waited until it walked by. I loved to see her sitting calmly while the other dog pulled and strained and whined to get at her. She even pottied and scooped it up into the plastic bag and threw it in the trash can. No, she didn't do that, but she was a wonderful dog just the same.

Through the years, we had welcomed other animals into our home, including several dogs from the pound and a cat or two. They all had had some good qualities but some issues too. One of the dogs had been a runner and would bolt and then carouse around the neighborhood for hours. It had been very frustrating trying to catch a creature that acted like it was running from a zombie and could easily outrun this particular zombie.

Our favorite dog before Oakley had been a petite little girl, six pounds, named Sugar. She'd especially loved Pud. She would cuddle up by him in his recliner and snooze for hours as he watched TV. She'd loved food too. One day when I'd picked her up to put her on our bed, I had been shocked that she seemed to suddenly be extremely fat. What had happened? She had always had tiny little pencil legs, but this day her body had become a firm, round barrel.

I'd investigated and found that she had gnawed a hole in the bottom of the dog food bag and had created her own secret food vending machine. We'd wondered how big she would have gotten left to her own eating plan. The food bag had been secured in a cupboard after that. As August had said, "Dogs don't have thumbs, so she can't open the door."

When the boys had been kids, we'd also had the discovery years of turtles, hamsters, snails, lightning bugs, and fish. Yes, Mom had been the primary caregiver of the small pets too. Surprisingly, the turtles had been the best pets of the container animals. They had always swum to the front of the tank when I'd approached to feed them. I'd thought that was pretty impressive for a turtle. The hamsters had been our least favorite, as they had just crawled into their homes, buried themselves in their cage shavings, and disappeared from view for days. In fact, one hamster had been dead for several days before we'd realized it.

Oakley and I crossed the street at the top of the hill and walked past the clubhouse. I looked to see if Pud was around; sometimes we caught him heading to the tenth hole. We didn't see him, but we waved to the starter. We meandered by the lake and then stopped and turned at the big rock. This was half a mile. I could really only walk about a mile; my knees complained when I walked too far. One of these days, I pledged to work on my weight and fitness. We walked back, downhill this time, stopped to check if the mail had come, and then went inside. Oakley and I each had a big drink of water.

I made my lunch from leftovers from the night before. I mixed the macaroni and cheese and vegetable soup together and enjoyed that delicacy. Then I melted cheese and onions on a bagel and polished that off. Oakley put her head in my lap and stood quietly, waiting for me to give her the last bite. I tidied up after lunch and then checked my tablet and social media.

I hurried upstairs to my work area to work on my photo project for a few hours. I turned on all my machines. Oakley sprang up a few minutes later and flopped on her side, with her legs straight, head pointing east, and tail stretched out to the west. Dogs enjoyed walks, playtime, and car rides, but they adored relaxing and sleeping as their owners sat quietly nearby. Oakley was my great reading and Pud's TV-watching companion. She helped me by lying peacefully nearby as I worked at my desk.

I finished scanning all the slides. There were about 1,200 slides that I wanted to save. I didn't scan all the multiples of Niagara Falls from my parents' honeymoon or dozens of cactus photos from a family trip out west, but I digitized every photo of my parents, sister, grandparents, and relatives, which spanned from my parents' wedding through our baby lives and growing-up years to high school graduations. I was elated when I completed that part of the project. I had basically relived the first part of my life.

I began the second part of the project, digitizing the print photos. I spent time sorting out the early photos. I visited each side of the family. I found photos of my young grandparents with their siblings, circa late 1880s. There were many photos of each grandmother in school and with her friends at the beach or at church picnics. I found photos of each young grandmother canoeing with her friends, and I was surprised that in New York and Ohio, young people in the early twentieth century apparently spent their free time in the same way. Another photo trend that fascinated me was that one hundred years ago, friends entertained themselves by creating comical reenactments. There were several professional photos of Grandmother Bertha and her girlfriends posed as a wedding party. One of the friends was the bride, another was the minister, several girls were dressed as bridesmaids, and Bertha was the solemn groom.

I devised a plan for the old photos. I handwrote and placed a label at the top of the scanner: "Grace Florence Angstrom, wife of Cyrus Pearson Eddy, mother of Evan

Eddy" (who was my father). I then placed approximately four to six photos about Grace on the scanner and clicked and whisked them into the computer. This seemed like a good way to memorialize the photos.

I made more labels: "Grace and siblings, Rob, Tom, Helen, Beth, September 1896," "Grace and friend," "Grace and Lindstrom cousins, Christmas 1910." I was fortunate that Grace had been persistent and had recorded identifying information on many of the photos. I found photos of relatives that I knew only as very old men, but here they were in their prime, dressed in jackets and hats and looking proud. I clicked Preview and then Scan, and they were stored in the modern way.

I worked liked this for several afternoons, with the dog snoozing by me and Pud at the golf course. After a week, I had completed the paternal side of the family from Grace's childhood to young adulthood to marriage to my grandfather and then the birth of my father. In the course of these years, the Eddy family had moved from the New York City area to the sleepier town of Logan, Ohio, when my dad had been a young teenager. I wondered what it had been like for my grandmother to leave the nexus of the United States to relocate to quiet Ohio before the Second World War.

As I worked on the other half of my family, creating labels for Bertha Zimmer Way and John Calvin Way, mother of Lois Mary Way Eddy, my mother, I basked in the pleasure that this project gave to me. I saw faces I loved—faces that were celebrating the milestones of marriages and births and large tomatoes in the garden and a new house and a fresh Christmas tree with tinsel and a child standing by her Easter basket for the first time. I found it calming and meaningful to systematically label the photos, place them in the scanner, and wait for them to be digitized.

After several weeks, I neared the finish. Once again, persistence and the "press on" drumbeat encouraged me to complete a long task. I was an archeologist who had uncovered the secrets of my family, an explorer who had transcribed the ancient hieroglyphics into understandable symbols. Little did I know that I was soon to be trapped in the underground tomb of an angry pharaoh.

As my photo project neared an end, I didn't foresee any problems. Instead, I mused at how much comfort I received from gazing at the special faces that meant so much to me. To someone outside my family circle, my photos would be nothing more than quaint or curious. But to me, these photos were elemental, profound, and cherished.

I thought back to when Pud and I had taken our two boys to Florida to visit his folks and had driven to Disney World for the day. Both our sons had always been very independent, so Pud and I had spent most of the day apart from each other. Pud had taken Zim on the rides he'd wanted to go on, and I'd palled around with August.

We hit a snag when August wanted to go on Space Mountain, a ride that was too scary for me. He said he could go by himself. He was about ten years old, so after some thought, I let him get in line. I told him I would wait for him where he exited the ride. After he had moved along into the mountain building, I went to the exit area, and I watched for over a solid hour. Every time a group came out, I quickly searched for his face.

At the beginning of my vigil, I rehearsed what I would say when he came out. "You rode it all by yourself! How was it? Wow, you did great!" But as the minutes ticked by, I looked and searched, but I didn't see the face I most wanted to see. Finally, I realized that an hour had gone by, and something was wrong.

I found a Disney worker, and because it was Disney, they quickly had us reunited. August had gotten cold feet at the last minute and left the ride. He hadn't come out the ride exit, so when he hadn't seen me, he'd known what to do and had found a Disney friend who had taken care of him. After a quick walkie-talkie communication from my end to wherever lost children ended up, I had been briskly walked to the lost and found, and we had been happily reunited. I never forgot that feeling of looking at the blur of hundreds of faces, one by one, waiting to see the only precious visage that I cared about. The meaning of life was found in the faces we love.

I was immersed in my photo world, but I did come up for air to see Pud each day in the late afternoon after his day of golf. I was a time traveler, having spent the afternoon in the 1920s or 1940s with my photo family and the evenings with my spouse in the twenty-first century.

Most nights, we took a bottle of wine and headed to the patio to relax and grill steaks or burgers. Our burgers were especially tasty, as we loaded them with American, cheddar, or pepper jack cheese, condiments, mayonnaise with interesting flavors, relish, onions, mustard, and jalapeño peppers. It was a whole food court on a bun.

As we sat outside, Pud updated me on his golf score and on the stock market. He told me regularly that he didn't like the appearance of the river birch trees, and I replied, as usual, that I liked the shaggy bark and sweeping branches. He occasionally stood and practiced his golf swing, and it looked like the YouTube videos had helped him. I told myself that what I loved about Pud was his solidness, dependability, and predictability. At least I knew that he would always be there for me and our house and family. We continued our string of balmy, low-humidity days, and it was relaxing to spend time together.

"I am about three-quarters of the way through the photo project," I reported one evening while we were waiting for the grill to heat.

No response. I poured us some more wine.

"Oh, photos. So how many did you have to do?"

"I would say about six hundred total. Some were too blurry or didn't show much, so I weeded those out. So, yeah, six hundred. I did over a thousand slides."

"Okay, so three-quarters done, so you have about 150 to do?" Pud asked.

"Yep, should take me another day or two." *Thank you, math guy*, I thought. "I am planning a big surprise with these photos."

Pud responded, "Should I put the burgers on? Oakley, do you, uh, want one too?"

I finished all the scans a few days later and texted August.

> All done with scans!! Will you be home this weekend to help me burn dvd disks? Ty ly

August sent back:

> Yep. Disks are easy.

On Saturday morning, August and I made sausage gravy and biscuits for the first time. Pud always ordered this when we were out to breakfast, so since I had August for support and guidance, I decided to surprise Pud with his favorite delicacy. Our first attempt wasn't bad. Pud recommended that we add more sausage, so we promised to adjust the recipe for the next time. August tasted the gravy and then put strawberry jam on a biscuit and ate that instead. I put honey on half of my biscuit and tried some sausage gravy on the other half. The honey won, so I made another biscuit with honey and shared it with Oakley.

Then Pud put on his red hat and left for the links. August, Oakley, and I climbed to my office and prepared to burn the disks. August was right; it was easy to insert a DVD, move the thousand slides to the burn folder, click Burn, and wait. I made a note of these directions while we waited.

"I still think you need a much bigger monitor," advised August.

"Well, you might be right. It's a lot of small photos for my tired eyes." The disk popped out. "Oh, let's look at it to make sure it's okay."

August went to his computer and inserted the disk, and soon hundreds of thumbnail images from the slides appeared. "Yep. Looks like there are 1,129 images here, so it looks good."

He clicked and opened a few to full-image size. I was thrilled to see a full-color photo of my mom holding me when I was a baby. "Wow, they look so clear."

August agreed. "Thirty-five-millimeter cameras were good back then. And Grandpa did a fine job with the focusing and exposure."

"Okay, thanks, hon. The slides are done, so I will try to burn the photos to a disk myself now. Will you be around awhile in case I need to scream for help?"

"Sure, but you can do it."

I went back to my desk and intently studied my directions, and soon I had another disk completed. I found August and asked him to check out the disk with the photos on them. I couldn't wait to see the photos on his big monitor, as some of the elegant ones from a century ago would look magnificent on his big screen.

August clicked open an image. Everything was blurry. He clicked on another; that one was blurry too. He kept going, and every image we looked at was out of focus. Little did I know that the black cloud had arrived.

"Oh no!" I cried. "What happened? What's wrong? Why are they all messed up?"

"Let me see." He kept checking and thinking.

"The slides came out fine. What's wrong with all the photos?" I whined.

"I think there is something wrong with the scanner controls. Let's adjust those, and I also think the scanner may have had trouble focusing on all your written labels, and it changed the adjustment on your photos."

This time, there had been a train wreck around the next corner. I had been so excited to finish the project, but now half the project was worthless. August checked and worked and tested the photos by scanning some them again. I couldn't believe that all the photo images were junk. The slides looked great on the computer.

"Okay, I changed the controls, and you should separate the photos so they scan separately. They seem to be turning out fine now."

I peeked, and yes, they did look fine the way he did them.

"Okay, so I have to do the photos all over again? I have to scan hundreds of photos again?"

"Yes, but then they will look great."

I took a moment to compose myself. Sometimes it wasn't so much fun to be persistent. This was one of those times. Wouldn't it be easier to give up? But what about my surprise? I had to rescan them. What had Grandma Eddy said? "It's a great life if you don't weaken." I would stay strong and press on, and I wouldn't let Grandma down.

18

Around the Next Corner

Several years earlier, I'd encountered one of my most exciting around-the-next-corner happenings. It had been a bright and sunny day. There had been no clouds in the sky, and the azure of the sky and the royal blue of the water could have been on the same paint sample strip. I was spending one of the last hazy days of summer at a community recreation park, waiting at a picnic table for Zim to get off work as a lifeguard.

The last days of summer gave me the same feeling as Sunday night before a workday, a sad, soulful melancholy. I took a break from my book—I was rereading *The Color of Water*—to ponder the fading of summer and consider what autumn might bring. Out of nowhere, I had an idea. I should get a new car. *I should get a new car?*

Yes, I firmly decided, *I should.* August and I shared a vehicle; that was why I was waiting to pick him up. He was campaigning to take the car back to school. Our spare jalopy was getting so old I didn't feel safe driving it. I understood it made sense at this point to keep it until it died, but I didn't want it to flatline alone twenty miles from home. Pud and I could share our sedan, which was in decent shape, but what would I drive when he journeyed to all the golf courses? I really wanted, needed, to have my own drive—a car without dropped french fries, empty protein shake bottles, or fast-food trash; a car where I could always find my phone charger and the radio was set to my channel. Case closed.

I had time before Zim's shift ended, so I decided to walk to the snack shop, get a shake or cone, grab some Wi-Fi, and look online for cars. What appealed to me? Why not get a small car? I wanted something cute and economical to scoot around town in, and most important of all, a compact would be too tiny for my big boys and husband to comfortably use. It would be all mine. Ha!

I walked the long way on the path at the edge of the woods to the café. I passed young kids on scooters and big, panting Labrador retrievers, kite flyers, and bench sitters. I reached the end of the walkway and cut though the parking lot to head to my hangout.

Suddenly, I experienced love at first sight. I turned the corner, and there was my something exciting. I was paralyzed with passion. There, in all its splendor, was the car of my very recent dreams. It had a tiny European body, and it was white with some type of stripes and stunning chrome accents. Accompanied by the swell of symphonic sounds, I slowly walked closer. The stripes were a distinctive red and green, and "Fiat 500 by Gucci" gleamed in chrome. "By Gucci," I whispered, "a darling car and one of my favorite designers." I looked inside at the modernistic dashboard. The seats were black leather with a Gucci stripe for the seat belt. The wheels and the rest of the trim were couture.

I rushed to the snack shop to get on the Internet. Even if I had to go to New York or Los Angeles to obtain such an amazing car, I was flying there, first class. I took my tablet out of my tote bag and Googled *Fat 500 Gucci*. The search engine assured me that it was ignoring my typo and searching for *Fiat 500 Gucci*. I thought, *Hurry, hurry*.

One of the first sites to appear was for a Fiat dealership ten miles south of Cleveland. So close! I clicked on the site and scrolled through the available cars. Light blue, black, red, sport package, and then on page 2, twenty images per page, I found it: a new white, hardtop Fiat 500 by Gucci, only driven to the Cleveland Fashion Week. It was a limited-edition car of five hundred.

"What are you doing?" Zim had found me. He was sipping on a strawberry smoothie.

I handed him my tablet.

"Look at this car. I have to have it. What do you think? Would it be good for me?"

He looked and read. "Yeah, that would be good. You need your own car. And it's a special version."

"Okay, I agree. So what should we do?"

"I am going to be around Cleveland tomorrow, so I will stop by and check it out."

"Okay, and if it looks good, put a hold on it until I can come. I can get there the day after tomorrow."

I got in line at the ice-cream window and ordered a double-espresso soft-serve ice-cream shake to celebrate the sudden incarnation of my dream vehicle.

Zim was a son of few words, but he was solid and dependable, just like Pud. He stopped by the Fiat dealership the next day, as he had promised, and texted:

> This is the car 4 u. Told them you would be in tmrw. Can u come at 2, they will hold til then.

Yes!

Zim dropped me off, and I arrived at the dealership the next day at 1:43 p.m. I strolled past the cars in the front lot, precious toy cars in festive colors. Then I whispered a prayer and walked into the showroom and saw my baby, all primped and ready for me. The rest of the showroom faded to black and white, and my car glowed in a celestial light. I slowly walked around it and soaked in its wonderfulness, the special chrome headlights and body trim, the leather, the Gucci.

"Are you Mrs. McAntic?"

"*Yes!*"

"Your son said you would be stopping by. Good to see you and glad to help you. Do you have any questions?"

"I love it."

"Well, it's a little celebrity around here. It was displayed at the Cleveland Fashion Week at the convention center, and Miss Little Italy rode in it during the Feast of the Assumption Parade in August. It's a limited edition, and we won't be getting any more."

"*Yes!*"

"Do you want to test-drive it?"

"*Yes!* I mean *no!* I just *want it!*"

I woke up enough to tell him I would buy it as long as I wasn't pressured at the closing to buy warranties or service agreements. I wanted to sign and drive.

"That's exactly how we operate here. We are here to help you."

I drove my little sweetie home. At every stop, people

took a second glance at my darling and waved approval. It was the most special thing I had ever bought for myself, and it had fallen into place so easily. Sometimes in life, everything worked out. I'd wanted a car, I'd seen the perfect car around the next corner, and I'd bought it.

But sometimes, life was tougher. Like parts of my life right now. Scanning the photos had turned out to be difficult. Handling an absentee golf spouse was even more difficult. *Press on, one day at a time.*

Once I'd realized I had to rescan the photos, I'd taken a big breath and committed to doing the project the right way. August showed me a better way to place and scan the photos. I enjoyed seeing my young grandparents again, and the newly scanned images looked so clear and engaging that it ended up being a pleasure to redo the photos. I showed August the new electronic images, and he agreed that the tone and clarity were excellent.

I worked in my official office at least two hours a day. After three determined weeks, I finished this supersized project. I was happy the piles of photos were digitized correctly and relieved that I had accomplished the task, but I was also sad to say good-bye to my relatives. I had enjoyed greeting them each day.

I put the last of the photos back in their archival boxes and tidied my desk, and the dog and I went down to the family room to see if Pud was ready for happy hour. Pud had already been to the basement and selected a wine, a bold cabernet sauvignon, and he had placed some blue cheese and almonds on a plate.

"All done for the day?" he said.

"Hi. Actually, all done, period. The scans are all done perfectly and saved, and I have all the slides and photos on disks."

"Great!"

It was a bit drizzly and cloudy, so we sat on our couch and relaxed as the TV analysts reviewed the day's bulls and bears.

"What are you going to do now that you are finished?" asked Pud.

"Well, I have a special surprise for the photos. Other than that, not sure. Oh, I know one thing we have to do is get back on track with the RSVP project."

"Okay, so what do you mean?"

"Well," I summarized, "we have visited Robin and Chester and Annie, Lindsey, and Erik. We have seen Buddy play basketball, and we were invited to his engagement dinner. Hopefully, we can take Maddy and him to dinner at some point. So that leaves Byron."

"What's Byron doing?" Pud asked as he reached for some more cheese. He gave Oakley a crumble that fell off his plate.

"The trouble—well, it's not *trouble* for him; it's trouble for *us*—is that he is in grad school in Boston until January. I doubt we can get there. And remember I texted him about dinner, and he said he was busy. So maybe we will have to take him out when he is back in town, like over the holidays or sometime next winter."

I reached for more cheese and slid closer to Pud. I made sure my thigh touched his thigh. Pud stared at the TV. He grabbed the remote and rewound the show.

"Who is that guy? It's not Phil Mickelson. Who is it?"

I glanced absentmindedly at the TV, but I was thinking about my thigh. Pud pushed away from me and slowly creaked up and headed to the bathroom. When he came back and refilled our glasses, I said, "We haven't had many opportunities to get to know him."

Pud settled into his recliner, and Oakley jumped up to the ottoman and settled right by his feet. So much for my thigh movement.

"Phil Mickelson? Who are we talking about?" replied Pud.

"Byron. He's the one we need to connect with."

"I don't really know him."

"I agree. We've only known George's kids a few years." Byron and his sister, Lindsey, had been lovingly welcomed into our family when Sibby had married their dad, George. They didn't live at home any longer, so we only saw them on holidays. That had been one of the reasons we'd created the RSVP Project—so we could get to know everyone better. That was why I wanted to take Byron to dinner; I didn't want to lose track of him. I figured a solution would show up.

"Well, at least I can e-mail Byron and tell him we are thinking about him. I'll find out how school is going and remind him that we will get together with him whenever he is back in town."

"Sounds good. What's for dinner?"

I texted Sibby to get Byron's e-mail address. While I waited to hear back from her, I checked my e-mails. Ads from department stores, electronic retailers, and streaming services were all flicked to the trash can. Next on the list was an ad from Meal4U.com. I opened the e-mail, which contained enticing photos of meals and a 20 percent off coupon to use on my first order. *Is this a new recipe site?* I clicked on 'Yes, I want to be a gourmet cook!' and was redirected to their website.

The website was welcoming and easy to navigate. I learned that every week I could order meals from a list of menus. I would be sent a box of fresh and seasonal ingredients, already portioned, with photo recipe cards.

It was touted as a convenient way to cook "chef-designed recipes at home." *Interesting.*

Just then, Sibby got back to me with Byron's e-mail address. I wrote a short, friendly e-mail to him.

> Hi Byron, this is Auntie Charli writing to let you know that we are thinking about you and hoping all is well with you and school.

Oh, that sounded too formal. I wanted to sound cheerier and warmer. I deleted that attempt.

> Hi Byron, this is Auntie Charli.

Hmmm.

> Sibby and your dad have been keeping me posted on you and your school life and I hope it's all going well.

Too stilted. Delete that. Obviously, I did need to get to know him better.

> I hope it's not too cold up north and that all is going well. We are thinking of you.

Better, but still not quite right. I figured I would switch the load from the washer to the dryer and then try again to write a decent e-mail. *No, just do it now. Don't procrastinate. Just babble something and send it,* I thought.

> Hi Byron, this is Auntie Charli and Uncle Pud. Did you know that this is "Write to

> Your Long-Lost Nephew Day?" Not sure if it's a national holiday yet, but today seemed like a good time to find out how you are doing and let you know we love you and hope you are thriving at school. I know that grad school can be intense, so we are sending positive energy your way. We would love to take you out to dinner when you get back to town. We'll keep in touch. Love and Good Luck!!

I reread it quickly and hit Send. It felt good to reach out to Byron, even in a very small way. I jumped up to do the laundry, and while I was up, I looked through the fridge, as Pud was right; it was time to cook. My fridge inventory indicated that it would be helpful to have one of our famous leftover meals. A leftover meal was when the chef—meaning me—put various storage containers of odds and ends on the counter and encouraged all takers to create their own meal. I usually tried to make something fresh that would tie it all together, like a salad or macaroni and cheese, and of course wine always helped make it a serviceable and palatable meal.

Would that Meals4U idea be fun? More tasty than a leftover meal? Would it be handy to get a box of interesting ingredients all ready to prepare? I wasn't sure about Internet meal service for our family. *Wait, would that be a neat idea?* I considered. *Yes, I'll do it!*

I would send Byron a Meal4U box. Since we couldn't take him out to eat right now, we could send the meal to him. At least he would know we cared. I figured he wouldn't mind cooking or he could have a friend help him with it. And Meal4U sounded trendy and cool—maybe not right for me but good for a young person. I was excited about my idea. I would get working on it as soon as I convinced Pud to help me eat these chef-inspired remnants. Pud came up behind me and gave me a hug.

Pud claimed the leftover ham loaf and fish sticks for dinner, and I stirred the lonely brussels sprouts into the pasta Alfredo and enjoyed my creation. Oakley finished up the tuna salad.

"Maybe I could start a business like Meals4U and send my leftovers to subscribers each week," I mused.

After we cleaned up the kitchen and took out the trash, I settled down with my coffee and tablet and decided to send Byron another e-mail.

> Byron, hello again! Pud and I want to take you and a friend out to dinner, but we may not be able to schedule it until you are done with school. So, in the meantime, I plan to send you a subscription to Meal4U.com, so you can enjoy a different approach to a meal. You should be getting an e-mail from the site soon. Love and bon appetit!

I continued to relax with my tablet, and I scrolled through my social-media news feed. I saw on a post that my friend Brenda in Indianapolis and her daughter, Andrea, were taking off on a seven-day eastern Caribbean cruise. Oh, how nice. How fun to go on a cruise with your daughter. *Next week? What's going on next week? That sounds familiar.*

Then I remembered. Next week was when Pud was going away on a weeklong golf outing with his friends from the racing world. They planned to meet at a race in Alabama and then golf the rest of the week. And who was going with him to golf? Yes, Brenda's husband and Andrea's husband were also going on the outing.

I read the comments on Brenda's post about the cruise and found out that, sure enough, she and Andrea were cruising because their men were golfing. "We needed a gals' vacation!" read one comment. Andrea and her mom were cruising the Bahamas while the men were crushing the ball. That added a different twist to my internal golf drama.

The next week came, and Pud left on his junket. I stayed home alone, pondering my golf situation. At the start of my first happy hour by myself, I opened a Riesling gewürztraminer, as Pud didn't favor the sweeter wines. The spice-and-sweet fruitiness of the wine was evocative of my mixed feelings. I found it intriguing that Brenda and Andrea felt that they deserved a vacation or at least chose to have fun together while their guys were away. Did I feel that way?

I wasn't happy that Pud had left me, especially since the golf plan was presented to me as a fait accompli, but I also didn't feel that I needed a quid pro quo. Pud and I had traveled this past winter, and I'd never minded staying home, my oasis in the universe. As I enjoyed my second glass of wine, I came to two conclusions.

First, based on my friends' comments and posts, I wasn't the only person who reacted to their husband leaving on a bro golf trip. Second, I would finally talk to Pud. I promised myself that I would discuss my feelings about golf with Pud when he got back from Alabama. It might not be a "come to Jesus" meeting, but we would certainly have a showdown. Or at least a session, or at the very least a small chat, depending on how hardy I felt. Maybe I could just e-mail Pud or text him?

Pud returned from his golf week suntanned and satisfied. We spent his first evening back enjoying a carefree happy hour on the patio. Even though it seemed I could see a big neon sign flashing *Talk to Pud! Talk to Pud!*, I ignored it. I didn't want to interrupt our wine and chat or wreck his first night back.

But the next day, I had to finish some board minutes and reports, and I didn't want to interrupt my deadlines by getting into it with Pud. The day after that, I forgot about my promise to discuss golf with Pud. When I remembered a few days later, I yelled at myself for procrastinating. Why was it so hard to me to discuss the golf problem with Pud? I set a firm deadline. I would tell Pud how I felt by the end of the weekend.

19

Mr. Mulligan

When Pud and I had been newlyweds, I'd gone through a phase where I'd referred to him as Mr. McAntic when I was laughing and chatting with my friends. Sometimes I'd even called him that to his face. When we had been younger, he'd seemed to be so much older than I was. I'd thought of Pud as grown up and mature and responsible.

"Devil may care" had been the catchphrase, motto, and aspiration of my group of friends. We'd delighted in being free spirits, trendsetters, and nonconformists. Mr. McAntic had not been a madcap man about town. I had been awed, amazed, and even a little fearful of him.

After a year or two of marriage, I'd stopped calling him *mister*. It had taken only a few times seeing him hanging on every episode of big-time wrestling or scratching his underwear for me to forget about his stuffy persona. He also had loosened up as he'd read to the kids or laughed while we'd tried different flavors of caramel corn. At times, though, I still caught glimpses of him as the calm, cool, and collected boss.

I was now faced with one of those mister moments. The weekend was here, and my deadline for talking to Pud about golf was at hand. We had driven an hour up to the Sandusky Bay area to eat at our favorite sushi place. I planned to talk about my golf dilemma on the drive home. I reasoned that obviously we would both be together in the car, there would be few distractions, and I might stay calmer. I hadn't started my speech, though. I continued to put it off. Part of the reason I couldn't get the words out was because life was actually going pretty well now. Ever since our romance had heated up, it had been easier for us to be together. Yes, the golf trip had surprised me, but why rock the boat now?

Today was a case in point. We had enjoyed a pleasant day together so far. On our way to the sushi/hibachi place, we'd passed a country grocery store that had a homemade sign posted: "Lisa's wine tasting, today, 4–6 p.m." The small parking lot had been packed, and cars had been jammed on the roadside. We were not generally spontaneous and flexible, but we decided to stop. After a longish debate on the correct place to park in the lot—"Too small, too tight, not by that old truck, too far"—we made it inside. Past the community bulletin board crammed with notices and the meat counter crammed with kielbasa, we found a card table with green tickets on it. We looked around, and then a spry older lady scooted over.

"Sorry to keep you waiting," she said. "I took a break and tried some wine."

"No problem at all," we chorused.

Pud said, "Wine sounds good. What do we need to do?"

For ten dollars, we each received five tickets. We were

directed to the back of the store, where we found a hubbub of voices and bodies clustered around a silver folding table with four white wines and four reds displayed. With our first tickets, I selected a Riesling, and Pud tried the Just Naked Zin. He smirked in a cute way as he ordered his selection. We sipped. Both wines were satisfactory, and we headed to the next table, a round wood circle on a barrel, and munched on the array of corn chips and orange cheesy snacks.

We made small talk with a cluster of couples, and soon we were discussing area restaurants. An older gent suggested, "We really like this old hut by the dock. What's its name?"

No one in the group could retrieve the name, but they all agreed it was right on the bay by the dock and that it had great perch and walleye. One of the ladies followed up with a puzzling statement. "You can't get food or stay there."

"Oh," said Pud. "You have to bring your fish and they cook it for you?"

Pud's remark clouded the issue even more, but we finally teased out that they meant it was a carryout place, although there were a few picnic tables, and it definitely had the best fish and potatoes.

After this heroic conversation, Pud and I headed back to the wine table. I noticed a bottle with the unusual name of Charorange. I picked it up. The redheaded wine pourer said, "It's orange and chardonnay. No one bought it when I had it on the shelf, so I decided to use up the bottles today, and now that I've featured it, everyone wants to try it."

"Are you Lisa?" I asked. "And yes, I want to try some Charorange."

Lisa confirmed that she was Lisa.

"This is our first time here. Very fun wine tasting," I said, thanking her.

We sampled a few more wines. The Charorange was not

what you would find in Napa Valley, but it was serviceable and would probably be refreshing on a hot summer's day.

We gave our remaining drink tickets to the fans of the fish shack on the dock and drove on to our sushi destination. When we got to the restaurant, we were later than our usual time and were confronted by a spirited full house. There was a thirty-minute wait for the sushi bar, so we decided to crowd into the lounge. We snagged a cozy place at the bar and ordered. Even though we preferred a quiet and sedate dining experience, it was fun to be in the midst of the surging and ever-changing throng.

Our sushi had been delicious, as usual, and my chopsticks had been well behaved. We were well beyond our early sushi days when our first daring attempts had been limited to California rolls. We'd grown a tick braver when we added volcano sauce to the bland avocado and crab rolls. Now we were adventurous and ordered deluxe rolls with spicy tuna, salmon, eel sauce, roe, aioli, and Sriracha, although we weren't as advanced as Zim; he favored the thin slices of raw fish known as sashimi, and the last time we'd treated him, he'd relished the raw octopus.

We'd finished the ginger and bantered with the bartender. Now we were on our way home, and I needed to start the golf topic within the next forty-five minutes. We had just entered the Ohio Turnpike. I didn't want to spoil our mood of close companionship, but I was determined to stick to my plan.

"You know, I finished the slide-and-photo project, and now I am working on my special surprise."

Silence.

"I had a great time exploring all the old photos, and now they are all on my computer."

Forty minutes left.

"Oh, I forgot to tell you, but all that wine reminded me tonight that Harlan called, and they brought back wine when they were out at the Sonoma race. He wants me to come to the office to pick it up," said Pud.

"Oh, that's nice. I hope it's a good one."

"I am sure it will be expensive," Pud told me.

"Great. I did kinda like that Charorange wine tonight. For a cheap wine, not bad."

Thirty minutes left. I changed the satellite radio from the Love channel to the Bridge. *Did those station names have a hidden meaning?*

August texted:

> The dog threw up. And her ear looks funny.
> Take her to the vet!

I replied:

> Ok, ty. Ly

I told Pud about the dog.

Twenty-two minutes left. I had to start talking about golf.

Pud intoned, "Why won't that truck pull over? They need to have a law that trucks can never run in the third lane!"

Nineteen minutes left.

"Since gas prices have gone down, it's like we're getting it half price now. On this big SUV, it's saving us like thirty-seven dollars a fill-up," said Pud.

Seventeen minutes left. *Maybe the governor will call and give me a reprieve.*

I stopped fiddling with my purse and took a deep breath. "Pud, I have been wanting to talk to you about golf.

Remember when that guy in Florida told you that golf is a religion? Well, I don't think it should be that important. Last summer, you golfed every day you could, and some of those were long days when you guys went out of town. That was your first year of retirement, so I didn't say anything, but this year is starting out the same way. It's like a full-time job for you. I want you to spend more time at home, please."

No, I didn't say that. I thought it. I could never say all that. Fourteen minutes left.

"Tonight was fun," Pud said.

Thirteen minutes left. Now or never. We exited the turnpike.

"Pud, have you ever heard this saying? I read that Bill Marriott—you know, the founder of Marriott—said that the reason he kept on working when he was older was that his wife told him she 'married him for better or worse, but not for lunch.' Well, I'm not like that. I want you home for lunch. I like doing things with you. So, I guess I am saying I was wondering if you could, I don't know, can we talk about golf?"

Pud looked straight ahead. "I golf. You read books. It's the same thing."

"Well, it's not, really. And I guess I feel like I am second to golf."

Pud continued to look straight ahead. "Golf is my hobby. You're my wife."

Then, possibly due to the stress of the moment, my crazy switch flipped on. I began to talk like the lady on that family TV show in an extremely exaggerated accent. "I want tooooo speennd tiiime wiz you. I looovve you. Just theeenk abooout it."

I stopped. I turned off my craziness. Pud chuckled nervously and kept looking straight ahead.

When we were two minutes from home, he said, "I'll check how Oakley is when we get home."

We pulled in the driveway. Time was up. Darn it. I hadn't accomplished anything.

I went to our bedroom, propped up my pillows, and began to read. I had a glass of root beer float vodka to cheer me up. I held my e-reader, but I was really reviewing the conversation—or pitiful attempt at conversation—that I'd had in the car with Pud.

Okay, really, reading is nothing like a whole day of golfing. First of all, I read at home in my spare time. I am here if anyone needs anything or wants to talk. Second, I don't go away for a week with my friends to read. But obviously Pud loves to golf, and he is going to keep on golfing.

I slammed my fist on my leg. No more negative thoughts! I clinked my ice cubes and drank some more. Oh, that root beer vodka was delicious. *It's like a job for him. You know, that's it. That's what bugs me the most. Pud treats it like it's his livelihood, like it's a top priority. To him, golf is nonnegotiable. So that's where I'll start. I'll talk to him about his schedule each week and go over what I would like to do with him or what activities we have planned.*

I hadn't come through with a big epiphany. After all my months of fretting, my solution was a tame one. Had I let myself down? Not really. We had made some positive changes this past year. I would press on with my small steps. Pud had been the one to think of the dinner idea. Together, we had planned the trips and dined with the young relations. We had even expanded and planned other events.

And we had grown closer this year. *Wait, why do I keep thinking about growing closer? Why do we need to grow closer? Haven't we always had a strong bond?* I paused and considered. I had assumed we were connected, but I could see now that for years we had lived parallel lives. Pud and I had been legally married for over thirty years, but due to his intense travel schedule, we joked that we had actually been together for only five years. Were our communication and relationship skills only five years along? Were we emotionally like newlyweds? Sort of like dog years? Was that why we needed to learn to grow closer, because we hadn't had as many opportunities to bond our hearts throughout the years?

I clicked open my e-reader. Pud came in and got ready for bed. I didn't fall asleep right away.

Why is it so hard for me to discuss touchy things? Is it because I like everything to be peaceful and smooth? Or is it because I always see so many sides to every issue or problem? Or do I just need more practice? It's best to keep moving forward. Or it's best to roll over and pull up the blankets.

Pud got up to go to the bathroom. When he came back, before I could analyze anymore, I blurted, "Hey, how about if we at least talk about when some of your important golf outings are, so I know what to expect?"

"That's fine," he mumbled.

At least I said something to Pud about his golf schedule. Okay, this is really enough thinking. I turned over, cuddled into Pud, and as usual said, "Another great day!" Except this time, I whispered my nightly blessing in my horrible fake accent.

20

I'm a Mixing Bowl

After I awoke and greeted my new gift of a day, I checked my tablet and found several texts and e-mails that I eagerly opened.

> Hello, thanks for the Meal4U. Jen and I will roll up our sleeves, fire up the stove and try some soon. I am in school or TV production about 12 hours a day. Byron

I replied:

> Our pleasure! Send me a photo if you can please and I will pretend we are eating together. Hope to see you soon, Auntie Charli

A new text message:

Coming back

The text was from Zim. He had been rambling around the world since last January. He had participated in an internship-abroad program in Australia. He'd stayed in a hostel and secured a position with a television production company. I was excited for him. When you were young, it was a good time to explore. I'd gone to Paris for a semester as a sophomore in college, and it had been a great experience on many levels: baguettes for breakfast, walking the Rue de Rivoli and seeing the impressionist paintings at L'Orangerie, buying doughnuts fried in a tub of oil at the Tunisian shop, drinking cheap wine, and riding the last metro back to my lodgings.

About once a week, I would send Zim a text along the lines of:

How are you? Exploring Sydney? Love you!

Within days or so, I would receive a reply:

Fine Yes

About once a month, I would break down and plead for more information:

Hi, when you have time, I would love to hear about what you are doing! Hope all is well! Love you!

After these pleas, he would usually message a photo—his group at Sydney Harbor Bridge, snorkeling at the Barrier Reef, a barbecue at the beach.

His internship had ended in April, and he'd decided to stay an extra month to travel more with his friends. After that, he'd planned a long trip home via Europe with friends he had met in Australia. They had stayed with various acquaintances, and every so often we'd figured out where he had landed when he'd used the credit card. I was proud and envious that he handled the world so well. Now, in September, it looked like he was headed back to home port.

Zim:

Plane arrives 8:10 pm.

Me:

What day?

Zim:

Sat

Me:

Do you want us to pick you up?

Zim:

No thanks. Friends from Columbus are-going to stay in Cbus w them 4 awhile.

Me:

Ok, ly. Safe travels and keep in touch!

Zim didn't send any more texts, but I couldn't keep up the cool-mom attitude. I added:

> Come home and see us as soon as you can.
> Miss you! Ly

Pud was golfing, so I sent him the great news that Zim had texted and was coming back to Ohio. We hadn't seen him for so long. It still might be a while before we actually saw him, but at least we would now be in the same state. Maybe he would make it to Buddy's wedding.

Sibby had been surfing the tsunami of wedding preparations. I'd ended up being swept along with her, and I was exhilarated by the ride. The wedding was in a month, and we were cresting toward shore.

One Saturday, a day that was so summery it was hard to imagine that we even had seasons like autumn and winter, I attended a lovely shower for Maddy. It was given by family friends of the bride and was truly worthy of a glossy magazine spread. Maddy and Buddy's dream was an outdoor wedding with a reception in a barn. According to the Internet site where everyone "pinned" their wedding preparations, barn nuptials were very popular, and Sibby had shown me many photos of casually bohemian-elegant affairs. The shower, however, was white gloves and party manners.

In the hearth room of the kitchen, on granite counters that were continents, not peninsulas, were photo-shoot-quality Caesar, cobb, and antipasto salads. I loaded my plate with a variety of fresh-from-the-oven breads and rolls, a fruit mélange presented in a Waterford crystal bowl, and cheese and charcuterie displayed on a marble platter. The desserts and bakery were showcased like a French patisserie and featured pastel frosted cupcakes, each swirled to identical perfection.

Every time Sibby and I attended a shower together, at some point, we always yelled, "I'm a mixing bowl!" This was our hilarious tradition that harkened back to one of Sibby's own bridal showers. At her shower, the guests had played that game where the hostess taped a card on your back and you mingled and asked questions to discover what bridal item was written on your card. It was like that WordUp! game Pud and I had played at Robin's surprise party but without smartphones.

At Sibby's event, the category had been "kitchen." One dear old church lady who had come with her daughter had been having the dickens of a time guessing what was on her card. At long last, when we had been getting ready to leave and everyone had forgotten about the silly game, she'd figured it out and yelled, "I'm a mixing bowl! *I'm a mixing bowl!*"

Sibby and I could still dissolve into teary laughter when we revisited that moment. In addition to Maddy's shower, there were many other wedding events on my calendar now, and because I was always updating Pud about my plans, he in turn had become more considerate and forthcoming about his golf schedule. He was still on the golf course most days, and I still missed him and begrudged being a golf widow, but it was a start.

I found Pud on the back step cleaning his golf shoes, red hat on, getting ready to start his day.

"Hi, hon. Today I am meeting Sibby at the linen store to help her pick out what she needs for the rehearsal dinner. Oh, and tomorrow night, we are going to a sampling at the caterer's, so I won't be home for dinner."

"Okay, have a nice time. Don't worry about me; we are golfing all day tomorrow up at Kirtland, so I'll eat there."

"Sounds good. I am home the rest of this week, but I know next week Sibby is picking up her dress and then going to the last fitting of the bridesmaids' dresses, and I think there's a night they are all working on the favors. So I will be doing some of that."

"Okay, love you."

I didn't think Pud could have passed a quiz on what I had just told him, and I wasn't sure he had listened at all. Then he surprised me.

"Should we, uh, be doing something, a dinner or something?" he called out over his shoulder as he strapped his clubs on his golf cart.

"Wow, you mean for the wedding? That's a neat idea. Let me think about it!" I shouted to him.

He waved and headed up to the course.

I was pleasantly invigorated by Pud's idea to further the wedding festivities. Earlier in the summer, I had thought about planning an event. I decided to revisit the concept I had come up with then and check it out with my sister.

Sibby and I had a blast at the linens store. It was the first time I had been in such a unique place with a wonderland of a showroom. There were ten display tables, each decorated in a different theme. The most prominent display featured the popular barn motif with big and little red checks galore and sunflowers and vegetable displays entwined through the table settings.

We wandered wide-eyed throughout the store and viewed the other exquisitely presented tabletops for every mood and occasion, including modern, royally elegant, Hawaiian, fifties diner, Scheherazade, and Jazz Age themes. Displayed on all the walls were linen samples in every style, fabric, color, and tone. It was more fun than Disney World.

"Sibby, I had no clue that there were so many ideas and items to choose from. What are all these things?"

"I know, I love it all," she said. "You can have coordinating tablecloths and napkins. What you are pointing to is a chair cover; you would coordinate that with your linens. You can even pick different actual chair colors, like silver or gold. And see how you can select the china to match the charger? The charger is that big plate thing."

"Amazing. All that plus all the centerpieces too."

What was even more fun than looking at all the concepts was that Sibby and I could create concepts on our own blank table. We swooped around, grabbing whatever pretty colors and interesting patterns caught our eye. We relived childhood fantasies—princess, playing house, and tea with teddy bears—all in one glorious design revelry. As we placed a navy-and-green chevron tablecloth on our canvas and searched for a coordinating china pattern and napkins, I was inspired to tell my sister about my own plans for a family event.

"Oh, Sibby, I had an idea about hosting some kind of dinner for Buddy, Maddy, and our families, but after seeing all this, it's overwhelming what can be done, but I do want to have everyone over."

"How sweet of you, but you don't have to do anything. Here, can you reach the teal napkin with sparkles? I want to see how it looks with the plain teal tablecloth instead of this chevron thing."

"Okay, this one? So I came up with an idea, and I thought—"

"Should I lay the napkin on the plate flat or fold it?"

"Um, let's see the folded. I would like to have something special for all of us."

"No, it doesn't look right with this charger. Oh, is that my phone? What were you saying?"

Sibby clicked open her phone and greeted Robin. At the same time, the manager approached Sibby and told her that the china she was considering was not available on her date. She followed him to the other side of the store to see some other patterns he recommended. I finally got it through my head that this wasn't a good time to tell Sibby about my plans. So I texted her.

> Tell me a date that would work for a late afternoon or evening patio party. I want to get us all together. Zim is coming home, plus the wedding, so we have a lot to celebrate.

From the other side of the store, I heard Sibby's phone ping, and a few seconds later, she rushed over.

"He's coming home. Oh, yes, let's get together. I can have something. I am busy and not sure how to fit it in, but I can plan something and have it at my house."

"No, no, no. I want to do it; just tell me a date. I have a good idea for a fun get-together—at least I *hope* it will be fun!"

The linen store was closing soon, so Sibby and I finished our playtime, hugged good-bye, and parted.

As I drove home, still overflowing with ideas from the linen center, I outlined my plans for the patio party. Somewhere on the Internet, I had picked up the idea to have a red cup celebration. Those ubiquitous red cups, used for beer and other beverages at casual parties, symbolized a time of casual, happy fun. The gathering I envisioned would celebrate Zim's return, Buddy and Maddy's wedding, and even our dining visits with the young cousins, as well as all the other happy milestones our family had achieved or would soon come to pass: graduations, new jobs, and moves. A red cup celebration encompassed all the joie de vivre I wanted to share with my family.

I pulled into our garage, and Pud was right behind me on his golf cart.

"Perfect timing!" he said.

"Yes! Hi, hon. How was your day?" I hugged him as we walked inside together, arm in arm.

"It was good." He took off his red cap and threw it by his computer. "I'll get us some wine, okay? Red or white?"

"Let's have white. And meet me on the patio, please. I want to tell you about this party idea I have. Well, you actually had the idea!"

I let the dog out and waited for Pud. I walked around the patio, studying and planning my red cup celebration. The patio was a new addition to our home. For several years, I had planned to remodel our kitchen. I'd gone to home design shows, stores that helped with kitchen redos, looked at magazines, and lusted after friends' kitchens. I'd drawn layouts on the back of printing-mistake paper, measured, and had Pud and my boys plan out the space with tape and lots of furniture moving.

I'd brought home samples of granite and composite counter materials, cabinets, and flooring. I'd even met with a contractor to get an estimate. But I could never quite pull the trigger. My current kitchen space was awkward. Every design change I contemplated did not improve the situation significantly, and given the big price tag of a kitchen project, I grew wishy-washy about continuing.

Then one weekend, August and I were outside playing ball with the dog. He mentioned that he had seen people in our area start to put in grand outdoor living areas with paver stones, built-in bars and grills, wood-burning fireplaces, and even pizza ovens.

"Yes!" I exclaimed. "That's it. I never could get a kitchen plan going that I liked, but you're right; I could create an outdoor kitchen and family area."

"We would love it, Mom." August walked and marked off areas while he gestured. "We have plenty of room. Think how you and Dad would like to grill and sip your wine after Dad golfs and have friends come and sit by the fire."

"Oh, that sounds so nice. And you and your friends can use it too. Wouldn't you all like that?"

That was the spark that led to the majestic outdoor stone fireplace that eventually was the star of our patio. After August planted the idea of an outdoor enhancement, I explained it all to Pud and then plunged ahead. I immediately called the landscaper we had used and got the plans rolling.

The landscapers, Dan and Mark, assured me they could have it done by Labor Day. Great! By Labor Day, the only thing that had been accomplished was that a front-end loader had been parked in our driveway for a few weeks. I begged and pleaded, and by November, two days before the first snow, the pavers were done, and the bar took shape. It took them most of the following summer to finish the hardscape, and then the next summer was spent placing all the landscaping. Finally, after several summers of labor, we were able to enjoy our beautiful, calm, and tranquil patio.

The patio was where I learned to like scotch. By the time the area had been finished enough for us to sit outside and use the fireplace, it was chilly, even with a fire, so I said to August and Zim, "What would be good to drink out here, since it's still rather cold?"

Zim had suggested, "Hot chocolate."

August had said, "I will get the perfect drink. Scotch. It will not only warm you, but you will see that the smoky smoothness will blend perfectly with the ambience of our environment."

He had been right, and now I always savored scotch by the fireplace flames. Pud drank hot chocolate with Zim.

I finished my circuit of the patio, and Pud came, and we tasted our wine. That first sip was always the best. What was next best was savoring a glass with your husband on a mild, comfortable evening, accompanied by gorgonzola cheese. We had prime seats for the approaching sunset. I eagerly told Pud about the red cup celebration, describing how special it would be to have our family all together, celebrating all the joyous recent milestones, outside here, eating and drinking.

"Fine; whatever you want to do. Sounds good to me. These new bar stools are really comfortable."

I kept prattling to Pud about possible food choices and the guest list. "What am I nattering about? We need to pick a date!"

"You may not, uh, like this idea, but why don't we invite everyone that we've had dinner with this year, not just our family? What did you call this? A happy hour party?"

"Red cup celebration. And I like your plan, I do. Let's try to have it before the wedding, but we could have it afterward if we are inviting everyone; it's not just about the wedding but about cheering on all our loved ones."

I texted my sister later that night, and we agreed on a date two weeks after Buddy's wedding. She knew that Buddy and Maddy planned to come back to her house to pick up their wedding gifts. The red cup celebration of our family, I was now calling it, would be a good way to welcome them as an "old" married couple and also a fitting way to introduce then to our friends. We decided on the third Saturday in October, hoping it would be a breathtakingly beautiful Indian summer day and not a typical time of icy rain.

I planned to spend the rest of the week creating and then e-mailing the invitations to the red cup celebration of family and devising a menu. It turned out that I would have an unexpectedly fun partner in the culinary department.

On Sunday night, my message alert dinged. I received a text with photos from Byron:

> Cooking 101.

He included a photo of the recipe directions from Meal4U. I squinted and read "Vietnamese Beef Pho with Thai Basil." The next photo showed Byron and his friend—who I figured was Jen—with the ingredients arrayed before them on their counter. I could make out some of the labels: "top round steak," "ginger," "Thai basil," and "Thai chili paste," along with beef broth, rice noodles and other interesting herbs and spices. The last photos showed their meals, completed and expertly plated.

I texted:

> Well done and looks delicious! Was it hard?

He replied:

> no it was fun thank you

I decided to be brave and check out Meal4U again. Byron's food looked so delectable and professional, could I try it for us at home? I might get new ideas for the menu for the red cup celebration of family.

The website for Meal4U informed me, "We believe food should be really fresh and really real." Made sense to me; I wanted my party to be really real. I clicked on the menu tab and scrolled down the recipe cards. I liked that they sent all the ingredients, including the precise amounts of some of those pesky herbs and spices that could be hard to find. Sometimes I didn't attempt intriguing recipes because

I fretted about going on a *Raiders of the Lost Ark* hunt for a tricky spice.

Okay, clicking further, what recipe should I try? Squash, ricotta, and sage tartines with apple salad? I might like it, but my guys wouldn't try that, and they also wouldn't like spaghetti squash with kale and creamy parmesan garlic sauce. It would require a heavy dose of sauce to hide the kale. Seared fish with chermoula, citrus, and potatoes sounded promising, although I didn't know what *chermoula* was. I read the recipe and learned it was a traditional Moroccan herb condiment that Meal4U would teach me to concoct. I finally settled on the braised chicken with potatoes and massaman curry, figuring that chicken was basic enough and that the massaman, a mild Thai curry paste, would be palatable. I clicked and ordered it for Wednesday delivery.

On Wednesday, my Meals4U, or should I say my Meal4Me, arrived promptly at 4:05 p.m. in a sturdy and well-insulated container. Pud was edging the sidewalk as I lugged in the box.

"I'll help you with that when I finish!" he shouted.

We unpacked all the cute little bags and containers of food. Pud seemed hesitant about the contents of the actual meal, but we had fun getting it all organized. I copied Byron's idea and took photos of the cooking process. On a whim, I sent photos of our meal experience to Byron.

> You inspired us to cook! Here is our Cooking 101

After cooking and eating our braised chicken and potatoes, Pud and I weighed in on the experience. We agreed that the appeal of getting the box and decoding how to cook the meal was entertaining.

"This would be fun to do on a weekend as an activity. And it's a good way to try something we wouldn't usually make."

Pud replied, "Well, for sure don't make this again."

I told Pud I would let him help me pick out the next meal. August stopped by to pick up some computer parts and tried a few bites. He thought it was cool that we were trying something so modern.

Later that night, Byron texted back:

> Good for you!!!

I asked:

> Have you tried any other meals?

He replied:

> Soon, busy exam schedule now.

I texted:

> Ok keep me posted.

Thus began an entertaining cycle of cooking exchanges with Byron. Jen and Byron next attempted vegetable biryani with potatoes and peas, and this time, he sent a video of Jen boiling the water for the rice, timing it for exactly seventeen minutes, and prepping and then baking the vegetables. I now knew that Byron was studying TV and radio production, so his video seemed professional.

I wasn't able to undertake a video production, but I replied a few days later with five photos of our next cooking enterprise, cod with pickled grapes and summer succotash. My gang liked the succotash, and I listed it as a contender for the red cup celebration menu.

Byron replied, "Ha!" when he saw the photo of me holding a knife with a bulky paper towel wrapped on my cut finger.

I texted:

> I know bad knife skills. But the succotash
> was worth it

Byron's next entry was flat iron steaks with artichoke-potato hash, purple asparagus, and caramelized shallot. Byron and Jen gave this meal high marks:

> Loved the vegetable hash better than we
> thought.

I texted:

> Would the Artichoke Potato Hash be good
> for my Red Cup party?
> Not sure if everyone would like it.

The hash didn't make the menu cut, but I was having a blast cooking and communicating with Byron.

The next weekend, August and I created frisée and farro salad with warm goat cheese. Pud declined to try this meal. It was not 4Him. August wasn't keen on it, but he relished the opportunity to show off his cooking skills. I was impressed with his deftness and told him so. These new recipes with exotic ingredients had ratcheted up the tastiness of my ordinary meals.

I sent Byron another digital gift card for the meal service.

> Here are some more dinners until we can meet and enjoy a special restaurant together. Keep on doing well in the kitchen and the classroom! Proud of you! Love, Uncle Pud and Auntie Charli

My e-mail dinged. It was Zim! He replied to my red cup celebration of family invitation with his usual economical communication:

> coming.

I hastily replied:

> Great, so glad you can come. Can't wait to see you! Love, Mom and Dad

21

Red Cups in the Sunset

People were everywhere in my house, milling in the hallways, racing up and down the stairs, sitting on the kitchen counters, jumping on the beds, and hiding in the closets. More crowds shoved in the front door, fell down the chimney, and climbed through the windows, yelling for food. They banged their cups on their empty plates and shrieked for more chips and cereal, creating a cacophony. My teeth fell out one by one and clattered to the floor. Where was the party food? Where were my platters of meat and vegetables and bowls of bubbles? *Bowls of bubbles? Oh, another crazy dream. Wake up!* "Thank you, God, for another beautiful day!"

Yet again, the hands of time had spun swiftly—sunrise, sunset, sunrise, sunset—yes, the days did swiftly flow. The red cup celebration of family was tomorrow. It was time to tackle all the last-minute preparations. No wonder my day had opened with another wild dream. I was equal parts excited and apprehensive about our event. We hadn't thrown a party this big in years.

Pud and I strategized after breakfast. We decided to pick up the cake, flowers, and a nice bottle of scotch for the young cousins to enjoy.

"Okay, so we get everything today. What do you want me to do tomorrow?" asked Pud.

"Good idea to go over the plans. Let's see. August is handling the bar. You and Zim are in charge of the grill. We can make the appetizers and other food tonight and tomorrow morning. So even though our party skills are a bit rusty, I think we are all set. I am getting excited!" I said.

"It seems like just about everyone could come."

"Yep, this is one of the biggest parties we have had." The only ones who couldn't make it were Andrea and Ryan, as they lived in New York, and a friend of Zim's.

"You might have time to fit a round in this afternoon," I suggested.

"Oh, that's okay; we'll see. And you have some kind of gifts or surprise?"

I told Pud I had created special gifts, but I hadn't even let him in on the secret. In possibly my greatest feat of persistence, I had pressed on and rescanned all 638 of the photos in less than two weeks, and it was well worth it. Thanks to August's help, his changes to the settings and procedures had resulted in clear digital images. I had three digital folders in my computer now: "Mom's Family," "Dad's Family," and "My Family." There were photos from as early as 1865; most of the images were from the 1880s to the 1980s.

Scanning the photos had been a good life lesson for me as I'd watched babies turn into schoolchildren and then young adults who married, had babies, raised families, and succumbed to Father Time. Clothing, furniture, cars, hairstyles, and house designs all had changed through the years, but what I'd realized remained constant was the stability and love of the people and families pictured. Had my young grandmother with her high-button shoes and hair piled on her head believed like me that something exciting was always just around the corner?

I could see the pride of my other grandmother as she stood by her young husband behind the counter of his grocery store. Had she also been troubled by the long hours he'd spent away from home at his job? Tomorrow, part of my surprise would be to teach my family that while the days might be long, the years were short, and sometimes it helped to see the panoramic view of life. Problems and praises occurred in lives like the continuous and endless rise and crest of the ocean's waves. I prayed that the red cup celebration of our family would indeed be a gala of blessings.

"Yes, I do have something special planned. I have to say it turned out well, and I am really psyched about it."

"Good," said Pud. "You know what I am psyched about?"

"No, what?"

"Ice cream. Let's get our to-do list done and then go out for a treat. We can take Oakley."

"We can take Oakley, but we're having ice cream at the party."

"I can eat ice cream two days in a row!"

"Sounds like a plan."

We spent the morning tidying the house, hiding hats and shoes, and cleaning the bathrooms. Pud volunteered to pick up the party supplies by himself while I fussed with arranging the plates, napkins, and serving areas. I also answered e-mails, texts, and phone calls from friends and family asking again for directions and offering to help.

When we were done with our festive chores, we decided Oakley preferred soft-serve ice cream, so we drove to the Honey Hut and sat outside at a picnic table with our treats. Oakley finished her treat in three gulps and then entertained herself by licking the cup while Pud took a few more bites to eat his strawberry sundae. We were lucky that in the latter half of October it was still jacket weather and wasn't too cold to sit outside. The forecast was for about forty-five to fifty degrees for our party, so with a fire, we would be fine.

"Oakley, don't eat the, uh, paper," said Pud. "We need to go."

The red cup celebration of family—I always thought of it by its full name—was in full swing now. Sibby and I shared a lounge chair as we sipped dark beer, her favorite. We surveyed the scene. Family and friends were cheerfully mixing and mingling. Plaid flannel shirts and sock caps mingled with cable sweaters and corduroy slacks. The appetizers were displayed on tables inside and out, and the bar was open and featured a dazzling smorgasbord of flavored vodkas. We had flavors galore: iced cake, root beer float, kissed caramel, cotton candy, whipped cream, watermelon, coconut, many fruit flavors, and bacon for the guys.

I updated Sibby, with bits of gossip thrown in, on who was who.

Karen and Bill came to us bearing a colorful gift bag.

"How nice! Thanks, you didn't have to!" I said as I jumped up and hugged them.

"Open it now; here, we'll help you."

I reached down into the tissue paper and pulled out a ceramic cup, a red cup.

"We made them ourselves. We are getting good at cups."

I pulled out a second cup. "They are the red cups of our party! I love them. Thank you, and how cool that you made them!"

Most people clustered at the bar or perched around the patio with their friends. The racing group relaxed by the fire. Dan and Mark, on the seat wall with Buddy, Byron, and Zim, discussed sports.

"Our state is victory challenged!" I heard Byron exclaim.

Some of the golf guys were with Pud, supervising the grill.

"Half a gin and tonic, then you flip the burgers!"

I had Pud on a short leash, as I wasn't in the mood for any political harangues today. August had steady employment, explaining the vodka and mixing margaritas, mojitos, and martinis. The red cup part of the celebration was flying high.

Sibby and I finished our beers and went in to check on the remaining guests who lounged by the inside fireplace or watched sports. We restocked the appetizer plates and passed some to the inside guests and then took the rest outside. The fruit kebabs were popular with the ladies, and the guys liked the pretzel rolls with honey mustard, and everyone liked the seafood tower with jumbo shrimp, crab legs, oysters, and mussels. The calamari had been demolished.

I mingled with each group. So far, everyone seemed comfortable; an enticing bar was a hostess's best friend. I stopped by the sitting wall and greeted the guys. I thanked Dan and Mark again for their hard work in creating our patio paradise.

Dan said, "We finally got to meet your son Zim. He's been showing us photos from Australia and Europe."

The racing wives were discussing skin-care regimens as I joined them.

Jo explained, "I drink sixty-four ounces of water each day. Water is so therapeutic for your skin."

"I'd have to go to the bathroom all the time if I drank that much water," another gal said, laughing.

Jewel explained that she was experimenting with different body oils for her hair and face. Body oils led to olive oil and nut oils and Mediterranean diets.

I greeted Nicki and the other neighbor ladies. I wandered to the group of younger gals, Maddy, Annie, Robin, and Lindsey. I figured they wouldn't be talking about drinking gallons of water or bathroom visits. I was right and listened in as they each shared their graduation plans and job-search challenges.

They also relived Maddy and Buddy's wedding; everyone had loved their barn reception.

"I saved the mason jars for the next wedding of our family or friends, so keep that in mind," Maddy chirped.

She told the gals that she and Buddy were discussing whether to stay in Indiana after she and Buddy graduated. Robin pointed out that Texas looked like the next stop for her and Chester, and she encouraged Maddy to consider moving closer to them.

"We'll visit you wherever you go, you can count on that!" I told them. "How's married life going, Maddy?" I asked. "And once again, you were a beautiful, perfect bride!"

"Oh, it's wonderful. We've been so busy with getting settled and then right back to school. We aren't going on our honeymoon until next summer."

"Oh, what do you have planned, pray tell? And you know, you don't have to wait for your honeymoon to have fun, right?" I ribbed her, and then I scolded myself. Maybe I should slow down my red cup consumption.

She giggled. "Well, it partly depends on if we move

somewhere or not, and then we might combine it with house or apartment hunting. If we don't move, I think we want to go to one of those beach places in Central America, like Robin did."

August took a break from libation creation and put some more wood in the outside fireplace. I asked him if he thought we should bring out the rest of the food.

"I think Dad's about done with the burgers and those awesome Angus beef hot dogs, so we might as well."

He and Sibby came in to help me. I had a list of the food so I wouldn't forget to put anything out. The final, official menu included our favorite family foods, so we had a splendid mash-up of entrées and sides. I hoped everyone would have fun with the macaroni and cheese bar. Guests could choose lots of toppings: salsa or tomatoes, bacon, scallions, chili, and broccoli. We created another platter for the burgers and dogs with four kinds of cheese, sweet and savory condiments, pickles, relish, and more bacon. The summer succotash from our Meal4U adventures complemented the old standbys of baked beans, broccoli salad, and a roasted vegetable arrangement.

"Come and get it!" I called.

"Call me anything, but don't call me late for dinner!" one of the older golf guys yelled.

Everyone went through the food line and found places to sit. The crowd quieted down once everyone began eating.

"Where's the hot sauce?" yelled Pud.

"Oh, thanks for reminding me; I'll get it."

"That stuff goes on everything!" Sam added.

"What's in this vegetable stuff?" Pud called.

"Lima beans, butter beans, corn, peas, onions, green beans. I think it's all things you like," I consoled him.

"Suffering succotash!" Sam was an entertainer.

Zim stopped by. "I am going to give Oakley a hot dog, since she's being so good in her crate."

"Hot dog for the hot dog!" Pud's buddy exclaimed.

I brought a plate of food to Susie, Jim, and their girls. Susie was sitting at a small table with a girl on each knee.

"Hi, Michelle and Melissa! When we have time, I want you to look at some boxes. There are some toys and puzzles and books that are in good shape. They were games the boys liked when they were little, and you can choose any or all of them that look fun to you!"

Everything seemed to be under control, so I went in to get ready for my special surprise. I came back out about ten minutes later, and Pud and Sibby were starting to clean up.

"Attention, everyone!" I screeched. "I have a special surprise, so please stick around, and let's gather everyone from inside to join us. And please fill your red cup with your favorite beverage for the toast. We'll begin in just a few minutes."

Sibby and I moved six rectangular packages wrapped in brown paper to my trusty lounge chair, which I planned to use as a podium. When it looked like everyone had gathered outside, I began.

"Pud and I want to officially welcome all of you, our dear family and friends. Thank you for coming."

There were shouts of "Thanks!" "Fun!" "Great party!" "Where's the hot sauce!"

I smiled and continued, "I have a special surprise for some of our family, which I hope will encourage them. After we are done, please stay for dessert. Dessert will be a surprise for everyone!"

I heard Pud say in the background, "We need a flat tax rate, I tell you!"

"Pud, cough, cough," I chided. "All right, please raise

your red cup. Pud and I planned this red cup celebration of family to truly honor our young relatives and their accomplishments. We love you and are so proud of you! To our family!"

"Hear, hear!" the group affirmed.

Pud said, "I forgot to fill my cup. August, pour me something!"

Everyone chuckled.

I went on, "You all know Pud retired a year ago last April after forty-two years. Many of you warned us that retirement could be challenging, and it did take us some time to get our bearings. Pud had a great idea, and that really helped."

"My first great idea!" Pud called.

"Now that we had more free time, we decided to get better acquainted with the younger generation of our family. So we visited or connected in some way with each of them this past year. We took Robin and Chester, Annie, Lindsey, and Erik out to dinner, and we learned we all like scotch."

This remark drew hoots and cheers from the crowd.

"Here's to Johnnie Walker Blue!" Chester exclaimed.

"I agree," I went on. "And Byron and Buddy and Maddy, we reached out to you, but we know we still have to schedule dinner with you. We will, I promise."

"What's the surprise?" someone yelled.

"All right, I will get to the surprise. Another thing that happened this year was that I discovered two old suitcases in the basement, and they turned out to be stuffed with old photos and slides from my parents and grandparents—and Sibby's too, of course. Kids, these would be your grandparents and great-grandparents and their families."

"Oh, I want to see them!" Sibby burst out.

"Thanks to the massive technical help of August, I

scanned them all into the computer, and I made disks for anyone who wants them."

"Oh my! How wonderful," Sibby continued.

Pud walked around pouring red and white wine to any takers. I knew I should keep moving along.

"Seeing over one hundred years of our family gave me many things to ponder, and I am going to spend the next three hours telling you about these revelations."

Loud groans followed that comment.

"No, I am almost done; you will get your dessert. But I will share one thought. Looking at all the photos gave me a view of life from thirty-five thousand feet. I saw the sweep of lives and the important markers of those lives. Births and special birthdays, graduations, weddings, and memorable trips were all recorded and memorialized photographically because family love and events are what sustains us. Sometimes I forget that when I am struggling through life at ground level, the day-to-day view may not be as important as the long vista. Sometimes we all need to take our gaze off the ground and look to the horizon. The days are long, but the years are short."

"Yes!" "You're right!" "Well done!"

"Thank you. For each of the cousins, I have made a sixteen-by-twenty canvas print of an old photo, selected especially for you."

"Lovely parting gifts!" bubbled a wit from over by the fireplace.

"Ha! So here they are, and I want you all to know that I love these photos, but I cherish each of you even more."

Sibby and Zim helped me uncover the photos, and Pud arranged them so they could all be seen.

"Ohhh," the group murmured.

"I will start with the youngest. Zim, I had to give you a

photo of Uncle Heinrich Zimmer, who you are named after. He was a success in business and a friendly and generous man. Good luck in your career and life, Zim. And welcome home!"

Zim came forward, and I reached for the next photo.

"Annie, please meet Uncle Heinrich's wife; this photo was taken before they married. She is pictured in Hollywood in 1932. Somehow she ended up in California before coming back here. I know you want to travel too. Good luck, and we love you."

Everyone had crowded up by the photo prints.

"Buddy and Maddy, here is a photo of my maternal grandparents in front of their new house two years after they married. My grandmother adored my grandfather all her married life, so remember their love."

Pud yelled, "This is good, hon, but the dessert surprise is on its way!"

"Okay, real fast, then. Lindsey and Erik, I would like you to meet Uncle Bill and Aunt Hannah; this is their hardware store on Long Island, 1922. Good luck with your education and careers. Now for August, I am sure you remember my dad, who was a pioneer in the computer field. I wish he and you could have talked about the tech world. Here he is in a room full of giant computers. He would be so proud of your achievements.

"Robin and Chester, I like how you take time to have fun together and with your friends. Here is my dad's mom at the beach, Coney Island, 1918, in her long swim dress, clowning with her buddies. Keep on growing together.

"Byron, here you go. These are some of my dad's cousins, circa 1935, dressed for success on the golf course. Good luck as you graduate.

"Thank you, everyone. And as my grandmother always said, 'It's a great life if you don't weaken.'"

I hugged each of the cousins individually, and then we had a big group hug. Pud led everyone else to our driveway to partake in the special dessert. We heard an infectious jingling tune, and the ice-cream truck arrived and pulled up our driveway. Everyone cheered.

Pud handed me a chocolate taco, kissed me, and said, "Good job, Mom!"

I brushed my curly hair out of my eyes and looked up at him. He kissed me again and gave me a firm and secure hug. I leaned my back on his chest, and he wrapped his arms around my shoulders like a comfy sweater. He rested his head on my head. This was my celebration.

Sibby was standing by the ice-cream truck. "Don't go away," she called. "I want to talk to you about all of this. It's overwhelming what you did with the photos. I will join you as soon as I figure out what to get. George, what's that you have? Oh, that sundae looks yummy. Did you choose butterscotch? And what's that, Robin, a soft serve with chocolate dip and sprinkles? Decisions!"

"Get a couple," said Pud. "I am. I had to have the toffee bar drumstick, but next I want the, uh, thing with the bananas."

After the ice-cream truck left, the party wound down, and by eleven o'clock, only Sibby and George remained. We curled up on the couch inside by the fireplace, ate from a half-empty bowl of chips, and summed up the whole evening.

George said, "This party was the best—good food and probably too much to drink, but what you did with the photos was beautiful. You are right about family and friends. Our bonds are so special. We never thought we would lose my first wife so suddenly."

"I told you we bought too much vodka," Pud interjected.

"We are blessed with good kids, so we wanted to support them," I said. "And you know another thing I was thinking about when I scanned the photos?"

"How did you ever do all that? I can't wait to look at these."

"Well, it's a good thing my mantra is persistence, because it did take some time. But I just wanted to share one more thing that I didn't have time to say earlier at the party. The love we have for our family is highlighted at a commencement ceremony. The regal walking music rings out. The long line files in, and the whole time, you are searching for that one precious person. As hundreds of young people march by, you are riveted, breathlessly waiting for only one face. Sibby, don't you remember how excited and thrilled you felt when you finally saw your child enter? And heard her name announced?"

Everyone shifted in their seats and looked at me quizzically. I plunged on. "Remember, Pud, like when we were at Disney? When we lost our kid, we were frantic. Even though there were a million other children there, we wanted August back safely."

Pud interjected, "August always got lost. I, uh, told him and told him to stick with us, but he would never listen. It's just like Congress; they never listen."

"Do you mean kids are not fungible?" George added.

I finished my thought. "I don't know if I am saying this right, but the touchstone of life is that we each are blessed with a powerful connection to the faces that are unique and dear to us alone, and these cherished faces and the love we feel is the vital power that guides us and keeps us going."

"God is the power, don't you think?" Sibby replied thoughtfully.

I felt so strongly about my idea, but no one seemed to be getting it. *Oh, well, press on.* "Sibby, stay a few more minutes, and let's look at some of the photo disks together on my laptop."

22

Companionship

It had been a week of minor mishaps and miscues. One day Pud hadn't been able to find his sunglasses and finally had realized he must have left them on top of the golf cart and pulled away and lost them. He'd also mixed up his eye appointment and gone on the wrong date and had to reschedule. Then he and I had gone out to dinner, and he'd left his wallet at home. I'd made a mistake too. I'd poured egg whites on my cereal instead of milk. In my defense, the cartons looked the same.

Pud was feeling down about all his goofs, so I decided to tell him a story to cheer him up—except I couldn't find him. I asked Oakley and then shouted through the house. The dog and I finally found him outside trimming back the perennials and the decorative weeds for the winter.

"Hi. I was looking for you. I remembered a story I wanted to tell you."

Pud was fighting with the trimmer and the trash bags. "I am trying to get this done. I'll talk to you later."

It was a good tale. When the boys were kids, the three of us had spent many of our summers relaxing with my folks at their cottage. Their place had been in a quaint, Victorian-era town, Chautauqua on Lake Erie. We'd enjoyed the chance to swim and fish, eat ice-cream cones every day, and play miniature golf and shuffleboard. The boys and I were on our own in the summer when Pud traveled, so we appreciated the chance for fun getaways.

Each morning of our vacation, the boys and I walked down to the coffee shop and bought warm, juicy cream sticks and cinnamon rolls. We took them to the pier and watched the boats cruise by on the lake. We dreamed about our "someday boat" as we ate our treats and gobbled crumbs that fell on our shirts. After breakfast, we spent the rest of the morning at the playground and browsed through the shops.

One morning, there was a commotion in the bookstore. A man was at the counter with his pile of books, and as he went to pay for them, he realized he didn't have his wallet. He searched each pocket in his shorts, and when he didn't find it, he walked around the store, looking at the floor and shelves. He grew agitated, so other customers began to help him search. His wife came in, and he asked her hopefully if she had seen his wallet.

In the midst of this gentleman's panic, the store manager came to the counter and asked what the problem was. The man explained that his wallet was gone. He and his wife thought back and remembered that he had last used it the day before right after lunch, when they had walked down to the pier and bought ice-cream cones.

The manager listened and said, "You should go to security. Last night, the officer was telling me an amazing story. Yesterday, around 5:00 p.m., a fisherman stopped by the administration building with a wallet. He had been scooping up his fish with a net, and he had been shocked to find a wallet in the bottom of the net. He turned it in, and Al, in security, said he had never had anything like that happen before. Go see if it's yours."

As the man and his wife hurried out to check, we shoppers exclaimed about the circumstances. Someone pointed out that fishermen and lifeguards often pulled out hats, jackets, and swim toys that people accidentally dropped into the lake, but the manager clarified this. "Yes, but that's when those things are still floating and can be seen. This time, it was a lucky scoop of the net."

We'd all waited to see how it all would turn out. Sure enough, about ten minutes later, the man and his wife had come back, and he'd held up a damp, leather wallet. "It was mine! And everything is still in it, plus some seaweed!"

This memory had stuck with me because it showed me that somehow everything usually worked out fine. That was what I wanted to tell Pud. However, today would turn out to be a time when the heavens did not align. All I had planned to do was to meet my sister; what could go wrong?

It all began when Sibby learned that Pud and I had finally planned our fine-dining event with Buddy and Maddy. Our plans were to drive over and see them on the coming weekend. My sister called and asked if she could meet me before we left because she wanted us to take over some more wedding presents to the new couple.

"Sure, no problem," I said. "We'd be glad to. In fact, I should have called you and asked if there was anything you wanted me to take to them."

"Oh, thanks, and thanks again for all you are doing for the kids. Okay, I can bring the gifts over … let's see, late

Thursday night, because we are going to an open house for my friend's book signing that night. We can make it after 9:00 p.m."

"That's a little late for us, and you don't need to drive all the way out here. Isn't there someplace in town we could meet?"

"Oh, I don't mind driving. You are so nice to take this over for me," said Sibby. "Let me check my calendar. Okay, I can also come Friday morning at 7:30 a.m."

"Uh, not sure about that time either. I guess I am like Goldilocks; one time is too late, and the other time is too early. Let's see. If you are around on Friday, I am going to be getting a mani pedi at eleven o'clock, and that's close to you, so why don't you just swing by, and we can meet and load the car in the parking lot?"

Long silence. Then Sibby said tentatively, "Uh, well, it's not real close, but I guess I could."

"It's pretty close, isn't it? Plus it's right by your grocery; you can combine errands. You always need something from the grocery; that's what I always say."

Silence again. "Okay, so I will meet you sometime after eleven on Friday. Oh, Annie is calling; I'll get off now, and I'll see you."

In hindsight, maybe I should have thought more about why Sibby was so hesitant about my plan, but I clicked off and went on to the next thing. I didn't realize that this plan was not going to click.

Friday morning, I arrived at the spa for my mani pedi before eleven, signed in, and then picked out my polish. After much debate with myself, I chose a vibrant purple for my toes and a neutral tan for my fingers. My technician fixed the water at my chair so it was warm and swirling. I adjusted the back massagers to pulse and settled in to relax. I made sure I kept my phone handy, in case Sibby called.

My feet had soaked, and the technician had scrubbed them, and still no sign of my sister. I leaned back to enjoy the foot massage and warm towels. The massage felt so comforting, except when the gal tickled the bottom of my foot. Still no Sibby. Where was she? My phone had slid out of reach, so I figured I would call her before the mani started.

It was almost noon, and the polish was going on my toes—it turned out to be a great color—when Sibby burst in the door and steamed over to my chair. "I texted you; I guess you didn't see it. Oh, I love that color. Nice shade of purple. Anyhoo, I got mixed up, apparently."

"Oh, good to see you. I was wondering where you were," I replied.

"Well, I thought you were talking about the salon by your house, not this one. So I went out to the other place, and then when I didn't see you, I tried to text you, but I finally figured you might be here."

"You drove all the way out there and then all the way back? Yeah, I meant this spa here in Fairlawn; it's so close to your house. I even mentioned the grocery."

"I thought you meant *your* grocery—and you are right; it *is* close—and it would have been a good plan if I hadn't messed up."

"Oh, you didn't mess up at all," I said. "I guess I didn't say the name of the place, because I can never remember it. I certainly didn't want you to have to drive so far. But all is well. We are finally reunited, Rose."

"Rose?"

"Oh, that was a lame joke from *Titanic*. Remember how Jack could never find her? Hey, while you're here, I am ready to start my mani. Stay and get one too. My treat."

We debated this a few minutes, and when the technician assured us she could fit her in, Sibby sank into the chair at the stand next to me. The unaligned stars and the universe recalculated. Everything did always work out fine.

"Good. This will give us more time to chat." I smiled. "I haven't seen you for … what? A few weeks? Since our last breakfast."

"Thanks, I needed to relax. And we are going to a sixtieth birthday party at the country club on Saturday, so it will be good to have my nails done. Thanks!"

"You guys are friends … or wait, you must be her mom?" interjected the technician.

Not again! People always thought I was her mother. Sibby was four years younger and many years snappier than I. Sibby was used to handling this situation.

"We are best friends and sisters."

"Oh, gee, sorry," said the nail gal. "Well, it's great how you have so much to talk about."

I liked how this place put little marble-type balls in the soaking water and floated flower petals. I fiddled and twirled the little smooth stones.

"So, do you know where you are going out to eat with Buddy and Maddy?" Sibby asked. "There aren't that many places near his college, are there?"

"We looked a little online but ended up letting them choose. I think the restaurant is called something like Urban Farmer. It's one of those locally sourced, veggie, sustainable, small-plates places."

"Well, have fun. This has been such a good idea for you to take everyone out to eat. Robin and Chester still rave, and they consider you their best friends. And Lindsey is always telling me about the next place she and Erik want to go with you guys. Oh!" Sibby continued, "I have to tell you again how much we loved the red cup celebration. I have told everyone about it. The food, the red cups, and the photos—"

Sibby's phone rang, and it was a friend wanting to set up a yoga time. After that call, Lindsey texted her, but Sibby had to put down her phone because the tech was ready to put on our polish.

"So where were we? Oh, how are your boys?" she asked.

"The boys are super. Thank goodness for texting; at least I hear from them! You and I were just talking about all the kids and dinners, and I have to say that this whole year has been a source of pleasure and satisfaction for Pud and me. I was looking for something for us to do together; we were so frigid when our retirement began. Focusing on all the kids and getting to know them better has been such a positive for us. We had a great time planning the trips and meals and then sharing the highlights afterward. Doing something special together also opened our hearts to each other too. Kind of like the Grinch; our hearts grew three sizes bigger."

"All my kids always say how much fun they have when they go out with you or hear from you. They all really like you."

"Well, I hope we have been a source of encouragement to them. We really are proud of them. You have super kids. I believe the dinners helped me the most. I not only received the gift of love and friendship from them but also grew from seeing how they handled their lives. And as a bonus, I developed a better perspective about my own life from spending time with them and also with all the old family photographs. The first year of retirement turned out to be a blessing."

"Wow, you should be a speaker; you say that all so well. But what do you mean about Pud and you?"

"Oh, it's not a big deal or anything. I think you and I have talked about Pud and what was bothering me before. Oh, I like your color. Would you call that coral?"

Sibby was waving at someone walking by the window of the salon.

"Oh, watch your nails," said the technician.

"Oops," Sibby said. "That was Cheryl, a friend I know from school. She and I worked on the PTO spaghetti dinner committee together."

"Oh. Well, I was just going to say about Pud … do you still want to hear this?"

"Absolutely!"

"I spent a lot of time the first year of his retirement stressing about how he was gone so much golfing."

"Oh, that's right. So that's better now?"

"In some ways. He still golfed most of the time this past summer, but he agreed to mark big things like weekend club championships on the calendar, and he discussed more of his plans with me. For my part, I tried to be more understanding. But can I tell you one more thing: I heard something interesting last week."

"I'm all ears."

"I was at a board meeting, and there's a nice older guy on the board, smart and well spoken. After the meeting, he was telling some of us that when he was fifty, he and a friend biked across America from the Pacific Ocean to the Atlantic Ocean."

"Really?" Sibby said. "Geez. How long did that take?"

"As I recall, they did it in thirty days. Oh, now I remember. He said that it all depended on how far you planned to ride each day. If you rode one hundred miles a day, you got done in about thirty days. If you rode fifty miles, it would take about sixty days. I liked that plan because that's how I would think about it."

The nail tech told us we were finished and directed us over to the drying area. She helped us carry our purses over.

"So just to finish this long boring topic," I said.

"It's not boring. What were you saying? Something about the ocean? Oh, wait, the bike-riding guy. Go on." Sibby stopped texting.

"Okay. He finished his story by explaining that he planned this transcontinental trip right before he married his second wife. She told him she was remarrying for companionship, so he had to commit to doing things with her. He agreed, but he told her he wanted to take a month to complete his cross-country bike dream first. After that, he would commit to being her full-time husband and companion. There's more. Wait until you hear what I asked him."

"What did you ask him, and do you think our nails are dry yet?"

"Probably not quite dry yet. So I asked him, 'You mean to tell me that once you pedaled into the Atlantic Ocean, you were done with your dreams? You never tackled another bike trip or golfed or hung out with the guys?'"

"Yeah, like I believe that," Sibby retorted. "What did he say?"

"He said that while he did his best to be a full-time companion to his wife, he also felt that two people did need some space and time apart and other interests to pursue, so throughout their marriage, he has worked on balancing things with his wife."

"Oh, he does sound like a nice guy," said Sibby. "Darn, I just whacked this nail on the table. How does it look?"

"Oh, you lucked out. It looks okay," I told her. "So he talked about balance in marriage, and that's what I keep thinking about for Pud and me. I plan to persist and press on and find ways to keep this time in our lives enjoyable for both us together, but I also need to realize that things can't change in a day. We are on our way to a closer partnership, but it will take time to make our retirement years what we both want them to be. Hey, thanks for listening."

"George and I will be there soon enough. You and Pud are so good together. I hope you have many years of … what did that guy call it? Uh, companionship?"

We both laughed.

"Do you think he actually was talking about something else?" Sibby asked.

"Like a very intimate and close type of companionship?" I murmured as I hummed "Embraceable You."

23

Amuse-Bouche

I inhaled the aroma of my second cup of coffee as I finished my morning reading. I reread a story on my social-media news feed that touched my heart. A friend had shared a story about a red flannel shirt, told by a wife who loved to iron. She described how she had learned to iron as a child and had become quite adept at pressing clothes. It gave her great pleasure to care for her family with her ironing skills.

She went on, "My husband is a godly, hardworking, faithful, kind, and caring family man and husband. He drives a truck and spends long hours on the road to provide a living for us. I take great pride in ironing the red flannel shirt that he wears when he is on the job. When he stops at a truck stop or gets to the end of the line, I don't want folks to see an old, worn-out guy. I want them to see a well-loved and respected man in a crisp, ironed shirt. I iron for him because I love him. I am so proud of him, and I give him the gift of my ironing."

This simple story resonated within me. I joyously added a new affirmation to my daily greeting. "Thank you, God, for this beautiful day, and help me show love to my family."

Press on!

CPSIA information can be obtained
at www.ICGtesting.com
Printed in the USA
FFOW05n0221310815